NEVER GIVE UP

A Christopher Family Novel

W. D. Foster-Graham

authorHOUSE®

AuthorHouse™
1663 Liberty Drive
Bloomington, IN 47403
www.authorhouse.com
Phone: 833-262-8899

Published by AuthorHouse 07/31/2020

ISBN: 978-1-7283-6798-9 (sc)
ISBN: 978-1-7283-6797-2 (e)

Library of Congress Control Number: 2020913137

Print information available on the last page.

Any people depicted in stock imagery provided by Getty Images are models, and such images are being used for illustrative purposes only. Certain stock imagery © Getty Images.

This book is printed on acid-free paper.

ACKNOWLEDGMENTS

I would like to acknowledge the following: Arthur and Shelly Foster; Steven and Linda Berry; my fellow Sounds of Blackness alumni; my Central High classmates; Shanasha Whitson; Kevin Moore; All God's Children MCC; Kim Riley; Audrey Banham Smith (my inspiration for The Look); Rhonda Byrne, Joe Vitale, Lisa Nichols; Patricia George, Angela Woods, LaTonia Williams, Sandra Nolen Johnson, Trudy White (my listening ears); Pamela Smith Alexander; Lynette Fraction; Luther College Black Alumni Association; Wyatt O'Brian Evans; Al McFarlane; Queer in Color; Blair Denholm; VSS365; Stephen Berry; Pamela Taylor-Berry; and my brothers and sisters in Christ at St. Peter's AME Church.

This book is dedicated

to Walter and to Edward Lee

and in memory of Dad, who encouraged me to be a storyteller.

AUTHOR'S NOTE

This is a work of fiction. Names, characters, places, and incidents either are the products of the author's imagination or are used fictitiously, and any resemblance to actual persons, living or dead, events or locales is purely coincidental.

THE BERRY FAMILY TREE

Everett Berry (Ernestine Henderson)(married 1921)
  Eldon Berry (Elaine Madison)(married 1945)
    Ellen Berry (Kenneth Grayson)(married 1980)
      Krystle Grayson
      Alexis Grayson
    Elizabeth Berry (Carlton Chandler)(married 1984)
      Dominique Chandler
      Sable Chandler
  Earl James Berry (Juanita Langston)(married 1948)
    Sylvia Berry (Clinton Lewis)(married 1973)
      Zora Lewis (Roy Garvin)(married 1996)
        Phyllis
        Gwendolyn
      Richard Lewis (Isaiah Holliday)(married 2005)
        Roshon
        Juanita
      Langston Lewis (Kelinda Watson)(married 2006)
        Kendall
        Kaleah
      Alice Lewis
    Deshawna Berry (Jason Randolph)(married 1977)
      Dallas Randolph (Nefertari Hines)(married 2011)
        Amina
      Orlando Randolph (Brendan Livingston)(married 2007)

Delancey
Denver
Lincoln Randolph (Jessica Lowery)(married 2009)
Robbin
Tulsa
Linda Berry (Prentice Delaney)(married 1974)
Sierra Delaney (Rashid Hines)(married 2002)
Earl
Destiny
Prentice Delaney Jr. (Trevell Ross)(married 2009)
Barack
LaVera Berry (Derrick St. James)(married 1978)
Ashley St. James (Shawn Yang)(married 2006)
Brooklyn
Tecumseh
Devon St. James (Dominic Robertson)(married 2009)
Delores
Linden St. James
Chauntice Berry (Jarvis Varnell)(married 1981)
Antonia Varnell (Quentin Lawrence)(married 2007)
Ava
James Varnell (Jonathan Bradshaw)(married 2010)
Jonah
Kira Varnell (Keith Hendricks)(married 2012)
Carter Berry (Julian Edwards)(married 1983)
Donna Berry-Edwards
Lillian Berry-Edwards

PROLOGUE: NOVEMBER 6, 2012

Prentice Delaney-Ross was on a high, cheering in campaign headquarters as news of President Obama's re-election "rocked the house." People were hugging, cheering, and shedding tears of joy all over the office. Several times he and his husband Trevell embraced and kissed and shouted. There were many good reasons to do so that night. Not only had the president been re-elected, but Maine, Maryland, and Washington voted in favor of marriage equality, and Minnesotans had voted down a constitutional ban on marriage equality. Having celebrated their third wedding anniversary barely two weeks ago, the victories were mind-blowing.

He had no doubt his stepbrother, Jerome Franklin-Edwards, and his husband Ariel were at home with their daughters soaking up all the amazing news, even as they listened intently to the president's acceptance speech. The same held true for the rest of his family, especially his grandfather, Earl James Berry. Grandpa had always been a huge supporter of President Obama, as well as a staunch ally for equality and a believer in justice. He had retired from the bench in 1996, but his reputation as Judge Berry and that of his lifelong friend, Elijah Edwards, Sr., continued to be influential in the circles they traveled.

"You know, when Barack grows up, he'll look back on this time and wonder what all the fuss was about," Prentice said some time later, after they stepped out into the hallway to be able to hear themselves upon the conclusion of the speech.

"I imagine he will," Trevell concurred. "Right now, he's probably sound asleep while his grandma and grandpa are keeping up with all the commentary." Indeed, Prentice's mother, Linda Berry Delaney Edwards, and his stepfather, Melvin Edwards II, had doted on their newest grandson, Barack Joseph Berry Delaney-Ross, from the very beginning.

Trevell's parents were no better. Although they lived in Green Bay, Tremayne and Darcelle Ross were regular visitors to Minneapolis, showering affection on their first grandchild. A former Green Bay Packer, Tremayne Ross often had an audience and he never failed to talk about his grandson. Trevell strongly suspected his father desired to see Barack make it into the NFL when he grew up. Even at the age of two, the brainwashing had already begun.

Prentice had witnessed this phenomenon, and he understood it well. Grandpa Berry was not above a little brainwashing himself, setting Little Barack's sights on an appointment to the Supreme Court. It was a challenge to the couple, diplomatically holding those respective ambitions at bay so they could let their little boy be what he was: a two-year-old who was just beginning to really explore his world.

Hand in hand, Prentice and Trevell strolled down Hennepin Avenue to the parking ramp, basking in the afterglow of victory, sharing smiles and waves with drivers and pedestrians on this brisk fall night. At one point their eyes met and Prentice felt his heart break out into a melody.

27-year-old Trevell had the total package—the matinee idol looks of a young Idris Elba, the solid build of a quarterback, and a well-spoken demeanor. Prentice himself had inherited his father's smooth Duke Ellington looks with a strong dose of Berry genes, which would make anyone stop in their tracks to see if he was real or fantasy. At the age of 28, at this moment he felt like he was on top of the world.

They reached the parking ramp near the Target Center, for the moment lost in their own thoughts. Prentice's mind kept going back to his Grandpa Berry. He and Grandpa Edwards had said President Obama really needed two terms to accomplish what was necessary back in 2008, and they had gotten what they asked for. He had to hand it to them; they never lost faith that this day would come. Jerome, in fact, said so, not only about the presidential election but all the other issues as well, at a time when none of it seemed possible. Grandpa Berry had known the history behind Jerome's "gift," all the way back to the time he and Grandpa Edwards were young men.

Though he grew up on Milwaukee's North Shore, a six-hour drive from his grandfather in Minneapolis, Prentice always felt a connection with the man. Like Prentice's late father, Prentice Delaney Sr., Grandpa Berry had both a passion for the law and the importance of family. Unlike the portrayals of so many police shows these days, he had never been so driven to the point where he totally sacrificed his family for the sake of his career. On visits to Minneapolis with his parents, Prentice was blessed to see that special side of him, the family man. As a grown man, when he and Trevell made the decision to move to the Twin Cities, he made it a point to spend lots of quality time with his grandparents. Witnessing the love, commitment, and devotion they shared after 64 years of marriage, Prentice hoped that he, too, would have that kind of a legacy to pass on.

They stepped into their Chrysler 300 sports sedan, listening to an Alicia Keys CD as they left the parking ramp and headed out into the streets of downtown Minneapolis. Cars were honking their horns and people were out celebrating, something unusual for a Tuesday night.

"You think Sierra and Rashid are still up?" Trevell asked Prentice.

"Sure. They wouldn't miss this for the world. The only reasons they weren't at campaign headquarters was because Destiny was sick and it's a school night for Little Earl," Prentice replied, picturing his sister and her husband watching the set and simultaneously calling everyone they knew.

"You know we're going to be going through this with Barack in a few years, just like they are."

"True. Anyway, since Barack is spending the night with Mom and Mel, let's stop by and see Grandpa and Grandma."

"Aren't they in Chicago visiting the Christophers?"

"They were, but they wanted to make sure they were home for Election Day, so they could vote. I'm sure they're up for the occasion."

"OK, but just remember that we have grocery shopping to do tomorrow and I have an early meeting."

They passed Loring Park and the Walker Art Center before they turned off on Douglas Avenue, driving through the historic and posh Lowry Hill neighborhood. Just before they reached the Berry estate on Kenwood Parkway, they spotted a car driving away from it at high speed. "What's up with that?" Trevell wondered.

"I don't know, but I don't like it," Prentice replied to Trevell and the warning bells in his head. "Wait a minute. That looks like Grandpa's limo over there."

Prentice braked quickly and they bolted from their car. The road was normally quiet, but tonight it felt a little too quiet for comfort. His concern escalated to worry as strange shivers permeated his body. Ears alert for unnatural sounds in the cool night air, Prentice and Trevell slowed down as they approached the still Cadillac limousine. Would their worst nightmare become reality? Their eyes grew wide with fear as they stepped closer, their night vision revealing the bullet holes in the windows. Prentice's heart sank.

"Noooooooooooooooo!!" he yelled as Trevell frantically grabbed his cell phone to call 911...

Juanita Langston Berry

When I walked across the stage to receive my high school diploma in June of 1946, I never dreamed how my life would change, or the role that a young man named Earl James Berry would play in it. At that moment, I felt blessed to be a graduate from Vocational High School. It meant that I had a marketable skill. It also meant I didn't have to work in someone else's home for a living. Sure, one day I would marry. But in the meantime, I could be a secretary in an office, earning my own money, buying my own clothes and contributing to the family.

I met Dr. Maureen Moore Christopher, the wife of billionaire Allan Beckley Christopher, many years later; it felt great to have a kindred spirit since we both had parents who were teachers. In Minneapolis, though, African American teachers stood out more by virtue of a small minority population. My mother, Phyllis Barclay Langston, taught at Warrington Elementary School, while my father, Paul Laurence Dunbar Langston, taught over at Harrison Elementary School. After I was born at what was then Hennepin County General Hospital on August 27, 1928, the doctor told Mama she couldn't have any more children. However, Mama and Papa took this as God's will and to be grateful for the child they did have--me, Juanita Sue Langston.

Teachers, even today, are paid less than what they're really worth, but in the community my parents were highly respected. From our residence at 3656 Clinton Avenue, Daddy left early in the morning to commute to the North Side, while Mama literally walked across the street with me to Warrington. Their word was law, and my conduct

1

at school was under very tight scrutiny, not only there, but in the neighborhood as well. Ah, those were the days.

Aurelia and Donna Gray lived over on East 35th Street and 3rd Avenue South, but growing up I didn't know them that well because they were older than me. The Edwardses lived in the mini-mansion on the corner of East 34th Street and Portland Avenue. I'd see them at church, but I hadn't socialized with them to any degree. Not that I expected to, since the Edwardses had the status of being both socially prominent and having deep pockets of wealth by virtue of Melvin Edwards being a financial wizard. Then again, so many of us knew who everyone was in the community, even if we traveled in somewhat different circles.

I don't know what strings my parents pulled to get me into Vocational High rather than Central High, but they managed it, and for three years I would take the 4th Avenue Line trolley to downtown Minneapolis, where the imposing Art Deco building stood at South 11th Street and 3rd Avenue South. Unlike Central High, the building is still there today, only it was taken over by Hennepin County and renamed Century Plaza. Thanks to the discipline my parents taught me, my grades were exceptional and I graduated with honors. After commencement, we celebrated at the senior class party until the wee hours of the morning.

It took a little longer than I thought it would to land a secretarial job, but I never gave up. I made it a point to look and conduct myself professionally, always looking for ways to improve my efficiency. Mama and Daddy held out the hope that I'd go to college and get my bachelor's degree, but I was a young woman who had plans of her own, which I would talk about at length with my friend Cassandra Weldon. A taller version of Betty Grable, Cassandra was a fellow Vocational High graduate who worked in the stock room at J.C. Penney's, while I worked in an office building a few blocks down near the Foshay Tower, the tallest building in the city at the time.

I was working late on a Thursday evening in December (December 12, if memory serves), making plans to do a little Christmas shopping before I went home and hoping my parents wouldn't be there yet. I was dressed more for a brisk fall day, since that December was mild and still "green" at that point. I locked the office door and headed down to the end of the hall. Normally I was out the door at five, but that night I saw a young man leaving an office with a mop, bucket, and cleaning supplies. He didn't see me at first as I stood there waiting for the elevator, but when he turned around our eyes met.

"Hi," I heard him say.

"Hi," I replied just as the elevator door opened and I got on. As the door closed, I saw him look at me again and give me a smile. I don't even remember if I returned his smile, but on the trip down I found myself hoping that I had.

As I shopped for presents at Dayton's, then while I waited for the trolley, and during the ride home, he piqued my curiosity. During dinner with my parents, I found myself distracted. While I listened to the Hit Parade on the radio, I couldn't get his image out of my mind. I wracked my brain in an effort to place him. I wasn't sure if he was familiar, but his image was a delight to the senses. I had estimated him to be 6'0", in contrast to my 5'6". Even in a custodian's work clothes, he was one well-built man—I had no doubt he must have been an athlete in high school, and probably kept that way in the military. His deep brown complexion was rich, and his raven black hair a curious mixture of curly and wavy. Could he possibly have Native American blood in him somewhere? As for his smoky gold eyes, I saw intelligence and pure animal magnetism in them, a sense of knowing exactly what he wanted.

My dear—if a woman wasn't careful, she could lose herself in that man, but the trip would be filled with nonstop enjoyment.

As the Ink Spots serenaded me with "To Each His Own," I got up from my bed and stood in front of the floor-length mirror in my bedroom for an appraisal. From Mama I had inherited a healthy hourglass figure and a thick head of shoulder-length, dark brown hair which was currently hot-pressed into submission. Papa had given me smooth, medium brown skin, his engaging smile, and his passionate but wise eyes. People who see me today would consider me an older and darker-complexioned version of the Fifth Dimension's Marilyn

McCoo. I've laughed about that, since she's young enough to be one of my daughters. When the group hit the charts in the late '60s some people would ask me, "Are you sure she's not your niece?" Nobody I ever dated had given me an argument about my looks, and Papa was always there to guard my virtue—with deadly weapons if necessary. In my self-appraisal, I already visualized my "mystery man" standing next to me in the mirror.

No, there was more to that brief exchange of greetings than met the eye, as far as I was concerned. I was full of questions, questions I hoped to have answers for soon. Of course, at 18 a girl wants those questions answered yesterday. Had I seen him before? Where did he live? What was a man like that doing in a custodian's job when he was clearly capable of so much more, if his eyes were any indication? And how would I fit into the picture? Better yet, how did I want to fit into the picture, if there was one?

Back in those days a woman who considered herself a lady would never do the unthinkable and throw herself at a man, not like today when so many girls line up to audition for the role of slut. As I thought about him over the next couple of days, the thing to do was find out who he worked for and his hours, unless divine intervention brought him to me. I had so little to go on that I didn't even consider talking to Mama and Papa. Cassandra, however, was another story.

"He sounds luscious," Cassandra said as we talked on the phone the next evening. "So, have you done anything to find out more about him?"

"Well, not yet. I thought about staying late today, but that would have been too obvious. Monday might be a better time. How are things going with Vince?"

"Smooth as silk. We're going to the movies tomorrow night. But back to this dreamboat of yours. How does this affect your plans as a professional secretary?"

"It doesn't. I want both, at least for a while. What movie are you going to see?"

"*The Postman Always Rings Twice* is playing at the Orpheum. It's supposed to be good."

We continued to discuss film noir movies we'd seen in the past. For us, seeing women in power in such movies—down to the knives in their nylons and guns in their minks—was utterly fascinating, not to mention the way they led their male victims down the road to destruction. Not that we would even consider that as a surefire way to get a man, but we loved the sheer entertainment value.

Sunday, of course, had the Langston family in St. Matthew's African Methodist Episcopal Church for worship. I always made sure I looked good for church. On that day I wore my best grey wool suit with matching pumps, having pressed and curled my hair into a chignon with victory rolls, something similar to Ingrid Bergman's hairstyle in the cocktail party scene of *Notorious.* We were always there before services started because Papa was one of the trustees and Mama taught Sunday school. I hadn't really decided what I wanted to do at church since I graduated, but I knew that at some point I had to do something.

Service attendance had been increasing since Thanksgiving and the start of Advent, so the church was nearly full when it was time for service to start. Because I tried to stay as focused as much as possible on the service itself, I usually didn't look around at people who came in late. Today was no different. I took out my Bible to follow along with the Scripture lessons and soaked in the sounds of the choir, looking forward to the Christmas program that afternoon.

Rev. Walker gave an inspiring message about the "reason for the season" that day, and after the benediction we stopped for a few minutes to chat with other members. I happened to look over at one of the exits for a moment and caught a glimpse of someone leaving. My mouth dropped slightly. *What's he doing here? Is my mind playing tricks on me?* I decided that was it; I'd been thinking about that man for the past few days, and now I was imagining him showing up everywhere. Still, when we returned later on for the program, I found myself wondering if he would show up.

The church was packed for the Christmas program, and it was wonderful. Our choir and a guest choir from St. Andrew's concluded the program with the "Hallelujah Chorus," and afterwards we gathered in the dining hall for fellowship. I felt a little disappointed that Mystery Man hadn't made an appearance, but the time for praise and worship had been well spent.

As I waited in line to get a plate, I saw Lillian and Melvin Edwards holding court with their friends. They were a "power couple" long before the phrase was coined. Mama and Papa exchanged pleasantries with our pastor, while I wished that Cassandra would have been there as she'd promised to be. I was pleasant and polite to the women who were serving, and I talked to the people nearby about the program. I filled my plate and found a seat when I realized I had forgotten to get some punch. When I got up to do so, I stopped in my tracks. My heart fluttered in my chest. When did it suddenly become more difficult to breathe?

"Aren't you…"

"Yeah," Mystery Man said, and that brilliant smile of his came out in full wattage. "You're the woman from the hallway."

"But…I feel like I know you from somewhere."

"Well, if it helps, I'm Earl James Berry. I've been away at college. And you are…?"

"Juanita Langston."

"Langston…Langston. You know, I think my father knows your father. Probably from the NAACP and the Urban League. Didn't you go to Central?"

"No, Vocational. I just graduated this past June."

"It figures. If you had gone to Central, I would definitely have remembered someone like you." I must have been smiling, because there was an extra twinkle in his eye. "Would you like some punch?"

Remembering my initial mission, I answered, "Yes, thank you."

"Coming right up. And if it's all right with you, I'd like to join you."

"I'd like that." I was downplaying my response to his flirting as much as possible, even though I wanted to scream *"Yes!!!!!"* from the rooftops.

From that day on, we talked on the phone and took time to socialize at church. Our first real date, though, took place on New

Year's Eve. Even though it was a house party and we were double-dating with Earl's older brother Eldon and his wife Elaine, I made it a point to look my very best. I had saved up enough money from work to buy a formal gown that would show off the sophistication of a young woman, and the sweetheart bodice and padded shoulders did the trick for me. Of course, accessories are everything, which meant that Cassandra and I shopped for the right pumps, evening bag, gloves and earrings, followed by a trip to the beauty salon for an upswept hairdo.

Earl was prompt, not only coming to the door but coming inside so my parents had the opportunity to give him the once-over. "You're Everett Berry's son, aren't you?" Papa asked, after introductions were made.

"That's right, sir." Earl gave Papa a confident handshake.

"So, where are you two going this evening?"

I wished Papa hadn't embarrassed me with that question—I was 18, for heaven's sakes. But Earl was a gentleman and he answered, "We're going to a house party in the neighborhood. My brother Eldon and his wife are going with us."

"Well, you take good care of my daughter and drive carefully, Earl."

As we walked outside to Eldon's car, Earl took his opportunity to tell me, "Juanita, you look sensational." My dear, if I were a white woman my blush would have been quite obvious over his compliment. On the drive over to the party on 41st and Portland Avenue, Eldon and Elaine made small talk with us as Eldon navigated the streets with the heat on full blast to combat the subzero temperatures outside. I loved the way Eldon and Elaine finished each other's sentences from time to time; from the way they spoke to each other, they were very much in love. The family resemblance between Earl and Eldon was unmistakable. As for Elaine, I did believe there was a grain of truth in that saying, "everybody has a twin somewhere," but I never made the connection with Elaine until 20 years later, when I first laid eyes on Nichelle Nichols as Lt. Uhura on *Star Trek*.

The party was in full swing when we arrived; a lot of the people there were either people Eldon and Earl knew from school or familiar faces from the neighborhood. I was introduced, and while we mixed and mingled, Earl caught sight of someone.

"Hey, Eli!" he called out. A tall, striking young man with a familiar air looked around for a second, saw Earl, and immediately approached us with his date in tow.

"Earl! What's going on?" he said as they exchanged a hearty handshake.

Earl regarded him with a big grin and a clap on the back. "Just came by to bring in the New Year." I could tell from the body language that Earl and Eli had to be best friends, probably for years. "Oh, let me introduce you to my girlfriend, Juanita Langston. Juanita, this is my ace, Eli Edwards."

I was stunned that Earl would give me the title of "girlfriend" this early on, but I was not complaining. "Hello, Eli," I said pleasantly. "And who is your date?"

Eli, ever the gentleman, turned to her. "Earl, Juanita, I'd like you to meet Marion Wells. Marion, this is Earl James Berry and Juanita Langston."

After the introductions were made and conversation started, I couldn't help noticing that Marion was gazing at Eli with a starstruck possessiveness mixed with calculation. Eli had those pretty-boy Edwards looks, highlighted by his high-yellow complexion and curly brown hair that any woman would love to run her fingers through. Obviously, he inherited them from his father, and no doubt they attracted women like butterflies—or moths.

At the same time, though, I was sure Marion was carefully hiding the dollar signs in her eyes. I had never been formally introduced to Eli until that night—well, other than seeing him at church—but I hoped Marion was merely his date for the evening and nothing more serious than that. If it was, I could only imagine what his mother, our reigning society queen, would do to that woman. No one messed with Lillian Christopher Edwards.

8

From the way the party was going, 1947 rolled in sooner than we thought, and we made our toast with club soda. Earl and I exchanged our first kiss amidst the celebration of the New Year, and it was breathtaking. I could feel the heat of his passion, and something in me answered that heat. Sure, I'd had young men kiss me before, but I hadn't felt the kind of desire I felt when Earl's lips met mine. This was something entirely different.

Years later, as our family grew, I would think about that kiss at different times. It was all I could do not to touch my lips in his presence for the rest of the night. During the party, I caught the amorous way Elaine looked at Eldon on several occasions and thought to myself, "There's no turning back when you fall in love with a Berry." The Berry brothers possessed a mesmerizing charm. When he brought me to my doorstep and kissed me again, leaving me with the taste of him in my mouth and a heat in me that defied the freezing night, I was well on my way to doing just that.

"So, Juanita, when are you going to invite your new beau over for dinner?" Mama asked me the next morning at breakfast. "We'd like to get to know him better."

Leave it to Mama to pick up on such things. I must have been glowing—that's what she said I did whenever a young man caught my interest. "Well, how about Saturday?"

Papa and Mama exchanged a look before Papa said, "Fine. We'll expect to see you and Earl then."

"How did you…"

"We do have eyes, Juanita. Every Sunday since the holidays, it's been written all over your face whenever you and he are in the same room."

He had me there. "Well, Papa, he is going places, and I am no fool," I said defensively. "You've always said the Twin Cities needs more Negro lawyers."

Papa nodded in agreement. "True. The same thing goes with school principals. But we can talk about that when he comes to dinner."

Over dinner, I was quite proud of Earl when he outlined his plans to become an attorney. My parents were very shrewd when it came to sizing up a young man. Fortunately for him, Earl spoke with confidence and not conceit, intelligence and not raging hormones. His support of me and my career ambitions really put him in solid with Mama. Papa, of course, took him into his study for a "man-to-man talk," which was always a tense moment for a guy who was considering courting me. From experience, not every guy survived that interview. When they came out with Papa smiling and patting Earl on the back, I could finally release the deep breath I had been holding.

A week later, I was a guest at the home of Earl's parents, Everett and Ernestine Berry. I drew on all the poise, deportment, professionalism, and manners Mama had taught me. It didn't take a rocket scientist to figure out where Eldon and Earl got their looks and magnetic personalities from when I saw Dr. Berry, not to mention their ambition. Indeed, he had worked hard to become one of the very few Black dentists in the Twin Cities at the time, and he was grooming Eldon to join him in the practice. I could only imagine how many women flashed him seductive smiles before and after they had their teeth cleaned or examined. Mrs. Berry, though, was the one I really had to impress, and I knew it. She and I had a long talk that evening. Only Papa's advice to "be yourself" helped me survive the grilling—I mean interview—and receive a blessing from the Ella Fitzgerald lookalike.

I learned to appreciate our courtship, largely because we had to make whatever time we had together count. With Earl away at college and me working, we became very creative about our dates, planning them in our letters and over the phone when he could afford to call. And yes, I became a lovesick woman, but being that way made me more efficient at work. Despite the fact that being around Earl made me want to fan myself on numerous occasions, I still had my dreams of using my skills professionally. And when Earl had to go back to school after a break, I had a captive audience in Cassandra, with whom I could share just about everything. During a double date with

10

Cassandra and Vince, Cassandra pulled me aside. "Earl doesn't just sound luscious, he *is* luscious. Juanita, you got yourself a good one."

I remember well when school let out for the summer of 1947, for it began the onslaught of days that roasted a person where they stood and balmy nights. The heat sent residents in droves to the city lakes or up to the cabins and resorts of northern Minnesota. At home, our windows stayed open, the fans were on around the clock, and cold beverages were always on tap. It amazes me when outsiders gripe about the cold Minnesota winters without even entertaining the flip side of the coin. On the other hand, the summer did have its benefits, what with Earl back in town and us working in the same office building again.

One of the activities I enjoyed was when Earl could use his older brother's car—a 1940 Dodge coupe—and we'd go for drives. Back in those days there were very few developed suburbs around, like Robbinsdale, St. Louis Park, Columbia Heights, Hopkins, and the Country Club section of Edina. The interstate highway system wouldn't begin construction for another nine years. Osseo was a stand-alone town along U.S. Highway 52, as were places like North St. Paul off Highway 36, White Bear Lake on U.S. Highway 61, and of course, Stillwater's niche on the St. Croix River.

Farmland abounded, it seemed, once we left the city limits of Minneapolis and St. Paul. We'd see one-room schoolhouses and towns that had that small-town feel to them. Of course, that was before they were surrounded by what would become the Twin Cities metropolitan area. I'd bring a picnic lunch for us to enjoy by a lake we'd happen to find, reminding us there was also beauty outside the city. Those trips also showed us, as we appreciated what Mother Nature gave us, that we could enjoy each other's company without saying a word.

July 25 was a day that left me wilting when I got off work to board the streetcar. That Friday was filled with one fire after another which had to be put out in the course of the office day while the ceiling fans seemed to do nothing but circulate the 97-degree heat. I had been at my desk wishing our boss would get up off some cash and invest in an air conditioner. The only saving grace to the day, as I rode home, was that Earl was taking me out to a movie that evening, and the theater did have air conditioning.

We relaxed comfortably in the cool and the darkness of the theater, watching Humphrey Bogart and Lauren Bacall in *Dark Passage*. Afterwards, rather than ride the bus, we chose to walk home from downtown. That was one of the benefits of living here back then—one could walk home in peace. The three or four miles didn't seem like a great distance when you considered how quiet and beautiful the walk was—except when you had to cross Lake Street.

By the time we had reviewed the movie, our days, small talk, and sometimes enjoying peaceful silences we had reached Nicollet Field. There were a few couples around sitting on benches, but we found one for ourselves, savoring a breeze that came up.

"Juanita, I've been thinking a lot about us."

"You have? What have you been thinking?"

"How good we are together."

"Really?" I said, with a little coyness in my voice.

"Yeah, really. I don't know if I ever told you this, but I fell in love with you that night when New Year's came in."

My heart was full with the love I felt for him. "Oh, Earl. You felt it, too."

"Not only that, but I think you're an absolutely amazing woman. Remember that song in the movie?"

"Yes."

"Well, that describes you, too. Beautiful, smart, fun to be with, and marvelous. Just the kind of woman I want to spend my life with." A breeze went up, but Earl went down—on one knee. My hands went to my face, overwhelmed with emotion when he said, "Juanita, I love you so much. Will you marry me, be my wife, have our babies, and share a life with me?"

My mouth refused to function, so I nodded in agreement. It all seemed like a dream until Earl took my hand and placed the engagement ring on my finger. I finally managed to answer, "Yes. Yes, I will, Earl." When he got up and sat beside me with that gleam in his eye, I knew what was coming, and I was more than ready for it. His kiss was torrid, heated, and filled with happiness, and I for one didn't want it to stop. Until, that is, we heard the sound of a throat being cleared nearby.

We looked up and saw a police officer staring at us as though we were having sex in the park, and he looked like he was ready to haul us in. Earl, quick on the uptake, told him, "Officer, this is my girlfriend. Actually, she is now my fiancée. I just asked this wonderful woman to marry me, and she said yes."

The police officer's expression changed as I gleefully flashed my ring. "Oh. Well, in that case, good luck to you both." Giving us a wink, he walked away.

After he left, we laughed, and Earl took me in his arms again. "Now, where were we? Oh, yes..."

On Saturday morning, I floated out of my room to the kitchen to help Mama with breakfast. "Well, how was the movie, Juanita?" she asked me as she put bacon strips into a frying pan.

"Great movie, Mama. Of course, there was a happy ending for Bogey and Bacall," I sighed, grabbing a bowl and breaking eggs for scrambling. "Where's Papa?"

"He's in bed reading the paper. He'll be in soon." She looked up from the pan and went to get some bread. "Oh, I tell you, the last time we had a summer like this was in 1936, only it was much worse. Asphalt was melting all over the place. Temperatures stayed over 100 for days on end."

I nodded while I stirred the eggs. "I know. You wouldn't let me outside to play very much that summer."

"Of course not. It was like that over most of the country. But still..." Mama dropped the slices of bread and stared at me.

"What, Mama?"

"What...is that?"

I followed her line of sight to my hand. Putting the bowl on the counter, I played nonchalant. "Oh, this? It's a ring."

"I know it's a ring, Juanita. But when did you get it?"

I gave Mama a grin and replied, "Last night…when Earl proposed to me."

Mama—my cool, calm, collected, schoolteacher Mama—screamed the house down. I couldn't help but scream with her as she hugged me, and we were caught up in the joy of the moment. It was enough to bring Papa in. He looked at us and asked, "What has gotten into you two?" I calmed down just enough to hold out my hand. His eyes locked on the ring and said, "Oh. *Oh.*" His face broke out into a megawatt smile as he embraced me. "Earl is a fine young man, Juanita. I hope he makes you as happy as your mama and I have been."

"He will, Papa, he will." I beamed, wiping tears from my eyes as Mama and I finished preparing breakfast and they both pressed me for details of the evening.

There was no way I could hold this in for 24 hours without telling Cassandra. I practically flew over to her house to give her the happy news shortly after lunchtime. Once she saw my ring, we had a screamfest, and with good reason. She and Vince were getting married on September 27. My best friend would become Cassandra Weldon Martinelli, and I was to be her maid of honor. Both of us were now engaged! In my excitement, I gave her a recap of the previous evening, after which we discussed more of her wedding plans, including her bridal shower and dress fitting. Later that day, Earl and I visited his parents and gave them our news, which pleased them for two reasons: both of their sons would be married, and it increased their chances of having grandchildren, something near and dear to Mother Berry's heart.

During our engagement period, Eli promised to be Earl's best man and—thank God—he had the good sense to dump his latest girlfriend. Marion, the girl I met at the New Year's party, hadn't made it to Valentine's Day. There was one other girl, but she wasn't worth mentioning, judging from some of the conversations I accidentally overheard between Eli and Earl. I suspect, though, that Eli's mother probably chewed them up and spit them out just before he did.

That fall, however, Eli met Donna Gray, and it was love at first sight. Not only that, Eli's parents were solidly behind their relationship. Mr. and Mrs. Gray had given their hearty approval, and as for Aurelia, she always had a flair for the dramatic. The ironic thing about it all was that unlike numerous women in the community, Donna had not set out to land Eli, never mind his pretty-boy looks, his mind by IBM, and his deep pockets of family wealth. The romantic in me loved it. As for me, I had fallen in love with a Berry. There was no turning back, and I was exceedingly happy with my lot.

The fact that our engagement came during Earl's senior year in college wasn't lost on me. I felt frustrated sometimes when Earl got bogged down with his studies because I wanted him to spend more time with me. On the other hand, in order for him to get into law school he had to pull down grades and Law School Admission Test scores that put him in the top one per cent of the class. I really missed him while he was away at school.

When he came back, I wanted us to spend as much time as possible together. Instead, when his first school break came, he spent the first part of it at the U of M library without even calling me. I thought I would scream. A few days later, he came by to take me to dinner. I was ready to read him the Riot Act and did, slamming the door in his face. He walked down the steps with his tail between his legs, while I went straight to the phone and ranted to Cassandra about him.

The next day I had calmed down enough to steaming level, and we had just finished having dinner when there was a knock at the door. Earl was standing there with his hat in his hand. I stood there giving him dirty looks, refusing to let him in. That's when he said, "Juanita, I made a mistake not seeing you as soon as I got back, and I'm sorry. Dad and I had a talk the other night, and he told me something I'll never forget."

"Oh, he did? And what was *that?*" I snarled, with crossed arms and narrowed eyes.

"Can I come in?" he begged.

"Whatever you have to say, you can say it right here."

"All right. You know that Dad's a dentist, and there are times when his practice gets pretty busy. However, what he told me last night was this: to never, *never* sacrifice your family on the altar of your career. Yes, I want to be among the best attorneys in the country, but without you to share that success with me, it would be meaningless. I give you my word, Juanita, I will always keep our family first."

I pondered his words in silence for a good minute—I wanted him to suffer just a little bit longer—before I uncrossed my arms and let him inside. Mama and Papa saw us and made some transparent excuse of going to the grocery store and left. When I was sure they actually did leave and weren't listening at the front door, I turned to Earl. "Maybe—just maybe—I did overreact a bit yesterday. The thing is, we need to talk about these things. The better we communicate, the stronger we are as a couple."

"Wise beyond your years, aren't you?" he said with a little smile.

"Could be." I found myself smiling back. "Mama always said I had a lot of good common sense. I accept your apology, Earl. You realize, of course, that I will hold you to it. Now, there are two things you can do right now to make it up to me."

"Sure. What?"

"First, kiss me. Next, take me to see that new movie that came out—*Sorry, Wrong Number.*"

"I think I can manage that," was his sexy reply as he wrapped his arms around me and went in for that kiss.

I wanted to savor every moment of June 26, 1948—my wedding day. Mama was in her glory as mother of the bride, and Cassandra was a stunning matron of honor; her new husband, Vince, was sitting on an aisle seat in the sanctuary, totally enamored of her when she processed down the aisle. Donna was among my bridesmaids, what with Eli standing up for Earl as best man. Mama, in schoolteacher fashion, had "the talk" with me about my wifely duties in the marriage bed a few weeks previously. Cassandra, being a newlywed of nine months, told me what I considered "the real deal," and it certainly sounded nothing like a duty to me. The sheer anticipation of the delights of the wedding night, in fact, had me fanning myself at the oddest moments.

As part of our wedding ceremony, Papa lent me one of his prized possessions—a book of poetry autographed by his namesake, given to him by his parents. Before we said our vows, Earl and I each read a poem from it to each other, something that made the day even more special. In my satin and lace wedding gown with an eight-foot train, my hair styled into a sleek pageboy, surrounded by our wedding party, our families and intimate friends, Rev. Walker pronounced us husband and wife. As for the kiss, suffice it to say that my toes nearly curled in my ankle-strap pumps.

Earl definitely put in the time and money to give us a honeymoon in the Cayman Islands. Prior to that, the only beaches where I had ever spent any time were on the city lakes or along the Mississippi River. Spending time on the Seven Mile Beach, something I'd only seen on postcards or inside books, was romantic and breathtaking. We saw sights like the Pedro St. James Museum and the nature walks of Cayman Brac. Being able to share that with Earl was wonderful, and we made sure we took plenty of photos. Shopping really wasn't his cup of tea, but he put up with it for my sake. As for the nights, well…

I'd experienced plenty of Earl's kisses by the time we reached our honeymoon suite, and I was ready for a whole lot more. From the persistent erection I felt when he held me close, I knew that so was he. Slowly, and I mean slowly, he undressed me, planting heated kisses on each spot that he bared. I felt warm and dewy in my feminine core. Of course, I couldn't let him have all the fun, and undressing him was a treat. Seeing how aroused he was, and knowing I was the one to have that effect on him, had me heady with confidence and boldness, which was confirmed by his deep moans as we rubbed our nude bodies together.

I loved the way Earl licked and caressed my breasts, sucking my nipples to distraction. I didn't think that a woman could feel pleasure when a man put his head down between her legs, but my

17

husband proved me wrong, in an extremely satisfying way. The fact that I made a lot of sound during lovemaking really turned him on. When he was pumping and thrusting inside me, steadily increasing the tempo, I moaned and screamed my head off like the hooker in *Ruthless People*. And when the crashing waves of orgasm swept us away, there was no doubt in my mind that Earl and I would be doing this for a long, long, long time.

When we returned from our honeymoon, grinning from ear to ear, both of us went back to work. With Earl's aspirations of a law degree in the works, it would take both of us working for a while to achieve that end. Yes, the Baby Boom had already begun in the U.S., but Earl and I agreed to wait a few years before having children—at least, until he graduated from law school and passed the bar exam. Although they wanted grandchildren, Mama and Papa didn't have a problem with our decision. Mother and Father Berry weren't pleased about it, but they had no choice in the matter. I suspected their attitude stemmed from the fact that Eldon and Elaine had been married for three years and they were still childless.

We set up housekeeping in an upstairs duplex at 3847 Second Avenue South, in the days before the houses across the street were torn down to make way for Interstate 35W. Earl had saved up enough money to buy his first car, a 1939 Ford sedan, which made getting around much easier. While he hit the books and cleaned office buildings, I had moved up to the position of office manager at work.

We spent our free time with family as well as our friends, Eli and Donna. That summer, when they announced their engagement, I shouted with delight for them. I had to laugh when Donna told me about Aurelia's big scene when they broke the news—typical for Aurelia. Earl kidded Eli as he shook his hand, saying, "Well, she's got you, man, eight ways from Sunday." It was also a sad time for me as well, when Vince and Cassandra moved to Seattle because of a job transfer. I knew I'd miss Cassandra. Still, ours was a friendship that endured, through letters, phone calls, and periodic visits to one another until Cassandra died unexpectedly in 1993.

Eli and Donna's wedding was the social event of the season in 1949, and we were honored to be part of the wedding party. There was no question of who Donna's matron of honor would be—any woman who dared to usurp that position would have been looking down the barrel of a .45 in Aurelia's hand. As for best man, Earl considered it his sworn duty to return the favor for his best friend and running buddy.

In the fall of 1950, we were well settled into married life. Earl was into his final year of law school, I had received an excellent appraisal at work, and my parents had geared up for another school year. My mother-in-law was singing the "Grandbaby Blues," since neither Eldon nor Earl had given her one yet. There were times when we dreaded going over to their house for dinner, knowing where the conversation would go. When Mother Berry came by to visit, she'd look at our spare room and sigh, "That would make such a lovely nursery." I really felt sympathy for Elaine, who had had to endure this from her longer than me.

On the other hand, Mrs. Edwards was giving her annual fall party, and we had been invited to attend. Going to one of her parties was always a treat. We never knew who might turn up there; as Eli would say, "Mother has her methods." That year her special guest was Benjamin O. Davis, Sr., the first Black general in the U.S. Armed Forces. Considering the fact that the Armed Forces was officially desegregated the previous year, his attendance was timely.

Donna had really come into her own as part of the Edwards family. I, for one, was happy for her and for her relationship with Mrs. Edwards. She was patient and understanding when I shared my own feelings about my mother-in-law situation, which had me taking aspirin for the headaches I got after a visit from her. That evening, though, it was time to forget about all that, and my eyes lit up when I saw how Donna was decked out for the party.

"Donna, you look fabulous."

"Thank you, Juanita. I love your dress, too. Where did you get it?"

"Oreck's. Once I saw it, I knew it would be perfect for the party."

Donna looked toward the other side of the room, where Mr. Edwards and Earl had their heads together. "You know, I think Melvin has something planned for Earl."

"Really?" I beamed.

Donna nodded and lowered her voice. "I overheard Eli and his father talking the other day when we were here. Once Earl graduates, doors are going to open for him. But don't let on that you know. Just act like it's business as usual."

"You'd better believe I will." I smiled at the prospect of Earl's career taking off like a rocket. "And when he makes his announcement, we want you two to be there to celeb...."

"Juanita, are you all right?" Donna asked me, her eyes showing concern.

"I don't know...I feel...I feel..." Ladylike or not, I knew I had to run to the bathroom in a hurry. Charging through the crowd, I jerked open the bathroom door. No sooner did I lift the toilet seat when I tossed my cookies. When my stomach had nothing left to heave up and I flushed the vomit, I was aware of someone behind me. "Oh... Mama," I sighed, wondering what her knowing look was all about.

"Are you all right now?" she asked, helping me off the floor.

"I don't think I could eat a thing tonight." I held my stomach and looked in the mirror. "I look ghastly. I don't get this. I never throw up."

"Well, you may be doing that...for a short time, anyway. But it looks like your career plans are going to change."

I wiped my face and pulled out my lipstick. Before I applied it, I thought about what Mama just said and turned to her. "What does my getting sick have to do with my plans?"

Mama gave me that knowing smile again. "That was the first sign."

"Of *what*?"

"That I was pregnant with you. Juanita, I would strongly suggest you go and see your doctor, but I'm sure he'll tell you the same thing," she said, giving me a gentle hug.

I was in something of a fog when we came out of the bathroom, where Donna was waiting in the hallway. "Are you all right? You look strange."

"She'll be all right," Mama said, glowing. "All it is…well, I'll let her tell you." As Mama walked off into the crowd, I could swear her feet weren't touching the ground.

Donna took me over to a couple of vacant seats, ready for a revelation. "All right, Juanita. What's going on? Why did you rush out of here so fast?"

I happened to see Earl some distance away talking to Mr. Edwards. He nodded at me, and I smiled and gave him a little wave. I turned back to Donna. "Well, I got sick."

"Sick?"

"Yes. Mama says it's morning sickness."

Donna's eyes lit up with glee. "Oh, Juanita…"

I felt myself caught up in the moment and I beamed as I said it out loud. "I'm going to see the doctor as soon as possible, but…I'm going to have a baby."

Donna gave me a big hug. "Have you told Earl yet?"

"No, not yet. Mama had to tell me just now. As soon as I see my doctor, I'll tell him. I can hardly wait. Now, will you promise not to tell anyone? Not even Eli?"

"Cross my heart. Aurelia won't even be able to get it out of me. Can I get you something to eat?"

"Please, no. Maybe some club soda."

After Donna went off for refreshments, Mrs. Edwards happened to walk by. "Hello, Juanita," she said with the graciousness of the reigning society hostess she was.

"Mrs. Edwards," I said. "This has been a wonderful party."

"Thank you. Your mother said you were a little under the weather this evening."

"I was, but I'm better now. Much better."

"Good." She leaned in close and lowered her voice, giving me the same knowing smile Mama wore. "At this time, it's very important to care of yourself." My jaw dropped in surprise. *How did she know?* "Don't worry, Juanita. Your secret is safe with me until you're ready. I know Earl will be positively delighted when you tell him. Congratulations."

As Mrs. Edwards walked off to work the room in regal hostess style, I sat there with my mouth still open for about 10 seconds before I remembered to close it. Was there anything in this town she didn't know about? I could only be thankful that Mr. and Mrs. Edwards were staunchly in our corner. Powerful friends like that don't just drop out of the sky, and heaven help the persons who had the audacity to cross them.

That Monday I took time off from work to see my doctor to be tested. Over the next few days I'd grown more certain than ever that I was pregnant, and the test was merely a formality. Earl was getting a little curious about my decreased appetite for breakfast, so I was anxious to get my results as quickly as possible.

On Wednesday afternoon of the following week I came home from work and prepared our dinner. I knew Mama would probably be waiting by the phone after she came home from school, but first things first. Earl appeared fatigued, what with work and his studies, so I had some of our favorite songs playing on the phonograph. As we ate and talked about our day, Earl gave me a tired but gratifying smile.

"I had a talk with Mr. Edwards the other day," he said.

"Really? How was it?"

"It was better than I ever imagined. He told me about an opening in the law firm that represents him. In fact, I met with them today, and they're interested in bringing me on board once I pass the bar."

"Honey, that's wonderful," I beamed. "I always knew you had what it takes. And our children will know it, too."

"I know they will, when they get here."

I gave my husband a fat smile. "Like next spring, for example?"

Earl's mouth dropped. When he was able to form words, he said, "Baby, did you just say…" I nodded, still smiling as Earl leaped from his seat and took me into his arms.

When we went to visit his parents and broke the news, Mother Berry literally shouted for joy, almost like women in Pentecostal churches do when they "get happy." She was on the phone to all her friends proclaiming her expected grandchild in moments. At church, she eagerly shared the news with the church mothers. Mrs. Edwards never let on that she already knew of my condition when Mother Berry told her; she merely gave me a gracious hug and a smile of congratulations. That was the beginning of an even closer relationship with my mother and my mother-in-law, complete with many pearls of wisdom and advice about expectant motherhood.

Donna and I talked on numerous occasions about what it would be like if our kids united our families. I was excited for Donna when winter came along, and she found out she too was pregnant. When we got together, we could discuss pregnancy and babies nonstop, in addition to her sister-in-law Debbi's upcoming wedding. In March of 1951 I went on maternity leave, which was just as well since the snowfall that month was relentless. Mother Berry was a constant visitor during the week. So was Mama, after school was out and she got Papa squared away with dinner. Of course, there was friendly disagreement about what I would have. Mama and Mother Berry were certain I would have a girl, and Papa and Father Berry were equally certain I would have a boy. Earl was also betting on a boy, which left me playing the role of diplomat.

March, in weather sayings, went "out like a lion." Easter Sunday came on March 25, and the 20 inches of snow that was on the ground was enough to discourage any Easter parade. That people actually made it to church was a miracle in itself, what with so many people snowed in. It was no surprise that the schools were closed the next day, either. With my due date practically around the corner, I was concerned about making it to the hospital. So was Earl, and it showed by the vigor with which he kept the sidewalks and the driveway cleared, and the car in top running condition courtesy of Lucius Gray's mechanics.

With the onset of April, we started to breathe easier. Temperatures crept above 32 degrees and combined with rain to melt the snow. I was in what was called the "nesting stage" that happens during the last month of pregnancy and it showed up in the amount of cooking I did—enough to have both families over for dinner. Earl and I were also speculating, at this point, on the possibility of the baby's arrival on April 17, Earl's 25th birthday. His response was, "Now *that* would the best birthday present of all."

I had been feeling somewhat out of sorts during the second week of April. My doctor told me the baby could come at any time, so Earl stayed close to home. On the afternoon of April 10, I had been resting, drinking tea, and listening to the radio while Earl sat at the dining room table studying. It had rained earlier during the day, but the weather reports predicted storms later in the evening. I walked to the nursery, looking longingly at the crib with the anticipation of seeing a baby in it when the phone rang.

"Honey, it's Donna," Earl called from the kitchen.

I plodded over to the telephone and picked it up. "Hi, Donna. How's everything?"

"Fine. Eli's taking me out for my birthday next week."

"Sounds like fun," I said, remembering that Donna's birthday was the day before Earl's. "Did he tell you where?"

"No. He wants to surprise me."

"The way that man worships the ground you walk on, I have no doubt he'll do it up right," I said with a chuckle.

"Have you been able to get that man of yours out of the books long enough to take a break?"

"Yes, thank God. He took me to the movies the other night."

"Good. What did you see?"

"*The Day the Earth Stood Still.* The movie had a great storyline."

"That sounds like something right up Eli's alley. I think I'll put a little bug in his ear."

"Great. We can compare notes. So, how's the baby?"

"Good. The doctor said everything's fine, but he kept checking for heartbeats."

"Why?"

"Because I'm so big for six months."

"You're not having twins, are you?"

"No. Every time I go, it's the same results. Lillian told me from the git-go that I'd have a big baby, and I'm starting to believe her," she sighed. "But what about you, Juanita? I half expected you to be in the hospital by now."

"I know. I'm ready for it all to be over. But Mama and Mother Berry keep saying to be patient, and the baby will come when it…" My breath stopped when the back pain hit.

"Juanita? Juanita?"

I tried to stifle a groan, but I was unsuccessful against the strange pain that coursed through me. According to Mama, that meant only one thing. "Donna, it's time to go."

"Are you sure?"

"Well, I felt these twinges about 20 minutes ago, but they're stronger now."

"Girl, you'd better go. Tell Earl to let us know what happens, OK?"

I hung up the phone and made my way into the dining room. "Earl."

He heard the funny tone of my voice and looked up. I nodded in answer to the question in his eyes. "OK, let's get this show on the road," he said, doing his best to stay calm as he called the doctor and left messages for my parents at their schools.

As we went out the door to the car, I heard a pitiful meow near the steps. When I looked over to my left, I saw her. Her black fur was plastered to her body from the rain, and I knew she had to be cold and miserable. Our eyes met, and my heart melted. I bent over—at least, as much as I could—and extended my hand. Cautiously she approached me, sniffing my hand before she allowed me to pet her.

"Honey, we need to get to the hospital," I heard Earl say with urgency in his voice.

"We can't leave her out here," I insisted. "Besides, the doctor said we could wait until the contractions are 10 minutes apart. The least we can do is dry her off and give her something. Now could you please go inside and get a towel?"

"But honey…"

25

"Please?"

Baby or no baby, Earl knew when he was fighting for a lost cause. He sighed in resignation and went inside, while I scooped up the cat and followed him. While Earl was standing there looking at his watch, I fussed over my new friend and dried her with the towel. In a burst of intuition, I told Earl to get the cardboard boxes we were going to throw away, along with some dirt I was going to use for plants. By the time we finished setting up a makeshift bed and litter box and left her with a saucer of milk, I had another contraction. This time, Earl wasn't taking no for an answer. With my suitcase in hand he helped me out to the car.

Our respective parents arrived just after the dinner hour, so I was told. I, however, was in the maternity ward, experiencing the kind of pain you simply cannot describe. Meanwhile, the thunderstorms had kicked in, the kind reminiscent of 1930s horror movies from Universal Studios.

These were the kind of labor pains I hadn't bargained for when I signed on to the ranks of motherhood. 22 hours of pain, screaming, and torture. It was like being the heroine in *Werewolf of London*, when she laid eyes on her mad-scientist husband after he turned into a werewolf. My thoughts at the time were far less fearful; I would have ripped the werewolf to shreds and dumped the remains into a vat of molten silver. Between the storms outside and the storms in labor and delivery, my family whiled away the hours in the waiting room in anticipation of the big event.

My parents normally didn't miss days at school, but the impending arrival of their first grandchild was a notable exception to their rule. As for Mother Berry, a tyrannosaurus couldn't have run her out of there—she probably would have roasted it on a giant spit if one had come near her. And so, when I gave birth to Sylvia Lois Berry at three p.m. on April 11, 1951, the Berrys and the Langstons were all there to get their first glimpse of her through the viewing glass.

Later, Earl came to my room to see about me and he got to hold his seven-pound, seven-ounce daughter for the first time. I heard the awe in his voice when he talked to her, the smile on his face and the tenderness in his eyes complimented by tears of joy. I could understand it, because I was crying, too. In later years, when people saw the brilliant attorney in the courtroom, I knew they wouldn't be able to picture the sensitive side of him when it came to his children. I knew, though, and so did those closest to him.

It was a joyous time of celebration for our family when Earl passed—or should I say, aced--the bar exam that June. On that particular day, after I put Sylvia down for her nap, Elaine and Donna came by. Donna was eight months pregnant but looked like she was ready to go to the hospital any minute. We had been getting all the juicy details from her about the scandal that Claudette Jennings caused when she soiled her evening gown at an Edwards party when Earl came home. Earl was bursting with excitement at his good fortune, topped by a meeting with Melvin Edwards that set his legal career off to an amazing start. As he regaled us with the events of his day, I remembered the conversation Donna and I had the previous fall, beaming with happiness for him as Donna gave me a covert wink.

The only thing that exceeded Earl's satisfaction with his career as an attorney was watching our family grow. It seemed as though all the wives in the community were either pregnant or nursing; then again, we were living in that period of history known as the Baby Boom. Even Ethel Waters, the cat I had taken in as a pet, had a litter of kittens every year until she was 10. My having Sylvia only served to whet Mother Berry's appetite for more grandchildren. Fortunately, Earl's passion pole never shot blanks, and his amazing ardor in the bedroom kept a certain smile on my face. The fruits of our love were Deshawna in 1952, Linda in 1954, and LaVera in 1955.

With that many children born so close together, it was necessary for me to resign my position. I had made good money, and it went into our savings account as part of our nest egg. Fortunately, Earl's new salary more than made up for mine when I became a stay-at-home mother. Seeing Mama and Mother Berry's delight when they had the opportunity to babysit—and spoil—our daughters was gratifying, yet I couldn't help but feel for Eldon and Elaine at family gatherings.

Sure, Eldon was doing well, being in practice with his father and now Dr. Berry in his own right. However, I knew how much they wanted children. They loved their nieces, and to see the pain in Elaine's eyes as the years went by was heartbreaking.

Our family was doing well during the summer of 1956. Earl's law practice was prospering, and with my office and accounting skills the books reflected and furthered that prosperity. On top of that, he had made partner in the firm. As a criminal defense attorney, he won and lost his share of cases, but I knew that came with the territory. Investments we made through Edwards Enterprises were reaping dividends. We had moved into a comfortable three-bedroom house at 3728 Third Avenue South, across the street from Bryant Jr. High School and a block away from my parents. Our 1953 Buick sedan was still in very good condition, but with four children it was time to get a second car. As blessings would have it, Debbi Hendricks' husband Woody was a car salesman, and he gave us a good deal on a 1955 Chevy station wagon.

It was a good thing we did, for soon afterwards I came home from an appointment with Dr. Bradford, beaming as I told Earl, "I'm pregnant." Donna, of course, was thrilled for me when I gave her the news; so was Debbi, since she was five months pregnant with her second child. Eli, who was there at the time, had a funny look in his eye. When he came out of it, he said cryptically, "You're not the only one who has news, Juanita. Your brother-in-law is going to be a very happy man soon."

I flew over to their house to see Elaine. She was glowing. She was absolutely euphoric, raising her hands to God and giving thanks and praise. After 11 years of marriage, her doctor had given her the news she'd been waiting so long to hear. "I'm pregnant, Juanita. I'm pregnant!" she exclaimed. We went to visit them the day after she gave Eldon the news, and he still hadn't come off the ceiling. To celebrate the joyous tidings, the four of us went off to the movies to see *The Girl Can't Help It*.

Father Berry was in his glory with congratulations for Eldon. No one could keep the huge, ecstatic grin off Mother Berry's face, having both her daughters-in-law pregnant while her granddaughters lavished affection upon her. As Elaine and I got bigger and started wearing maternity clothes—which Elaine could hardly wait to wear—so did Mother Berry's grin. Eldon claimed well-deserved bragging rights along with Earl about the coming babies, not to mention that satisfied grin men get when the fruit of their love becomes evident. Mama just wore a fat smile through it all; I'm sure she felt compensated for having an only child by all the grandchildren she was getting from me.

It was truly a time of praise and great celebration for Eldon and Elaine when, on Valentine's Day of 1957, they became the parents of seven-pound, six-ounce Ellen Ernestine Berry. I can only imagine how many cigars Eldon passed out, but I wasn't surprised when I saw Earl, Eli, Woody Hendricks, and Jerry Edwards carrying a few extra ones around. Mother and Father Berry, I'm sure, told everyone they knew about their new granddaughter, putting emphasis on the fact that Ellen's middle name was in honor of her grandmother. Yes, Mother Berry was positively giddy. It didn't stop there, though. Two weeks later—to the day—Earl and I became parents to our fifth child, seven-pound, eight-ounce Chauntice Laverne Berry.

Our beautiful daughters were a joy to us even as they kept us busier than we ever dreamed, and in 1958 I was pregnant again. We were happy, of course, and started planning for another daughter to add to the Berry clan. January 25, 1959, however, brought us the unexpected. When I came out from under the anesthetic after my C-section, Dr. Bradford told me, "Congratulations, Mrs. Berry. You have a son—eight pounds, two ounces."

I was in shock, but the good kind. From what people told me, so was Earl at first. Afterwards, he was shouting like men do these days when they win $20,000 in the fast-money round on *Family Feud.* As for Father Berry and Papa, they felt vindicated. They nearly bought out the cigar store and generously shared the proceeds with their friends. For Papa, who had recently secured a position as an English teacher at North High School, my son's birth made it a banner year.

When Earl came to see me in my hospital bed and our son was brought in, he was overwhelmed. I knew he would never show favoritism when it came to our children, but there is just something about men and their sons. We had been so sure we'd have another girl that we hadn't considered any boys' names. However, as I saw Earl holding him the perfect name came to me.

"Earl, I just thought of a name."

"Name?" He appeared somewhat distracted; of course, that had everything to do with the baby in his arms. "Oh, right. He needs a name."

"Well, I thought we could name him Carter Woodson Berry. You know, after Carter G. Woodson."

"Hmm," he said. "The father of Black history. Hmm." I watched my husband as he processed the name through his legal mind. "Juanita, I like it. It has character and history behind it." I beamed as Earl declared to our newborn son, "Carter Woodson Berry, you have quite a legacy behind you."

On the evening of August 19, 1960 Earl and I, Eldon and Elaine, and Donna and Eli were gathered at Eldon and Elaine's new house at 4054 Clinton Avenue, enjoying a barbecue. It was a warm but comfortable summer evening. Eldon, like most men, considered himself a master at the art of all things that could be barbecued on a grill. Our children were playing in the back yard after they ate, while we sat back in the lawn chairs and talked. We had already discussed the movie we went to the previous evening, *Butterfield 8*, and now we were on to politics.

"So, what do you think Kennedy's chances are at the presidency?" Eldon asked Earl.

"Well, I know we're going to vote for him," was Earl's hearty reply.

"If we are, I hope this baby waits until after the inauguration to get here." Elaine rubbed her softly rounded stomach, partially concealed by her sleeveless maternity top. "I want to see what Jackie's going to wear to the inaugural ball after she has her baby."

I took a sip of root beer. "You know, she's going to set some fashion trends around the country."

"Anyway, I hope Kennedy makes some changes for civil rights," Eldon said, getting up to go inside the house. He came out after a minute and said, "Elaine, I'm going to get some more beer. Do you want anything?"

"Bring some Coca-Cola. We want to make some ice cream floats for the kids."

"Got it." Eldon gave Elaine a kiss, flashing a smile as he walked to the driveway where their 1958 DeSoto hardtop was parked. "I'll be back."

Donna, Elaine, and I continued to talk about Jackie Kennedy as a fashion trendsetter. Earl and Eli discussed the finer points of owning a Cadillac, in particular the 1957 Cadillac we bought from Woody at the beginning of summer. When Earl first saw Perry Mason driving that model on the TV show, he had to have one like it. There were times when it was wise to concede to one's husband—I benefitted from the deal with a 1958 Buick station wagon as an anniversary present.

We must have talked for a good twenty minutes or so, enough to notice it was nearing sunset. Carter had fallen asleep in my lap, so Elaine and I went into the house to find someplace comfortable and safe to put him down. Donna soon joined us with her youngest son Julian, who had also pooped out.

"I wonder where Eldon is?" Elaine asked. "At this rate, the kids will all be asleep by the time he gets back."

"It shouldn't be too long," Donna answered as she put Julian down. "The stores are going to be closing soon."

As time went by, however, we grew more concerned. Just going to get beer and soda shouldn't have taken Eldon so long. We talked on, but the atmosphere started to cloud over with unease. "Why don't I go down to the store and see what's holding him up?" Earl offered.

"That sounds like a good idea," Elaine said. "Sometimes he gets to talking with people in the neighborhood that come in the store."

We rounded up the kids and brought them inside as twilight made its appearance. Earl grabbed his keys and prepared to leave when we heard a knock at the front door. I saw the puzzled look on Elaine's face upon seeing the two men standing on the steps. "Yes?"

They identified themselves as police detectives and asked her, "Are you Mrs. Eldon Berry?"

"Yes, I'm Mrs. Berry. What's this about?"

"Mrs. Berry, we're here to give you some news," one of them said solemnly.

We didn't like the way he said 'news,' and the apprehension grew worse. "What kind of news?" Earl asked.

"Mrs. Berry, a man was shot and killed about an hour ago."

Elaine grew tense. "What does that have to do with me?"

"He was identified by his driver's license as Eldon Berry. We're sorry for your loss."

To her credit, Elaine didn't faint or scream—she was more stunned—but we could see how hard the news hit her. She clutched the door frame for support. I heard the tears in her voice when she said, "Where is he?"

"He's been taken to the morgue, Mrs. Berry. But we need to ask you some questions."

"Can't that wait until she's gone to identify him?" Earl adopted his take-charge stance. "You've just told her that her husband's dead."

"We're sorry, but we need to do this while things are fresh in her mind."

Earl's expression was strained, but his voice was strong and controlled. "I'm Earl James Berry. I'm his brother, and I'm also an attorney. We're going to the morgue. You can ask all the questions you want in the morning."

I grabbed Elaine's purse and handed it to her, still in disbelief over the grim report the police had given us. "You go ahead with Earl," I told her. "We'll stay here with the kids until you get back."

When they returned, I saw the pain and raw grief in their faces over the reality of Eldon's lifeless body lying in the city morgue. Elaine's tears came gradually after she sat down, with Eli and Donna doing whatever they could to comfort her. My husband held me in his arms. I could feel his body shaking with unreleased sobs, sobs on the inside. It seemed like untold moments passed before he could compose himself, saying to me, "Honey, could you stay here with Elaine? There's something I have to do."

"Of course," I agreed, knowing where he was going and how difficult it would be for him to deliver that horrible news. No matter what people think, there's never an easy way to tell parents that their child is dead, even a grown child. I noticed the older children standing around with confused looks on their faces. *Oh, the news. How are we going to tell them?*

Eldon's funeral was an ordeal we got through only by the grace of God. The senselessness of his death was lost on no one. People had so many good things to say about him as they expressed their sympathy to the family. Mother Berry had her head on Father Berry's shoulder during the packed service, the life force seemingly drained out of her. Earl's face had a grim expression on it, one that swore revenge on the perpetrator of this crime even as they lowered his brother's body into the ground. Eli and Donna, as well as the rest of the Edwards family, also attended the funeral and stood by us during that difficult time. I was grateful Earl had a friend like Eli, another rock he could depend on.

As soon as the trial date was set, the Berry family was there, with the Edwards family and my parents providing solid moral support. When the defendant was brought in, Earl's body tensed up and his jaws grew tight. My eyes narrowed as I took a good look at the vile, monstrous beast that had callously taken the life of my brother-in-law. In that instant I wished that Minnesota had the death penalty, but I had to settle for the thought of him rotting in a prison cell for the rest of his miserable life.

At the age of 37, Eldon had been struck down in the prime of his life. He had had so much to look forward to. With a wonderful wife like Elaine, the family he'd always wanted, plus an excellent career working side by side with his father, why did this have to happen to him?

I came to the trial whenever I could, but Earl and his parents were there every day. The case seemed cut-and-dry to us; the defendant was robbing a store and Eldon was killed trying to stop him. What could be clearer than that? Unfortunately, the defendant got off on a technicality.

I remember sitting there in the courtroom with Earl, Elaine, Mother and Father Berry, wanting to scream obscenities at the judge for a miscarriage of justice but too stunned to say a word. I glared at the defendant and his attorney congratulating themselves, hoping that they would be driven to walk into the Amazon River and become lunch for a school of piranhas. I didn't have to go far to see that same look in Elaine's eyes.

To say that the verdict left a bad taste in our mouths was a gross understatement. There may have been celebration about President Kennedy's election, but there was a pall over our family during the holidays. I could only imagine what it was like for Elaine, having a three-year-old child and pregnant with another, one who would never know his or her father except through others. Elaine's doctor had been concerned that the stress of Eldon's death and going through the trial could cause her to either lose the baby or go into premature labor. Her doctor, however, hadn't reckoned with the steely resolve of the Berry family to both protect and support Elaine and Ellen. In addition, the family stood firmly on God's promises of protection for them. We knew He never failed.

Earl had changed when it came to his work. He was tense, just "doing his job" without the passion. He often came home from work short-tempered and testy, to the point where the children were hesitant to approach him. I often had to intervene, and the tension between us could be felt. In addition to that, our sex life had taken a nosedive. The fact that Eldon's murderer had walked was eating away at the family. Something had to be done.

On New Year's Day of 1961 we were all in church, listening to our pastor's sermon. Earl was unusually quiet, hardly saying a word during fellowship time. That night, after all the kids were in bed, he turned to me and said, "I've come to a decision."

"What kind of decision?"

"About my work."

I was puzzled. "What do you mean?"

"I've had enough of being a defense attorney." He must have read the question in my eyes, because he added, "No, Juanita, I'm not giving up law. But I am changing it."

"But how?"

"Tomorrow, I'm having papers drawn up to have my partners buy me out."

"That still doesn't tell me how you're changing things when it comes to practicing law."

"Because I'm putting in for a position at the district attorney's office. I'm going to become an assistant district attorney."

I looked into his smoky gold eyes. Never had he been more serious than at that moment. "This change…it has something to do with Eldon, doesn't it?"

There was steely conviction in his voice. "If I couldn't get justice for my brother at the trial, then I can get it for others. The only way to do that is to become a prosecutor."

Tammy Wynette put out a song years ago called "Stand by Your Man." We spent half the night discussing the matter, but by the time we went to bed I was convinced that his decision was merited, and I stood by him. It was as though the negative energy Earl had been carrying around diffused, for he took me in his arms and made up for all those nights we had gone without.

Our family and friends created a shield around us. Melvin Edwards, in empathy with Earl's motivation, gave him a business referral that couldn't be ignored. We saw the move not only as a way to get justice for Eldon, but for Elaine as well. Eldon had left her well provided for and we all rallied around her when, on January 31, 1961, Elizabeth Regina Berry was born. Though it was a bittersweet moment, we all prayed Eldon could see and watch over his newborn daughter from heaven.

Earl took a passion to his new duties in the district attorney's office. When the children were in school, I would sometimes sit in on some of the trials he prosecuted. When he presented a case, examining prosecution witnesses and cross-examining defense witnesses, I often thought, *That's another one for Eldon.* He racked up an impressive record of convictions during the twelve years he served as an assistant district attorney. Of course, being one of the very few African Americans in that office, everything he did was closely watched.

I remember well a case in the spring of 1965 that he was on, the Sheree Madsen case. Sometimes I wonder if the weather was an indication of the heinousness of the crime, since it went to trial a few days after the supertornado outbreak on May 6 of that year. Child molestation cases didn't get the kind and degree of press they do today largely because of the reluctance to report them, but this one made it to trial.

The girl's mother made a very strong witness, and Sheree's testimony was damaging. I'm sure Earl was thinking about our children as he made his spellbinding closing argument. The jury was out barely an hour before they returned with a guilty verdict, and the defendant, Malcolm Wesley, received the maximum sentence. The accompanying press coverage solidified my husband's career as a crusader for justice. Our children in turn looked at him as a man who "put the bad people away."

Earl wasn't the only one in the family who made a change in career paths. Though Eldon left her financially well off, Elaine made the decision to go into the work force, and in 1964 she became a court reporter in Hennepin County. It was no surprise to me, and we were there to support her in whatever way we could, often having Ellen and Elizabeth over at our house until Elaine got off work. Shortly before she started working at the courthouse, she told us, "Even though I wish that scum of the earth would die in a vat of sulfuric acid, I can't spend my life being angry and bitter. Eldon wouldn't have wanted that, and I have to think of our daughters. What I can do is be a part of justice."

Her career flourished, yet Elaine Madison Berry never remarried. Call it "old school," but she's a woman who exemplifies the term "one-man woman." No other man, in her mind, could ever compare to Eldon Berry.

My husband didn't lose many cases when they went to trial, even on appeal, contrary to the tongue-waggers who spitefully considered him a "one-case wonder." I, of course, would remind him to take a breather so he could reconnect with his family and friends. Some of his cases were more difficult than others, usually resulting in tight jaws when he came home. His patience was tried when the case was shaky, and witnesses were unreliable.

However, his commitment to justice was rewarded when, on January 8, 1973, he was appointed by the governor to serve as a criminal court judge in Hennepin County. At Earl's swearing-in ceremony, we were all standing proudly behind him. As an added treat, Lillian Edwards held a celebration party in his honor, no doubt because of Earl's amazing skill, ability, and integrity, which encouraged Melvin Edwards to add his influence in securing the appointment.

Meanwhile, our children were growing up. They had varying complexions between mine and Earl's, but they all had their father's stamp on them in the looks department, especially his smoldering, smoky gold eyes. Sylvia, Deshawna, and Linda got my natural hair, while LaVera, Chauntice and Carter got Earl's curly-wavy hair. When it came to our daughters, they had inherited my build, and they ranged in height from LaVera's 5'5" to Deshawna's 5'9". I could see Earl would have his hands full when it came to their suitors; I had to admit they all could set men on fire without even trying. Earl, of course, nipped certain ideas in the bud when they were teenagers. All their dates were taken into his study, and when they came out, they often had the look of young men who'd been staring down the barrel of a .38 for the entire time. Carter didn't have Earl's height—he stopped growing at 5'8" —but he had everything else, which meant that some young man's heart would not be safe if he ever turned on that Berry charm. The one thing I hoped for as we raised them was that they would have good taste in men, and hopefully one or more of them would marry an Edwards, as Donna and I often talked about and earnestly prayed for.

1973 brought other changes as well. Deshawna and Linda were in college, and LaVera was an honor student starting her senior year at Central High. The investments Earl made through Edwards Enterprises reaped great dividends, and so we purchased a new home at 4128 Columbus Avenue, right next door to our best friends Eli and Donna. Moving day came on July 1, and not a moment too soon.

Our oldest, Sylvia, had graduated from the University of Minnesota that spring, and on July 28 she married Clinton Lewis, an up-and-coming employee at Christopher Electronics. Earl was a proud and sentimental father of the groom as he walked her down the aisle, and Mama and I were shedding our share of tears when she and Clinton said their vows. After our pastor proclaimed, "I now present to you Clinton and Sylvia Lewis," in the back of my mind was, *One down, five to go.* Yes, even before Bill Cosby referenced it in his standup comedy act once the children reached a certain age, Earl and I had set the goal to get them out of the house.

The pain of Eldon's death never completely went away for Earl, and unknown to me he had been keeping tabs on his brother's murderer periodically. On the morning of August 19, 1978, Earl called me from the courthouse. "Juanita, I need you to get the family together. We're going out to Fort Snelling."

"Sure honey, but why?"

"I just received some news."

"What news?"

"It's about that monster that killed Eldon. He died today."

"He did? How did you know?"

"Eli told me."

This was huge, especially when Eli Edwards was involved. "How did he die?"

Earl spat the words out. "Cancer. Untreated cancer. He died a long, slow, painful, agonizing death from it."

I had zero sympathy for the man who just died, but I understood the reason behind my husband's request. "I'll take care of it, honey. And I'll make sure Eli and Donna are there."

"Thank you," was Earl's grateful reply.

By six p.m. all the Berry family, along with Eli and Donna Edwards and their family, were gathered around Eldon's headstone at the Fort Snelling National Cemetery. Those of us who were old enough to remember that day back in 1960 found ourselves referring to it, as we heard Father Berry say, "Eldon, my son, justice has been served. What the courts couldn't do, a disease did, and your killer paid dearly for what he did to you and to this family."

"What I couldn't do as a defense attorney, I was able to do as a prosecutor for others," Earl added in acknowledgment. "I couldn't bring him to the justice he deserved, but a power greater than us did that for us today. Your death could have broken us, but instead we became stronger. I know you would have wanted that. And Elaine, Ellen, Elizabeth, all of us, love you and carry you in our hearts."

Elaine lovingly placed a bouquet of flowers on his headstone as we said silent prayers in memory of Eldon. Finally, finally, we had closure. Of course, it couldn't bring Eldon back, but a certain weight of injustice had been lifted from us when we left the cemetery.

I never thought I would find myself sounding like Mother Berry—or Mama for that matter—but after Sylvia and Clinton were married, I was ready for grandchildren. Donna Gray Edwards became a grandmother in 1971 and we loved to fuss over little Darrell when his parents, Eli Jr. and Sandra, brought him over. Back then I wasn't quite ready to claim that title. However, once Sylvia gave us our first grandchild in 1975, Zora Hurston Lewis, I wanted as many as I could get, and with six children that was a lot of possibility.

My children did not disappoint me as one by one they married and gave me grandchildren, who in turn gave me great-grands. Carter and Julian did drag their feet for a while, but they finally kicked in and gave me two granddaughters by 1998. In fact, my youngest grandchild, Lillian Juanita Berry-Edwards, is the spitting image of me. You know I've been eating that up! As for Donna, having great-grands by the time her mother passed away in 1993, the younger generations soon afterwards called her Madear. She loved it, and she has been that ever since.

Earl's reputation as a tough but fair judge kept him on the bench, and he was re-elected every time. His character and integrity as an officer of the court were well beyond reproach. Being the wife of a judge, one who was formerly a district attorney, I had no illusions about Earl having universal popularity. He had many enemies among the criminals he prosecuted as an ADA and sentenced as a judge. Some were more vocal than others, swearing they would get even with him, or that they would make him pay for putting them away. We wound up getting non-published telephone numbers after some of those individuals called our house, screaming all manner of threats and obscenities at him. Even when he reached the mandatory retirement age of 70 in 1996, he had criminals and deadbeats seeking revenge for, as they put it, "ruining their lives." The logic of that reasoning completely escapes me. These were the kind of people who never believe they're guilty, that it's always someone else's fault.

Not that Earl lived his life in fear after retirement. For him, it represented another phase in his life. He was in demand as a speaker, sharing the benefit of his wisdom and experience in the area of law and being one of those trailblazers here in Minnesota. He and Eli were always as thick as thieves, and when Allan Beckley Christopher was in town, they were off and running, ready to go fishing at the drop of a hat during the season.

When Eli saw the World Trade Center attack in a vision and the authorities and bureaucrats didn't believe him, Earl was there to support him in the aftermath of that fateful day in 2001. From time to time he would visit former staff and cronies at the Government Center, even witnessing a budding romance for our oldest grandson Ricky. When my niece, Dr. Elizabeth Berry Chandler, took over her grandfather's dental practice, Earl felt a deep sense of vindication that the legacy of Father Berry and Eldon would continue.

As for me, I have my own interests as well as a network of friends and in-laws like Donna, Aurelia, Elaine, Debbi Hendricks, and Maureen Christopher. And of course, there is that special time Earl and I have together that is sacrosanct. So, so much to be thankful for...

Juanita sat down on the bed, satisfied with the outcome of Election Day as she prepared for slumber. Eli and Donna had shared their time of celebration over at their mansion on Lake of the Isles Parkway, along with their contemporaries like Debbi and Woody Hendricks and Aurelia and Rufus Barnett. Allan and Maureen Christopher had called earlier that evening to share in the festivities and give them the happenings in Chicago. Not only that, the couples had the opportunity to celebrate and reminisce with Eli and Donna on their 63rd wedding anniversary that night. Truly it was a night of victory, celebration, and love.

She counted her blessings, thankful that she could still get around under her own power, for good health, a sound mind, wonderful friends, and a strong, loving family. She laughed to herself when Mr. Boone was called upon by Earl to take him to Starbuck's for coffee and a cinnamon roll after they dropped her off at home. Earl and his nightly craving. Oh well, that's my husband; he's not about to change on that subject. I just hope he ordered decaf so he can let me sleep.

She couldn't swear to it, but from the open bedroom door she thought she heard someone pounding on the front door downstairs, followed by Mrs. Bynum's footsteps as she went to answer it. The voices were unclear, and the conversation was short. The sound of someone running up the stairs with urgency disturbed her. What was going on?

The footsteps stopped with the figure of her grandson Prentice standing in the doorway, Mrs. Bynum behind him. As she looked from one face to the other, Juanita knew in her heart that something was terribly wrong.

Sylvia Berry Lewis

I know it is such a cliché for a story to start out with, "It was a dark and stormy night," but that's what the weather was like when I was born on April 11, 1951. Hey, we're talking about Minnesota weather—go figure. It's a good thing my parents aren't superstitious, what with the drenched black cat that showed up outside as they went to the car for the trip to Fairview Hospital. According to the family story, Mama insisted on letting her inside the enclosed porch and giving her a saucer of milk, even though she was in labor with me. Daddy reluctantly granted her wishes, if only to keep her happy and calm. When I, Sylvia Lois Berry, came home from the hospital five days later, our family also wound up with a pet. Why Mama named the cat Ethel Waters I'll never know, but from that day until she died 16 years later, Ethel was a beloved member of the family.

My siblings and I are part of the Baby Boom generation, and during the 1950s we were part of the community, living a comparatively normal existence. Daddy made a good living as an attorney. Mama, who had worked as an office manager until Linda was born, opted to be a stay-at-home mom in order to make raising six children work, given that we were born so close together.

August 19, 1960 brought a change to that existence. Deshawna and I, being the oldest kids, knew something was wrong that evening at Uncle Eldon and Auntie Elaine's home. Uncle Eldon had gone to the store and never came back. Strangers came to the front door and Auntie Elaine was upset; so was Daddy when they left. The adults left behind—Mama and Mr. and Mrs. Eli Edwards—were acting strange. We asked them what the matter was, but they wouldn't give us a straight answer—at least, not until just before the funeral.

Being nine years old, it was hard to process the fact Uncle Eldon was dead. Prior to that, the only experience I had had with death was when one of Ethel's kittens died the year before. I had heard about people that died, like Mr. Edwards' grandparents, but it's different when it hits closer to home. Everyone was so sad. I know Daddy was, too, losing his brother and all, but he was angry as well, sometimes to the point where us kids were scared to say anything to him. It would be some years later when I learned the whole story behind Uncle Eldon's death, and why Daddy was so determined to become a prosecutor. When I think about those early days in his new career, Daddy would go to work with a look in his eye, that of a man on a mission—or should I say, a take-no-prisoners attitude.

When I was in ninth grade at Bryant Jr. High, John Edwards and I became close by virtue of our membership in the Creative Writing club. When we attended Central High, we were often on the phone talking about some story idea or another, not to mention our English assignments. The thing about it was, Mama and her best friend, Donna Gray Edwards, kept giving us these funny little smiles, like they were in on some secret. Common interests being what they are, our friendship spilled over into dating when we started high school, which our mothers were really pushing. Daddy, on the other hand, would sometimes give Mama a look as if to say, "Back off, honey."

It reached the point where my writer's curiosity got the best of me. Sure, John was one fine-looking man in his father's image, and I liked hanging out with him, but…wasn't I supposed to feel something else? One afternoon, though, I eavesdropped on our mothers while they were chatting, and I wasted no time in running to John.

"John, have you noticed how our mothers act when we're together?"

"They act weird, that's what."

"Well, it's not just weird. I overheard them a little earlier. They're scheming."

"Scheming like with us? To put us together?"

I nodded. "They want to see us married one day."

John shook his head in disbelief. "You're kidding, right?"

"No, I'm not. I think this is something they've been planning since we were little."

"But Sylvia, aren't we supposed to feel...I don't know...walking on air, gazing into each other's eyes and all that?"

I sighed. "Like our classmates. The only thing is, we've been going out and all that, but I still see you as a good friend—not as a boyfriend."

John looked at me in that way of his and said, "You know something? I think that's all we're meant to be—good friends."

"Too bad, Mama," I spoke to an imaginary image of my mother. "Your plans won't work with us."

"Sorry, Ma," John added. "Save your meddling for my brothers." After a good laugh, he asked me, "So, how's your new plotline coming along?"

John and I both graduated from Central with honors in 1969, with him going off to Drake University and me to the University of Minnesota. I knew long before I set foot on campus that literature would be my major. John and I were confidantes and pen pals, writing to each other about our classes, people we were dating, all the movements of social change in the country, radical changes on campus, etc.

It was at the beginning of summer 1972, amidst the Angela Davis trial and the Democratic National Convention that made for news stories of the day, that I found myself sitting at one of my favorite spots on the Mississippi River, not far from the West Bank side of the U of M campus. Ideas for a novella were buzzing around in my mind. Pulling out my pad and pen from my bag I started jotting them down, endeavoring to get the words out of my head for later work.

I reached the point where I had to take a break, looking up and out at the river with a relaxed sigh. I had wondered in the past why this happened whenever I was near the river or the lakes, until one of my English teachers talked about a writer's Muse. Although I received inspiration from many sources, my primary source, or Muse, was water. I could have mellowed out there all afternoon, but I had promised to meet up with Deshawna and Linda later. At that

44

moment I happened to look down the path, and what I saw, to say the least, was intriguing.

He was definitely one fine brotha, and even with his slight limp his walk was easy. His huge Afro reminded me of John's cousin, Wayne Hendricks. It added three inches to his 6'1" stature, and the sun had given him the complexion of a burnished golden brown. He was comfortably dressed in a tank top, khaki walking shorts and sandals, and I hoped I wasn't watching him as though I was studying him. My intuition told me, *This man has a story*, and I wanted to find out what it was. As he closed the distance between us, his eyebrows rose in interest as he said, "Hello."

"Hello to you, too," was my reply as I took in his eyes—studious yet sexy. "Enjoying the day?"

"Given the length of winter here, any time you get summer days in Minnesota is a time to enjoy." That comment, true as it was, still made us laugh. "What about you?"

"I couldn't agree with you more. You speak like a native."

"Of course." He cocked his head and checked me out. "Born and raised. By the way, my name's Clint. And yours?"

"Sylvia. I guess it takes one to know one." Knowing there were only three cities in the state that had significant Black populations, I asked him, "Minneapolis, St. Paul, or Duluth?"

"St. Paul. What about you?"

"Minneapolis. So, what brings you down here?"

"I like coming down here to relax and forget there's a city around me."

That was a familiar sentiment for me. "I come here to write and get ideas to write about."

Clint raised his eyebrows again. "Really? Has any of your work been published?"

"In college and high school anthologies. I hope to have a novel published one day."

The way he rocked back and forth was manly and captivating. I wanted to know more. I was looking for an inroad to continue our conversation when he said, "You know, Sylvia, this is the first time

45

I've been face to face with a writer, and I've always been curious about how they come up with ideas and plots. Do you mind if I sit down?"

"Go right ahead, Clint. I'd be most happy to answer your questions."

Clinton Lewis, as I learned, was born on V-J Day in the Rondo neighborhood, and a 1964 graduate of St. Paul Central High School. He attended St. Cloud State University, graduating in 1968 with a strong suit in the growing computer technology industry. After doing a tour of duty in Viet Nam, he was hired by Mr. Edwards when Christopher Electronics opened its Minneapolis branch in 1971, where he worked in production. He mentioned in passing that he received his limp and a Purple Heart from injuries he sustained while in Viet Nam. The guardedness I sensed about his time there told me not to press the issue—at least, not for the moment.

By the time I had to go, Clint had my phone number and we had a date to hear Gwendolyn Brooks, who was scheduled to be in town to share her poetry in a couple of weeks. Later, on the way to the Roller Garden in St. Louis Park, I found myself thinking about Clint and our conversation by the river, to the point where I didn't hear what Deshawna was saying until I heard, "After we go skating, we're going to the White Castle for their famous alligator burgers."

Realizing what she said, my face went into a frown. "Have you lost your mind?"

"Finally, you're back with us," she chided. "Now where were you and who were you with?"

"Deshawna, what makes you think I was with someone?"

"If you could have seen the look on your face," Linda threw in. "He must have been fine."

"Not only fine, but hot," Deshawna noted, leering at me out of the corner of her eye just before we got off Lake Street and pulled into the parking lot. We quickly found a parking space and I started to get out of her car, but my sisters weren't having it.

"Oh, no you don't, Sylvia." Linda blocked my exit. "We're not leaving this car until you give us the story about this guy."

Deshawna crossed her arms. "Start talking."

I did my best to keep it on an intellectual level, since Clint's mind was what stimulated my interest in him. Linda and Deshawna appreciated all of that, but they had to know the physical description as well. We finally went skating, and the entire time we were there they teased me when dudes would come up and ask me to skate with them, and I turned them down. "Sorry, but she has a man," Linda would blurt out despite the warning glares I gave her. Even so, while I did my routines on the floor, Clint's intriguing looks and personality did a pleasant slow dance in my head, stimulating my curiosity.

Gwendolyn Brooks was inspiring and enchanting, an excellent choice for a first date with Clint. Afterwards, we sat down at a coffee shop in Dinkytown, discussing her creative genius and our favorite poems of the evening. When Clint took me home in his 1970 Ford Galaxie 500, we listened to what is now known as "old school" music like the Ohio Players, the Stylistics, Al Green, and Kool and the Gang. We were glad it was summer because our only R&B station, KUXL, signed off at sundown.

I knew from experience how Daddy made potential boyfriends wish they were facing the gas chamber if their motives were questionable. When I brought Clint home to meet him in August, I took a cue from Lauren Bacall's character in *Dark Passage*—I held my breath and crossed my fingers. I wondered how long it would be before he cross-examined him like a guilty defendant on the witness stand; he was a master at that.

Mama exemplified all the social graces that evening, while my sisters were glued to their seats, fascinated by Clint yet waiting to see how the evening would play out. The fact that I was 21 was a mitigating factor, so I was prepared to do what I had to if Clint didn't meet with Daddy's standards. Granted, Daddy didn't care for Clint's huge Afro. However, his military service and his credentials from Christopher Electronics scored major points by the end of the evening. When Daddy and Clint went off to the study to talk about their respective tours of duty, I knew I could breathe easily.

Fall came along, and everyone was back in school—me in my senior year at the U of M, Deshawna at Iowa State, Linda starting her freshman year at Marquette University, LaVera and Chauntice at Central High, and Carter at Bryant Jr. High. I had started work on my senior paper, gathering my notes to do a comparative study of writers of the Harlem Renaissance vs. contemporary Black writers. The Muse would hit me in streaks, and during those times I would have short stories coming out of my ears.

And of course, there was Clint. He loved to read my stories and give his observations as a reader. Slowly, he would share some of his experiences overseas. I admit I was on the outspoken side, that the U.S. shouldn't have gotten involved in something that had never been declared a war in the first place. At the same time, hearing Clint's side of the story revealed more about the raw deal so many returning Viet Nam veterans received. I was concerned about him when, one October night out of the blue, he had what I now know as a panic attack. The self-assured guy I knew had, for those moments, disappeared. When it was over, Clint seemed surprised I didn't turn tail and run. With what he had shared, I had concern, but not fear or pity.

"That's what all the other women did." He took a breath to better compose himself. "They backed off. Said I had too much baggage."

"Have you been getting help for it?"

"Yeah, I went and saw a shrink. I still see him from time to time. There's a group of us from my unit that get together about once a month or so. These attacks don't happen as often now. Maybe time is making a difference."

"I wonder if that happened to Daddy when he was in World War II."

"Sylvia, there's no way you can be in combat without being affected by it. You're there. You have a job to do, and you may or may not come back. Your dad knows; he's lived it. War changes a person in certain ways. Things you thought were so important before seem trivial when you return."

I moved closer to my man and put my arms around his neck. "I guess it does, Clint, for better or for worse. But know this. I'm in love with you, and I'm not going anywhere."

That experience changed our relationship. Our communication deepened, and Clint opened up in ways that he probably hadn't in a long time, but it was a slow process. I asked Daddy about his time in the war, but aside from some stories about comrades over there he wasn't forthcoming about what he faced on the field of battle. He did, however, have strong opinions about what Black men in the Armed Forces faced when they returned home after V-E Day and V-J Day in the 1940s. When President Truman issued the order desegregating the military in 1949, his comment was, "Took long enough."

On Christmas Eve, Clint and I were relaxing in his lovely stucco house on East 45th Street and Park Avenue, listening to Christmas carols with a jazz flavor and talking about the holidays. The whole Watergate incident was about to blow up in Nixon's face, but we chose not to dwell on that. At some point Clint got up from the sofa and grabbed a cassette, which he put into his eight-track player. "Would you like some hot apple cider?" he asked me with a little smile.

"Certainly."

While he was in the kitchen preparing our refreshments, I let the sounds of the Delfonics envelop me. I love those ballads of the early '70s, and he knew it; it put me in a mellow mood. He came out carrying a wicker tray with mugs of apple cider, molasses cookies, and cloth napkins on it, setting it down on the coffee table. "I trust this meets with your satisfaction."

I picked up a mug and took a sip. "Clint, everything about this day is meeting my satisfaction," I purred.

"I'm glad you said that, because..."

"What?"

"I wish I could do this the way I want to, but the results of my Purple Heart won't let me."

"What are you talking about?"

"Sylvia, if I could, I'd do this on one knee."

Anticipation of the best kind filled me at his last words. "Clint…are you saying…"

"You're a beautiful woman, Sylvia, and not just on the outside. You're smart, you're highly creative, and you're strong. You don't back down or run away in the face of a challenge. I don't know just when or how you did it, but you stole my heart. You're the kind of woman who will stand beside a man—not in front of him, not behind him, but beside him. I want to be that man—forever. The bottom line is, I love you, and I'm asking you…will you marry me?"

"When You Get Right Down to It" filled the room as I watched Clint reach into his pocket and pull out a diamond ring. I looked into the depths of his eyes and felt my eyes mist. We'd only known each other about six months, but in those six months I knew in my heart that this was the man I was meant to have. As far as I was concerned, our meeting by the river was no accident. With a peace in my heart, my lips formed the magic word: "Yes."

Daddy and I had some of our best heart-to-heart talks during my engagement. It was only two weeks after Clint and I made our announcement that Daddy took his seat on the Hennepin County bench, starting him off in criminal court. I noticed, though, that certain subjects caused a change in both men. With Daddy it was Uncle Eldon; with Clint, Viet Nam. Their eyes clouded over from what could only be painful memories, memories that only time could heal. I'd see Daddy and Clint together sometimes when that happened, as though they shared a silent understanding.

I wanted my sisters and my cousins to be in the wedding party but picking a maid of honor among them would be dicey. Mama and Auntie Elaine, however, came up with a novel solution and gathered all us girls together. "Since you're the oldest, Sylvia, let's try this," Mama suggested. "Regardless of when she gets married, the next of you in age will be the maid or matron of honor. So, Sylvia, Deshawna would be your maid of honor, Linda would be Deshawna's, and so on."

We thought about her idea for a minute. "Well, with so many of us, it does make sense." Linda thought for a few seconds. "But what about Chauntice?"

"Well, if they're agreeable to this, Ellen would be Chauntice's maid of honor, and Elizabeth would be hers," Auntie Elaine offered.

"That sounds good," Ellen agreed. "When we get down to Elizabeth, then what?"

"Hmmm. Sylvia, why don't you be Elizabeth's matron of honor?"

"Sure, Auntie." Us women were smiling and pleased with their solution until LaVera stopped everything with, "Wait a minute. We're forgetting somebody. What about Carter?"

"You never know, Mama. He just might marry Julian Edwards," I added with a mischievous smile.

"Hmm." Mama was quiet for a moment, and I knew the seed I planted had taken root. "Well, when the time comes, let's do it by lottery."

Yes, Mama may have waited until the wedding night to give it up to Daddy, but I simply couldn't wait that long—my needs were too strong, and Clint was irresistible. It was a miracle I held out for the ring, but now all bets were off as far as I was concerned. I had been pleasuring myself with vibrators to take the edge off, but they were no longer enough. Sure, there was a time to be demure and a time to be bold, and my Clint appreciated a bold woman. That being said, I decided to put my plan into action.

On a Friday, early in February, I left the campus, packed an overnight bag and drove carefully over to Clint's house in my 1968 VW Karmann Ghia. At this point in our relationship I had a key to his place, and my spending a weekend with him was nothing out of the ordinary. This time, I was warm with the anticipation of the surprise I had for my man. I got there first, and with the way the snow was falling, this would be a hibernation weekend he'd never forget.

I had plenty of time to take a relaxing bath with my favorite oils. The woman who owned the shop where I purchased them practically guaranteed they would kick in with my natural scent and have him panting for me more than he already did. Feeling sensuous when

I stepped out of the bathtub, I patted myself down with a towel. I applied light makeup to my face, and then picked out my Afro until it looked just right. Satisfied with the results, I prepared a light snack and chilled a bottle of wine in readiness, sure that we would work up an appetite later. I knew it wouldn't be long until Clint came through the door, and just thinking about him had me damp when I went into his bedroom and reclined on the king-sized bed.

I heard the front door open and close, feeling more aroused with anticipation. My nipples hardened as he climbed the stairs. When he came around the corner and stood in the doorway, dressed in his business attire, his pupils dilated when he drank in the sight before him—me, nude, laid out on the bed, the scent of sandalwood incense in the room, flashing him a delightfully naughty smile while massaging my ample breasts and stroking my clit. If that wasn't bold...

"See something you like?" I purred.

The bulge in his slacks grew bigger. "Better believe it, baby."

"I know it's winter, but I do believe you're...overdressed, Clint." I continued to stroke myself while he gave me a wicked grin. "Wouldn't you like to get more...comfortable? Perhaps I can help you with that."

"I just bet you can, Sylvia." I watched him come out of his clothes like a man eager to claim his prize.

When he got down to his drawers, which were barely covering his throbbing erection, I said huskily, "Don't take those off. Let me."

I crawled across the bed like a slinky cat to where he was standing at the edge. His eyes didn't leave mine as I pulled his drawers down with my teeth. When his freed shaft sprang up, it was my turn for my pupils to dilate—with lusty appreciation. "My, my, my."

"I guess that means you like what *you* see," Clint growled softly, his eyes a potent combination of lust and love as my feminine mound got wetter. "So, as Marvin Gaye sings, 'Let's Get it On.'"

Trust and believe, I had been preparing for this evening. If there's one thing I have it's a voracious appetite for reading, and a steady diet of romance novels gave me plenty of knowledge I could now put into practice. This bold Berry woman did not hesitate to take my man in my mouth, to stroke, lick and suck him to distraction. His knees buckled when he gently pushed my head off his pulsing length, afraid he would spend himself before we even started. Once on the bed, bewitched by the scent of my bath ritual, he proceeded to give me a dose of my own medicine, and was it ever good; my womanly folds certainly thanked him. Sticking his fingers into my wetness, he then proceeded to lick my juices off them, all the while giving me these lustful looks that promised further pleasure for me.

Seeing my man walking around naked and hard as a rock because of me filled me with the sense of my own feminine power as he picked up a cartridge of jazz music and put it into his eight-track player. I was so ready for him at that point I could have burst. When he got back on the bed, he was ready to take charge. I opened my legs in a red-carpet invitation, and in he went. The fullness of having him inside me was indescribable at the time, and all I could do was moan in ecstasy while he took me.

I wanted more and more, and soon I was rocking with him to get it. Between his kisses and my moans of pleasure, the heat in our lovemaking went up degree by degree. He really laid it on me, and I gave as good I got when I clenched my inner walls to drive him up one. As the tempo increased and we were damp with sweat, I got closer and closer and closer, until my orgasm swept over me like a crashing wave, followed by another, and still another. The force of my feminine walls clenching Clint's hot, driving rod of pleasure soon drove him over the edge, and he roared in release.

Some indeterminate moments later, when we managed to resume normal breathing, Clint held me in his arms. "You blew my mind, Sylvia. I will never get enough of you."

Feeling so sexy, so desired, so satisfied, I replied, "Well, thank you, kind sir. That certainly deserves a reward."

"Oh? What kind of reward?" he asked with that sexy grin, his manhood beginning to stir.

I ran my tongue gently over my well-kissed lips. "Let's do it again."

July 28, 1973 gave us a beautiful summer day, with Daddy walking me down the aisle in my empire-waist wedding gown and baby's breath in my Afro as my wedding party preceded me. I also have to say that Deshawna made a lovely maid of honor.

As much as I tried to think this wasn't a big deal for Daddy to give away his oldest daughter, deep in my heart I knew it was. There was no trace of the stern, no-nonsense Judge Berry that day, only the father I loved and respected. There were a few moments, when I looked over at him, where I thought his eyes looked misty. When Mama saw us, the look in her eyes was one of happiness mixed with knowledge of some secret about Daddy only they shared. Of course, there was the other important man in my life waiting for me at the altar, and I felt warm with love when our eyes met, and I saw the little catch in his breath. I still say men look sexy in tuxedos, and Clint was a prime example.

Daddy's connection with Christopher Electronics got my husband in the door and a little more attention from upper management. In addition, his expertise and his willingness to pay his dues furthered his career, as he and Eli Jr. honed their skills from the ground up. In the meantime, I had secured a position at Northwestern Bank by day. By night I had my time with Clint—which definitely put a smile on my face--and continued to write when I had time alone. I often submitted short stories for publication in various anthologies or freelance articles for magazines, and occasionally they were published. The prize for me, ultimately, would be recognition as a novelist, and Daddy's motto of "Never give up," aided by Clint's support, would keep me focused on my game plan.

Life has a way of "life-ing along," and Valentine's Day of 1975 found Clint and I reveling in the smoldering volcano of torrid passion. I boldly claim my woman's intuition that something was quite different about that night, and from the look in his eyes, during the intense afterglow following mind-blowing orgasms, he knew it as well. Seven weeks later, just after Easter, I noticed my bra was tight and a strange desire for cornflakes in the middle of the day. I happened to be visiting Grandma and Grandpa Langston with Mama on a Saturday afternoon that spring when my craving for cornflakes was overpowering. Mama and Grandma Langston watched me wolfing them down at the kitchen table, then shared a fat, knowing smile.

"What? What?" I wondered, slightly irritated at some inside joke I thought they were sharing.

"Sylvia, I do believe it's time you went to see your doctor," Grandma Langston declared.

"Why? I'm not sick."

"No, you're not sick, baby. You're pregnant," Mama beamed.

I dropped my spoon into the bowl and was rewarded with a splash of milk on my chin. "No way. No way."

That smirk on Grandma's face just didn't come off. "Cornflakes at three in the afternoon? How long has *that* been going on?"

"Uh…uh…uh…"

"I thought so," she said as though there was no other possible conclusion. "Now you go see the doctor and take good care of that baby. I'll just bet you knock Clint's socks off when you give him the news."

"And after you tell him, you can tell your father," Mama broke in. "That case he's been presiding over hasn't been going so well." I recalled the grim look on Daddy's face lately as she continued. "A grandchild on the way will be just the thing to lift his spirits."

When I came home from seeing my gynecologist the following week with positive test results, I broke the news to Clint. He kept saying, "You're kidding. You're kidding," thinking it was some belated April Fool's Day joke I was playing on him. When I handed him the test results, he sank into his chair and breathed, "Wow."

The next day we were visiting Mama when Daddy came home from the courthouse, ready to chew nails. He went straight to his study. About 10 minutes later he emerged, ready to eat dinner. Mama, however, had other ideas as she nudged me. I did my best to keep a straight face, but I couldn't—I was way too happy for that. I blurted out, "I'm pregnant," which effectively stopped Daddy from going into the kitchen. He turned around, and the expression on his face was that of one soaking in information he'd been blindsided with. Finally, a grin spread across his face as he approached me, his arms outstretched to give me a big hug. Clint, having recovered from the shock, had that particular grin on his face men have when they have staked their claim and were given the proof of said claim.

After 17 hours of medieval torture—labor was too mild a term to describe it—I gave birth to our first child, Zora Hurston Lewis, late in the afternoon of November 14, 1975. I'm the writer in the family, but Clint is an avid reader in his spare time. When it came to picking names for our children, he leaned toward famous African American authors, writers and poets. Given the number of females born into the Berry family, it was no great surprise that Mama and Daddy's first grandchild would be a girl, and thanks to Grandma Berry, everyone at St. Matthew's knew within hours of my delivery. It was some consolation to my husband that although Zora has my eyes and my smile, she has his face, and his face is definitely one I love to gaze upon.

When I became pregnant with our second child, Clint and I had come to an agreement about succeeding children—to honor Daddy, any sons we had would have my maiden name as a middle name. Needless to say, Daddy was thrilled when his first grandson, Richard Berry Lewis, was born on May 30, 1977, the Richard being in honor of author Richard Wright. In the course of conversation with my sisters I mentioned the idea, and they loved it. As a result, all of Daddy's grandsons have the middle name Berry, with the exception of Linda's son Prentice Delaney, Jr. Given the length of time between the birth of her daughter Sierra and Prentice, we could respect her wanting to honor her husband's wishes. To commemorate Langston Hughes and Mama, our third child, Langston Berry Lewis, arrived on June 5, 1980. Our youngest, Alice Walker Lewis, was born on April 8, 1983. I gained the most weight with her—which meant that I had barely enough time to fit into my dress for Carter and Julian's wedding in July.

I never gave up on my writing, even while Clint and I were working and raising our family. I called myself waiting until the right time to start a novel, until one spring day in 1979 when Clint told me, "There's never going to be a 'right time.' You're an amazing writer, honey. All you have to do is sit down and do it." With that feedback and Clint's promise to take Zora and Ricky for an outing, I jumped into my 1976 Buick Century and drove over to the river. I found my mind traveling in so many different directions, until it kept returning to one particular genre—romance. I loved reading romance novels in my spare time. It was easy to get into the emotions of the protagonists and their challenges on the road to true love. *But wait. Perhaps it's time to write what I want to read—stories featuring Black characters.*

Sitting on a bench near the confluence of Minnehaha Creek and the Mississippi, I gazed out over the water and visualized the characters in my mind. Grabbing my pen and notepads, the outline and character profiles poured out of me and onto the pages. My hero, the successful head of a department store chain and self-professed workaholic, afraid of love. My heroine, a public relations analyst called in to revamp the store's image and that of its CEO, who falls in love with him along the way. He bucks like a stag every step of the way, but the power of love and passion win out in the end. My working title was, *When Love Makes You Over.* When I left the river and headed home, I was energized and couldn't wait to get in front of my typewriter.

John Edwards had gone through so many changes getting his first novel, *Slade's Destiny,* published. It seemed as though there was a rejection letter waiting for him in the mailbox every week until a publishing company picked it up. For whatever reason, my getting published took a much shorter period of time once I finished the novel. Before that happened, Deshawna called me from Dallas where her husband was stationed, excited about a suggestion: "Instead of a drawing on the cover, have a photograph done for it. This is your first romance novel, so get the hottest male model you can find, a brotha so hot women will be fanning themselves before they get to the first page." When it hit the bookstores, I was astonished at the sales. My hard work in creating the characters, plus Deshawna's advice, had paid off.

One midweek summer afternoon in July of 2003 I was doing a rewrite on my latest romance novel when the phone rang. I normally didn't answer the phone while I'm working, but when the caller ID said "Daddy," I picked it up. "Hi, Daddy."

"Hi, Sylvia. How's the new one coming?"

"It's getting there. I should have the rewrite done for my publisher by the end of next week. What's going on?"

"I just dropped in to see some colleagues down here at the courthouse. You'll never guess who else is down here."

He knew he had me hooked. "Anyone I know?"

"I would say you know this person quite well. It's Ricky."

"Ricky? What would Ricky be doing at the courthouse?"

"As a matter of fact, your son is very friendly with one of the bailiffs here." Daddy's voice implied that much more than friendliness was at play. "I just chatted with them for a few minutes before they went off to lunch together. Don't be surprised if they pay you and Clint a visit soon."

"And how, pray tell, would you know that?"

"How do you think? Ricky has the Berry charm, and the young man in question, for all his macho, is drowning in it. I rest my case."

I sighed in defeat. He knew I would not rest until I discovered who the object of Ricky's affections was, given my track record when Zora first started seeing Roy Garvin. I was most pleased, of course, that Zora and Roy's union was a successful love match, resulting in marriage and my first two grandchildren. Would Ricky have his happily-ever-after with this man? "What does he look like?"

"All I'll say is, you'll find him fascinating when you meet him. I'll talk to you later," he said and hung up. I hated it when Daddy did that.

That Saturday afternoon, I heard a knock at the back door. "I'll get it," I heard Clint say. I recognized the sound of Ricky's voice and heard that of another man as greetings were exchanged and the group came downstairs to where I was sitting in the family room, watching a DVD of the stage version of *Madea's Family Reunion*. I looked up at the three men when they entered, and Ricky had an expression on his face I immediately recognized. "Hi, Mom. Mom, this is my honey, Isaiah Holliday. Isaiah, this is my mother."

"Nice to meet you, Mrs. Lewis. My mother loves your novels. She buys them as soon as they're released," Isaiah said.

My honey, eh? I never thought I would say it, but Isaiah looked like he could have walked off the pages of a Brenda Jackson romance novel. About the same age as Ricky, he stood at 6'5" with 240 pounds of solid muscles in all the right places, exuding a masculinity that would make man or woman whimper with desire. He had a full head of curly black hair, rich bronze skin, and a face—well, he could nearly pass for Shemar Moore's twin, had he been shorter. Yes, this man could certainly handle himself and keep order in a courtroom. "Thank you, Isaiah. I appreciate your kind words." The besotted looks that passed between him and Ricky only confirmed Daddy's prior assessment. "Have a seat. Would you like some juice or soda?"

"Juice is fine," he replied.

"I'll just be a moment." I went upstairs to the kitchen and prepared the refreshments, after which I grabbed my cell phone and speed-dialed Daddy. "All right, Daddy. You could have told me Ricky's new boyfriend looks like a walking romance novel."

"And spoil the surprise? I'll just bet you want to make him a character in one of your next books," Daddy snickered.

"Given that his mother is a fan, I just might," I said, chuckling.

"You have to admit, Ricky does know how to pick 'em. Trust me, this one's serious."

"All right, Daddy, I get the message. Clint and I will smoke him out."

I returned downstairs with the tray of refreshments, in time to hear the men laughing over something Madea said. Even as they were laughing, I noticed the continuing degree of eye contact between Ricky and Isaiah and the secret looks that had been absent with anyone else my son previously dated. Clint signaled me with his eyes, and while we all watched the DVD, we used our interviewing skills on Isaiah without his even knowing it.

After the way Jerome and Ariel Franklin-Edwards, Mel Edwards' son and son-in-law, raved about Winnipeg, that was all the incentive Ricky and Isaiah needed to go there and tie the knot. They did so on August 7, 2005. At their age, any excuse to travel was good enough for Mama and Daddy, followed by the extended family. From their wedding came even more good news—Langston proposed to his girlfriend Kelinda at the reception. I shouted with joy when she said yes. Surely, the time in Winnipeg was like a happy ending to one of my romance novels. I felt that special glow as I watched the happy couples—Roy and Zora with my two granddaughters, newlyweds Ricky and Isaiah, and newly engaged Langston and Kelinda--while holding Clint's hand.

As for Alice, I'm sure she was relieved that there was no bride at this wedding, because she certainly would have moved out of the way if a bridal bouquet was thrown. To this day, she says she never wants to marry. However, I've been writing about and witnessing the phenomenon too long. *Just you wait, Alice. It'll happen to you when you least expect it.*

I have been deeply inspired by my readers. With a fan base like that, it wasn't as hard as I thought it would be to add romantic mysteries to my body of work, and then mysteries. I enjoyed reading Erle Stanley Gardner's novels as a young woman, but I was moved to put my own spin on such mysteries. Thus, my heroine, Sherry Payson, was created in 2005. She is an always-savvy, brilliant African American defense attorney who almost never lost a case, largely because her opponents—and the perpetrators—tended to underestimate her. Taking it one step further, even if she did lose a case, she could turn things around and uncover the perp. I had always liked the character of Della Street, but this was the 21st century, hence I created Tevion Maurice Nelson as Sherry's confidential legal assistant. My cousin by marriage, Wayne Hendricks-Bell, was thrilled that I had based Tevion on him, and he gave me his blessings for Tevion to use his trademark phrase, "Honey hush." To round out Sherry's "dream team," rather than have a bachelor as a private detective, Sherry's husband Brandon would have his own lucrative private detective agency—and draw in the husband-wife dynamics to my stories.

Daddy was thrilled to be a resource person for ideas and authenticity. My brothers-in-law, Prentice Delaney and Jarvis Varnell, and my fellow Central High alum, Sandra Harrison Edwards, were also most receptive to my venture into a whodunit genre. I researched and researched, and I must admit it was both challenging and fun doing it, finding that balance of a strong murder mystery, the distinct flavor of characters of color, and an absence of stereotyping. Come to think of it, art almost imitated life when I remember that Jarvis is a private investigator and Chauntice is a corporate attorney.

My fan base started to increase with the first two mystery novels, but the one that put me over the top was *The Case of the Blackmailing Bitch: A Sherry Payson Mystery*. Copies of that novel literally flew off the shelves. Libraries galore placed it in their "new arrivals" section. E-mails came pouring in. My friend and acclaimed poet, Helen Powell Edwards, couldn't put it down. "Ursula Foxworthy was a character I truly loved to hate," she said with a malicious laugh. Zora and Alice told me, "You rocked with this one, Mom. It was so much easier to pick out who *didn't* want that bitch dead." Ricky and Langston said, "Mom, we have to give you your props. You kept us going until the very end." Mama, Mrs. Edwards, Mrs. Garvin and Mrs. Holliday wanted copies for their book club, to ecstatic reviews. At my first book signing for it, Wayne came up to me with his own brand of praise. "Cuz, I was ready to give the perp a medal for whacking that woman. Now I love me some Sherry Payson, but Ursula was a real piece of work. And as always, Tevion Maurice Nelson was fiercely on point."

I was already known and well respected in the romance genre, but when this book hit it was gratifying to receive acclaim as a mystery writer. When the awards started coming, I was humbled. I first gave thanks to God, and then my family and friends for the success. The Sherry Payson books became a series, which, like my romance novels, I dedicated to Clinton, my children and my grandchildren.

Daddy, of course, encouraged his network of friends, associates, and colleagues to buy at least one of my books, in particular the one where the character of the trial judge was loosely based on him...

When Trevell gave her the details of the shooting, she nearly froze in her tracks. "We'll be right there." Sylvia ended the call and rushed upstairs to grab her bag, flustered when she couldn't find it right away. After a second scan of the bedroom, she located it sitting on a chair in front of her vanity table and hurried out of the house. While she locked the door and set off to meet Clint in the car, she couldn't shake the thought running through her head. Oh, no. This is something straight out of one of my mystery novels...

Deshawna Berry Randolph

Daddy had two major goals once he graduated from law school: building a strong family and furthering his law career. Our history of births on stormy nights continued when I, Deshawna Therese Berry, came along on July 7, 1952. Mrs. Edwards and Mama were neck and neck at the time when it came to births, because Eli Edwards, Jr. was born a month later. I'm sure that was one of those bonding times between them.

Daddy's career did receive a boost with a good word from Melvin Edwards, Eli Jr.'s grandfather, but I wish that Uncle Eldon hadn't died along the way. With Sylvia and I being the oldest kids, we knew things that our younger siblings didn't understand at the time. I'm sure Mama and Daddy did their best to protect us. Daddy's mood through all the grief, however, was different—it didn't line up with the kind over someone who had died of some illness. We learned later that Uncle Eldon had been killed during the commission of a robbery. As a result, Daddy chose a different area of law, that of a prosecutor. As he explained it to us at the time, "My job is to put the bad people away and do it the right way, in a court of law."

Like Sylvia, I heard the conversations Mama and Mrs. Edwards had when they didn't think I was listening about uniting our families. Daddy didn't get involved in that—at least, not to the degree Mama did. I mean, what young woman these days wants her parents to pick out her future husband? If I liked a guy, fine, and if I didn't, fine. Still, that didn't stop our mothers from plotting. When I was in my senior year of high school and was voted a homecoming princess—and later queen—Mama gave her not-so-subtle hints. "Eli Edwards, Jr. would make such a handsome date for the homecoming dance." The fact that he had asked somebody else didn't faze her.

As for other guys at school, I was less than thrilled with the ones who stared at me like I was a prime rib entrée, and even less the ones that asked me. In Mama's words, they were "only out for one thing." Daddy, had he been at school to witness them, would have issued arrest warrants. So, being a resourceful Berry woman, I found a date that would keep everyone at bay—Lonnie Montgomery, Jr. After all, who is going to mess with a guy whose oldest brother is a sheriff, his middle brother a chief of police, and oldest sister is a court clerk at the Ramsey County Courthouse? On top of that, my grandmother's generation of women considered 6'3", amber-complexioned Lonnie a "fine, tall drink o' water."

Eli, Lonnie, and I have been friends from way back. We were all in Central High School's Class of 1970. When Eli started dating Sandra Harrison, she was accepted into our circle as a matter of course. Lonnie and I would hang out together, often commiserating when we were between boyfriends. Having back-to-back birthdays only strengthened our friendship. Eli's cousin, Wayne Hendricks, was a year behind us, but the Edwardses and Berrys are a pretty close-knit bunch, so it was natural that he was part of the circle, too. Lonnie was honors-student smart and laid-back, but Wayne...what he wanted, he definitely went after.

Daddy approved of my hanging out with Lonnie as well his being my date for the homecoming dance. Like the other young men before him, Daddy had taken Lonnie into the study to talk to him. Unlike the others, Lonnie didn't have the terrified look that so many other guys had had in that situation. After he went home, Daddy took me aside. "That young man will make an excellent escort for you. I know his father. He just came on board at the district attorney's office."

"You what? Why didn't you tell me?"

"You never asked. The Montgomery name is closely connected to law and order. Lonnie's parents, his brothers, and his sisters are all in some field of law and law enforcement. I'm sure you two have a lot in common, since he's as picky about boyfriends as you are." Daddy winked as he walked away, leaving me with my mouth open.

During the time we went off to college—me to Iowa State University and Lonnie to the University of Iowa—Daddy got his appointment to the bench. After Commencement Day in 1974, our career plans were set; I had a business degree and was learning everything about real estate, while Lonnie used his degree to start up his own direct marketing business. Meanwhile, Eli Jr. and Sandra had gotten married and had a son, so he went to work at Christopher Electronics while Sandra pursued her law degree. I was more than happy to keep playing the field. Lonnie, however, had a somewhat different situation with his family—they were ready to put out full-page ads to find him a partner.

One day a year later, Lonnie told me about Jake Morelli. I saw it coming ten miles away—he'd finally found the right guy for himself and his daughter Khadijah. I could well understand why; if I had been in his position, I wouldn't have brought any old dude around my child either. No, he'd have to be pretty special. Usually, one found Mr. or Ms. Right and then had kids. Lonnie, however, did it in reverse. Surrogacy was something very new in the '70s, and Lonnie was a trailblazer in that regard. With the help of his mother, an adoption attorney, Lonnie went out to California, found a surrogate, and became a father when Khadijah Iman Montgomery was born on Halloween of 1974. The part about Jake being his former physical education teacher sounded like something that could only come out of a romance novel—something Sylvia would probably write these days.

"Get outta here!" I exclaimed.

"It's true, Deshawna. He was my P.E. teacher during summer school at Bryant Jr. High."

"And he had no idea who you were?"

"No. Not until I told him on our first date. He was in his late 20s when I was a skinny little 14-year-old kid at summer school. Who would remember that?"

"Yeah, you have a point there. So how does he feel about Khadijah? Better yet, how does she feel about him?"

"He loves her. She was cautious around him at first, but after he found something for them to play with, she started to open up to him more."

"Well, Mama says it's one thing to find a good man, and another to do what it takes to keep him. You are going to introduce this dream man to me, right?"

"Of course, I am. And speaking of men, is there someone in particular on your radar these days?"

"I'm not ready to take that step just yet, Lonnie. But I will, trust and believe."

I finally did meet Jake, and he was everything Lonnie said he was, not to mention having a strong resemblance to the man we know today as Christopher Meloni, only with dark brown shoulder-length hair. As for me, I continued to selectively play the field while I studied to get my realtor's license. In fact, my first commission was for the house in Golden Valley that Lonnie and Jake bought in the summer of 1975.

I never thought I'd see the day, though, when I'd let someone fix me up with a date. That was before Lonnie introduced me to Jason Randolph. Oh, he was fine—Morris Chestnut *fine*--and there was a certain spit-and-polish about him that appealed to me. Of course, before our date I grilled Lonnie for background information, and he finally told me, "Jason's 27, he's from Omaha, and he's a first lieutenant in the Air Force."

"Really? And how did you happen to meet him?"

"He's one of Jake's friends." I started to protest, but Lonnie held up his hand. "No, Jason definitely plays for your team. We've been friends for a long time, Deshawna, and I have no doubt he's your type."

Yes, when Lt. Randolph came to my door for our date, he gave me a smile of appreciation, unlike other men who leered at me at first sight. I liked his confidence, and I wondered if it was genetic or something instilled by his military training. Either way, I found it attractive, and our first kiss sealed the deal. When, after a certain number of dates, I brought him over to meet my parents, I was keen to observe how he interacted with Daddy. I have to give it to Jason—he treated Daddy with great respect but at the same time wasn't intimidated by him.

"So, what inspired you to go into the Air Force?" I asked Jason the day after the dinner party.

"It wasn't a what, Deshawna. It was who."

"All right, then. Who?"

"My uncle. He was one of the Tuskegee Airmen. He told me about what their unit accomplished during World War II, and he showed me his commendations. It was more than enough motivation for me to enlist and become a pilot." He gazed up at the clear blue sky and sighed. "There's something about flying—being up there in the sky—that I can't really explain, other than that you're one with something bigger than you are. It just does something to me. On the other hand, when you're on a mission and troops are depending on you, you do it, above and beyond the call of duty."

"When you put it that way, Jason, it's like the way Daddy feels about law. It's a passion."

Jason turned to me with eyes of understanding. "Yeah. You get it. And the same goes for you, Deshawna. A house isn't just a house to you. You see it as a home for someone and finding the right home for the right client is your passion."

He understands. Jason went in to kiss me again and send me to a place I'd never been before. *Jason understands.*

At the time of the Bicentennial, Jason and I had been seeing each other for nearly a year, and I was doing well enough as a realtor to enjoy a beautiful two-bedroom apartment near Cedar Lake. I appreciated walking over and sitting by the water, as well as jogging or cycling on the path around the lake. Added to that was the extra perk of Cedar Lake's hidden east beach. Sure, people pay for the lake, but I'm worth it. It stood in stark contrast to Jason's housing on the base, and I made it as inviting as possible whenever he came by, which was often.

I still remember that day in July like it was yesterday. I had been on the phone with Linda, who had just given birth to her daughter, Sierra. She was elated about being a new mother despite a healthy dose of fatigue from late-night feedings. I was on a high from a successful closing on a duplex, listening to the latest Spinners album, and enjoying the air conditioning that made the 94-degree day comfortable.

When I heard a special knock at my door, I knew it was Jason. He stood there comfortably dressed in khaki shorts, sandals, and a Creighton University T-shirt, with a bag of groceries in hand—a 6'2" hunk of the finest quality. "Hey baby," he said warmly before I greeted him with a kiss. "Just point me to the kitchen. I'm cooking for you tonight."

"Oh, a man after my own heart," I said saucily as he headed in that direction. "Anything you need help with?"

"Actually, you can be in charge of the music while I cook."

The meal was exquisite, not only in the taste but in the presentation, as well as the care he took in setting the table. We shared our respective news of the day and basked in each other's successes. I offered to help with the dishes, but Jason insisted on doing the cleanup himself. *I'm sure there are a lot of men out there who could take lessons from him.*

By the time everything was clean and put away it was nearing sunset. Jason looked at me with that combination of desire and appreciation and asked, "Why don't we talk a walk over to the lake?"

"After a dinner like that, how could I possibly refuse, kind sir?" I replied, already taking a swim in the pools of his amazing brown eyes.

It was a little cooler outside as we crossed Cedar Lake Parkway to the pedestrian path around Cedar Lake. Other couples were out as well, walking and holding hands, enjoying each other's company. Before we knew it, we had reached the main beach on the west side of the lake, finding a grassy spot to sit just beyond the sand. There was something magical about the twilight, the mild breeze and— thank goodness—the low humidity, which combined with Jason's

intoxicating presence that night. It had all the makings of a night of...
expectations, and I was curious to see where it would lead.

A crescent moon made its presence known in the clear sky, while
Jason and I were wrapped up in a lingering kiss, the kind I could
share with him for hours. When we broke, his voice was low and
full of underlying emotion. "Deshawna, when I think about you,
when I think about us, I see the kind of happiness that will last
a lifetime. Each day I've gotten to know you over this past year
only strengthened those feelings. I know, with all my heart, that I
love you."

I don't know why, but I felt tears form in the corners of my eyes.
"I love you, too, Jason. So very, very much."

"And that, Deshawna, is why I want to build a life with you. It's
not easy to be a mate to someone in the military, but you're the kind
of woman who knows herself, stands by her man and yet holds him
accountable. So, I want to ask you an important question." He reached
into his pocket, pulling out a small box and opening it. My hands
went to my mouth when I saw the sparkle of the diamond in the ring
and a tear ran down my cheek. The realization of how ready he was
to take things to the next level had me shaking with joy. Holding up
the box, he looked me in the eye. "Deshawna Therese Berry, will
you marry me?"

On July 30, 1977, Linda preceded me down the aisle at St.
Matthew's AME as my matron of honor, followed by Daddy and me
to Natalie Cole's song, "Our Love." Jake was standing next to Jason
as his best man, with Lonnie among the groomsmen. Jason was so
breathtakingly handsome and distinguished in his dress uniform—he
had recently been promoted to captain. I thought I would faint from
pleasure. Or was it the anticipation of our wedding night?

By no means did that detract from the ceremony itself, saying the
vows that would seal Jason and I together for the rest of our lives, and
meaning them deep down in our hearts. Natalie Cole nailed it with
that song. Looking at him with all the love in my heart, and seeing it
in his eyes, "Our Love" belonged to us. Once our pastor announced us

married, I was more than ready for that kiss and the proclamation, "I introduce to you, for the first time, Jason and Deshawna Randolph." And as we processed back up the aisle, I couldn't help but notice the pleased look on Mama's face that said, "Three down, three to go."

I had to give it to Jason for ingenuity—he found all these steamy things to do with me short of actual intercourse during our engagement; that was something to be saved for our wedding night. Deep kisses that left me heated with desire. Giving me orgasms just from sucking my nipples. Going down on me, with me holding his head between my folds and yelling from the newfound pleasure. Taking his awe-inspiring tool in my mouth and driving him to madness that could only be relieved by his release—you know I loved that kind of power. But on our honeymoon in Samoa, the wait was over!

Already wet and achingly ready from the exquisitely sensual foreplay, looking deep into his lust-glazed eyes, when he made that first sure thrust inside my virgin walls, I was a goner in the best possible way. His thrusts inside me had me wanting more, and more, and more. Even so, his hands and mouth stayed busy, working their magic on my body, fanning the flames of my desire for him. I have no doubt that I left scratches on his back, hickeys on his neck, arching my hips back to him until I finally exploded in pleasure, clenching my walls around him as he released his seed deep inside me. He made me his. I made him mine. Floating on the exhilarating cloud of afterglow, we knew this was just the beginning.

We made love on a relatively secluded beach, which I will never do again because of all the sand that worked its way into my vagina. Fortunately, Jason is rather creative in those instances, and we made love in the ocean, as well as semi-public foliage. Of course, between the abundance of passion-laden moments, we took time out for sightseeing, souvenir shopping, dining and dancing. On the way home, Jason dared me to become a member of the Mile-High Club, a membership I gladly accepted.

A year later, Jason and I flew back to Minneapolis from Texas to attend Wayne and Theo's wedding at the Edwards estate. I was six months along with our first child, and when we had a moment alone during the reception, Lonnie checked me out and noted, "Marriage is certainly agreeing with you. Congratulations, Deshawna."

"Thank you, Lonnie," I beamed.

"When are you due?"

"The end of November, so I still have some time. He kicks a lot."

"He? How do you know it's a boy?"

"Jason is absolutely certain I'm having a boy, so I just go along with him for now." I caught a familiar look in Lonnie's eye. "All right, Lonnie. Spill. What's going on?"

The grin that Lonnie tried so hard to suppress burst onto his face. "Well, Jake and I are going to be parents again. Mama found us a surrogate, and the baby is due to arrive sometime around the middle of April."

"Awwwww. Congratulations." I gave my friend a big hug and an even bigger smile. "Have you told Khadijah?"

"Not yet, but soon."

"Speaking of family, now that you have another one on the way, isn't it time you and Jake took your relationship to the next phase—like tying the knot?"

Lonnie gave me a thoughtful expression. "You know, seeing Wayne and Theo saying their vows today did something to me inside. It was encouraging, inspiring. It reminded me of all the reasons I love Jake. And to be surrounded by family and friends...yeah. I'd love to be married to him."

I put my hands on my hips and gave him a piercing look. "Well, what are you waiting for?"

He lowered his voice to confidential level. "If I'm going to do this, I want it to be right. My business has a big convention coming up celebrating the new people and those who moved up to the next levels at the Radisson South at the end of next month. As soon as that's over, I'll pick out a nice, beautiful, quiet place for the two of us and pop *the question*."

"That sounds like a plan," I agreed, the romantic in me doing somersaults. "Good luck, Lonnie. And keep me posted."

Though Lonnie had things all planned out, Jake beat him to the punch by proposing to him at the convention, just before he made his speech near the end of the program, to a packed ballroom. Overwhelmed, Lonnie managed to say yes, and the crowd went up in cheers and rousing applause. When Lonnie called me the next day with his engagement news, the romantic in me jumped for joy—well, as much as a woman who's seven months along can jump.

On September 29, 1979, with Jason as their best man and Lonnie's sister Topaz as their matron of honor, Lonnie and Jake Morelli-Montgomery had a beautiful wedding and reception at the Radisson South Hotel. Wayne and Theo serenaded them with Marilyn McCoo and Billy Davis' "The Two of Us," which guaranteed waterworks of joy. The Montgomery and Morelli families were very well represented in an outpouring of love and merriment. Among the youngest of the guests were Lonnie and Jake's five-year-old daughter Khadijah and their five-month-old son Cesare. And of course, led by Daddy and Mama, the Berry family was there in force.

It seemed as though we moved around so much in the early years of our marriage, but with having a husband in the Air Force it came with the territory. Sometimes I thought I barely had time to get a realtor's license in one state before we had to pack up and move to another one. And then there were the times throughout our marriage when Jason's duties as a military officer required him to be away for periods of time. Being busy in my own career helped to some extent, but there were the nights, alone in our bed, when I missed him, his presence, his touch, the way he'd reach over and spoon me in the middle of the night. Getting a letter or a phone call from him made my day, and I know that my letters made his. When I wasn't calling my sisters, Lonnie, or my parents, the other wives (and a few husbands) of military personnel served as a support system, for which I was most grateful. Daddy had opened up to me about this aspect of military life, saying, "For those of us who were serving in World War II, next to the combat, the hardest part was being away from our families. We lived for those letters and photos from home, those things that reminded us why we were there."

When the boys started coming, Jason had the novel idea of naming them after whatever city he was stationed in at the time. My reply was, "Fine, as long their middle name is Berry and the name isn't too weird." With that matter settled, we got down to life as a military family and starting one of our own, which didn't take long.

Dallas Berry Randolph arrived on November 27, 1978, shortly after we had returned to Dallas from Thanksgiving with Mama and Daddy—of course, Daddy was thrilled over how much Dallas took after him. When we moved to Jason's next assignment, I was not about to have a child of mine named Canaveral, so when we were told we had another boy on March 7, 1981, Orlando Berry Randolph was the name of choice. It was Jason's turn to claim bragging rights, since Orlando was the spitting image of him. Two years later we were moved again, only this time it was a little closer to home. Medical technology had taken great strides over the years, and after an ultrasound was taken in my second trimester, we received our news.

"I don't care that this is your hometown we're stationed in," I said firmly, staring my husband down with my hand on my hip, "we're not naming our son Omaha Randolph."

Jason knew when to concede. He looked outside the window of my obstetrician's office on Dodge Street, thought for a minute and turned back to face me. "Well, how about Lincoln?"

I screwed up my face. "Lincoln?"

"Sure. Lincoln's the state capital of Nebraska, and it's the first name of the brotha on *Mod Squad*—well, the character he plays. Deshawna, you have to admit the brotha was cool, and we can call him Linc for short." His points made some sense and it was a better option than Omaha. Add on the fact I wasn't about to admit I had had a secret crush on Clarence Williams III, and I agreed. Four months later, during the early evening hours of May 28, 1984, Lincoln Berry Randolph made his debut on, of all days, Memorial Day, looking just like me.

Though I lived in Omaha and Linda lived in Milwaukee, we always made time to call Mama and Daddy between our periodic

73

visits to Minneapolis. I loved hearing Daddy's voice and listening to his stories about some of the cases that came before him. I swear, with some cases it was like having your very own live soap opera for the duration of the trial. By the time he talked to Jason and the boys and we ended the call, I felt as though we were part of the center of his world—and indeed we were.

Yes, Omaha was just a seven-hour drive from Minneapolis and a plane trip from Eppley Airfield was even shorter, but as the years went by, I grew increasingly homesick. I had a wonderful family, a husband I only loved more each day and my career, but the feeling never went away. By the time Jason had his 20 years in, he had moved up to the rank of colonel. When he came home one late spring day in 1989, I could clearly see something in him that hadn't been obvious before—restlessness. He finally admitted to me that he was ready to move on from the Armed Forces into another field, and a light went on in my head.

"You know, I was talking to Sandra Edwards the other day," I said as we entered our bedroom after the boys went to sleep, but only after we promised them they could watch their favorite *Star Wars* videocassette the next evening.

"Oh?" he asked as he took off his clothes.

"Yeah. Her law practice has really taken off. And she's so proud of Eli Jr. He's doing very well there at Christopher Electronics." I continued to undress as I spoke.

"I can imagine, what with his dad heading that office."

"That may not be for too long."

"What do you mean?"

"Allan Beckley Christopher has offered Uncle Eli a seat on the Board of Directors, so Eli Jr.'s in line to become regional manager, and Vickie Christopher is now the CEO. But you know Uncle Eli. He doesn't just hand someone a position, not even his own son. Eli Jr. had to have all the credentials and skills to earn it."

Jason nodded. "Got that right. Those technical and management skills are crucial."

"He'll need them, too."

"Why do you say that?"

Stay calm and keep it casual. Plant the seed, even though Jason's hot naked body is a major distraction and I can hardly wait to feel him inside me. "Sandra told me they're expanding that office, so Eli's going to need all the experienced help he can get. Anyway, he wants to prevent having to look at a ton of resumes, so if you know anyone who doesn't mind relocating to the Twin Cities that has those qualifications, just give him a call. He's doing this all by referral. Between their jobs and their kids, Sandra and Eli stay busy, but it's a good kind of busy. I still remember how they were back in high school..."

A month later, Jason came home from work just as I had arrived from showing homes and a closing in Sarpy County. "Hey, baby." He gave me an affectionate kiss.

"Hi to you, too," I beamed. "You're in good spirits today."

"Definitely. Where are the kids?"

"They're over at Carter Lake, fishing with your father."

"Good. So, you and I have some uninterrupted time. Come on and sit down." He took me by the hand to the living room sofa.

"So, what's this all about?"

"Well, it's about a career change."

"Career change?"

"Yes. You know I've talked about it for the past few months, and I know how much you miss being around your family." I started to speak, but Jason gently held up his hand. "Don't try to deny it. I've seen it in your eyes. Anyway, I've had some long talks with Mr. Edwards over the past few weeks. I sent him all my paperwork, and I received this fax today."

As I read it, my mouth dropped open. "You mean..."

"That's right, Deshawna. It's a job offer. He wants me to start in four weeks. I went in today to resign my commission."

Is God good or what? I threw my arms around my husband. Not only was Jason given the opportunity to do something he enjoyed, but with a highly lucrative salary and benefits package. The company already had people in it that he knew and respected, like Eli Jr. and my brother-in-law Clint. And we could go back to Minneapolis!

That evening after dinner I was on the telephone to Mama, who was excited at the thought of having us back home, so to speak. When she put Daddy on the phone, I heard the delight in his voice after I gave him the good news. "Deshawna, that is wonderful news. Having your family back here will be such a blessing. And you know I want to spend more time with my grandsons."

"Trust me, you will. They want to come see you at work."

"Well, you know I have no problem with that, as long as it's not on a school day."

I chuckled. "Just like you did with us when you were an ADA."

When Mama came back on the phone, we immediately started talking about finding the perfect house for my family. That very weekend we drove up to Minneapolis. While Jason and the boys enjoyed time fishing on Lake Waconia with Daddy and my brothers-in-law, Mama and I hit the ground running in search of a house. The first few homes were nice, but not quite what I envisioned for my family.

And then I saw it—this gorgeous stucco home in the Tangletown neighborhood, within walking distance of Washburn High School. If I was a master chef I would have salivated at the sight. Not only that, as I realized later, Carter and Julian lived a few short blocks away.

Once we moved back to Minneapolis, like our parents before us, we had "couples night" outings, including Lonnie and Jake, Sylvia and Clint, Wayne and Theo, and Eli Jr. and Sandra. Given the fact that we all had kids, the evenings usually ended around eleven p.m. Still, it was fun doing things like dinner, bowling, the movies, roller skating, or having get-togethers at our respective homes. And after they kicked in and had kids, Carter and Julian happily joined us.

I saw the changes in Minneapolis' population and demographics show up in my career as a realtor, and Daddy was a witness to them during his days in court. The African American population had increased, but from the outside, the increase consisting of people moving here from Chicago starting in the 1980s. The South Side community I knew growing up began to change not long after we returned, and the area between East Lake Street and East 36th Street became increasingly Hispanic. In St. Paul, there was a growing Hmong community. The LGBT community, though still having concentrations around Loring Park and Powderhorn Park, had shown disbursement to all parts of the city, fulfilling our then mayor's dream of having "a gay family on every block." Adding to the diversity came the Somali population at the turn of the century in neighborhoods such as Whittier and Phillips, mixing in with the Native American population that resided mostly in the Phillips neighborhood.

In the community, though, never was that diversity more apparent than at the Sabathani Community Center on any given day. I started going there at least once a month, remembering what it was like when I used to walk those halls during its days as Bryant Jr. High School, meeting people from the neighborhood who remembered me from my childhood and sometimes helping first-time buyers obtain home ownership.

I was glad the Open Occupancy Law had been put in effect when I was in high school, because it helped me immensely once we returned to the Twin Cities. One of my first commissions upon our return came when I found the dream home for my parents on Kenwood Parkway. Once they saw it, they were sold on the spot. Sure, we'd miss the house on Columbus Avenue where we spent part of our years as teenagers and young adults, but at this stage of their lives, it was great to see our parents in a home just for them—and have room to entertain their friends and family when they desired.

In my line of work, first-time buyers were something of a challenge, one that I shared with Daddy one day while my family had dinner at their new home. "Daddy, it saddens me when I see the condition of some houses around here," I said, sitting on the patio while Jason and the boys were playing in the yard, with Mama cheering them on.

"In what way?"

"I remember the times we'd ride around the neighborhood when we were little, and I'd see these beautiful houses. I've driven around there lately, and those houses look awful. It's as though the people don't care about them. They need paint, the lawns are patchy, the roofs need work, things like that. And some of them got new owners within the past two years."

"And how did you find that out?"

"I have my sources," I said to his knowing look. "The thing is, many of the new owners were first-time buyers. There's no reason those homes should have gone downhill like that."

Daddy sat back with his thoughtful-judge expression. "Probably not. Now, Deshawna, can you think of some reasons for that?"

I sat back for a minute in silence. "Well, I guess buying a home is one thing, but keeping it is another. You must have the knowledge of what it takes to have a home. Everything is the homeowner's responsibility. When you're a renter, if something goes wrong you can call the landlord or the maintenance crew of an apartment complex. If you have immigrant populations who have never owned a home before, they may not have the knowledge of how to take care of these things."

"Your point is well taken. You see the problem. Now what would be a doable solution?"

That was Daddy, putting the ball back in my court. "To better prepare the buyers for home ownership. It's not enough to teach them about budgets and mortgages. Giving them classes in home maintenance and finding good companies that deal in home repair should be part of the package." An image of Sabathani Community Center came to me as a light went on. "I'm at Sabathani a lot of the time where I meet the people I want to serve. I could offer monthly workshops in home ownership. After all, the more homeowners there are in a neighborhood, the more stable the neighborhood."

Daddy gave me a smile as I beamed with my plan. "You know, if you hadn't gone into the real estate business you might have been an excellent lawyer, like Chauntice."

"Thanks, Daddy, but with you, Chauntice, Prentice, and Sandra, we have plenty of law and order in the family."

It took some time to put it together, but once the word was out about my class, people started coming. Those who didn't speak English brought relatives who did. It felt good to see the results of the class when my clients started buying houses. Those who took my teaching to heart improved and increased the value of their homes, from my first successful homeowner in 1992 to one of my more recent successes, Nevaeh Jordan. I'd have to say that of all the students I've taught in that class, she was my star student. As it turned out, she was also a huge fan of Sylvia's novels. When the class ended, her mother was on hand, giving Nevaeh a congratulatory hug and thanking me for my help.

Once our sons were grown and out of the house, it seemed as though they were taking their sweet time in settling down. I was ready for in-laws and grandchildren yesterday, but I understood the logic when Jason explained to me, "It's better to take your time than to wind up with the wrong mate. It's not that men are afraid of marriage, honey. What we're afraid of is being in a bad marriage."

Daddy even added, "Times have changed since your mother and I got together. Instead of husbands and wives, you hear about 'baby daddies' and 'baby mommas,' and what I would call microwave relationships with unrealistic expectations. I've seen more couples than I cared to count wind up in court because they didn't take the time to know each other, and enough of those cases had tragic results."

Orlando, as it turned out, was the first to bring home someone he was serious about. When we first met Brendan Livingston, we could have sworn we were looking at a young Benjamin Bratt, only with a rich brown complexion and long, black curly hair. The fact that Jason and I were big *Law and Order* fans brought that point home. I was further sold on Brendan when, while helping me in the kitchen after dinner, Orlando told me with a little smile, "He wants kids."

"Really?" I couldn't hide the delight in my voice. "And is he the marrying kind?"

"We're taking time to know each other, but I have no doubt that he is."

After dinner, I couldn't help but notice the look on Brendan's face whenever he laid eyes on Orlando. During those moments I remembered something Mama said and smiled to myself: *There's no turning back once you fall in love with a Berry.* Later that night, when we were alone and feeling romantic, the look in Jason's eye once again confirmed that statement.

A year later, Linc called about coming over for dinner. He added, "I'm bringing a guest, Mom. Is that OK?"

"Sure. Who is she?"

I heard what sounded like a slight double take. "How...how did you know it was a she?"

"I was young once, Linc. So, who is she?"

"Her name is Jessica. She's really something."

Jason and I exchanged a look of understanding when Linc brought his guest over for Sunday dinner with the family. Standing beside Linc was a lovely, curvy woman with a flawless dark brown complexion, sporting a short no-nonsense hair style and a friendly smile. Conversation was stimulating as Orlando, Brendan, Dallas, and Linc welcomed Capt. Jessica Lowery into the fold. Jason took the opportunity to share his experiences in the Air Force, and Jessica and I had time for "girl talk" and the challenges military families face.

I was as happy as could be that two of my sons were safely and happily married off—Orlando to Brendan in May of 2007 and Linc to Jessica in February of 2009. I also gladly offered my services as a realtor to them, ensuring that their tastes and the homes were a good fit. Still, my mission wasn't completed.

Dallas continued dating different women...and dating, and dating, and dating. He seemed to have no intentions of settling down. That is, until my nephew Prentice's wedding in Davenport in October of 2009. Dallas had come stag to the wedding, but during the reception, Mama and I noticed him keeping company with a certain woman.

"Who is she?" I asked Mama.

"She looks familiar, but I'm not sure. Sierra, do you know who that woman is with Dallas?"

My niece took a good look. "Oh, she's one of Rashid's cousins. Her name is Nefertari."

"Interesting," I said. "I wonder if she lives up to being named after Egyptian royalty?"

Mama gave her a scrutinizing look. "I'm sure we'll be finding out."

The three of us watched them, particularly the way Dallas was acting. "Yes, we will," I stated. "He certainly seems to be taken with her, even though he's trying to hide it."

"And if he is, she doesn't stand a chance once he turns on that Berry charm," Sierra concluded.

"You think so?" I said, pretending to be innocent before Mama and I exchanged a giggle. "Well, Nefertari may fall for a Berry, but we will be having a talk with her the minute he brings her home."

Indeed, three weeks later as Jason and me, Orlando and Brendan, and Linc and Jessica sat down for Sunday dinner, Dallas brought Nefertari Hines with him to meet the family. I have to say, I liked her. Statuesque with exquisite sienna skin, long dark brown dreadlocks, and plus-size model looks, she carried herself like her namesake with the confidence and intelligence one admired and respected in Michelle Obama. And there was that look she gave him, which left me without a doubt that the Berry charm was fully in play. Nefertari was her own person, but she would always have my son's back. Even Daddy gave me an I-told-you-so look when I told him and Mama about Nefertari.

"See, Deshawna? All it took was the right woman to capture him," he said, exchanging a meaningful look with Mama. "How did he look at her at dinner?"

I gave a little chuckle. "Like a man who's fallen hard."

"Did he give her a title?"

I paused for a second. "When he introduced her, he said, 'This is my lady.'"

"Awwww," Mama gushed. "If this plays out like I think it will, you'll be gaining another daughter-in-law. And as soon as he proposes, you can help them find a house!"

Having my sons find their respective mates was a blessing, just like it was when Linda and Mel got back together, and Linda moved here from Milwaukee before they were married in 2009. I was worried about her, though. She'd had trouble from some man there who wouldn't leave her alone after Prentice passed away. From what she and Daddy told me, I had my doubts that the situation was over…

"These past two years have been nothing short of amazing," Jason declared while he and Deshawna picked up dirty dishes and silverware to put in the dishwasher. *"'Don't Ask Don't Tell' is history, Obama's been reelected…"*

"Minnesota voted no on that awful amendment," Deshawna added. *"And we have more grandchildren."*

"Yeah," Jason said with a smile in his voice as he thought about their newest grandchild, Amina Iman Randolph, born three days earlier and bringing the total to five. *"Dallas was beside himself. He had a grin on his face that absolutely refused to come off. You know how independent Nefertari is. I hope he doesn't drive her crazy."*

"Crazy how? You mean like roll out a red carpet wherever she goes? Refuse to let her lift a finger the way he did when she was pregnant? Give him some credit."

"Well, perhaps he'll use some moderation. Still, that was going on ever since they found out they were expecting a girl." Jason gave his wife a look of mock chastisement. *"Besides, do you remember what you were like with Delancey, our first grandchild? When Orlando and Brendan told us they had a daughter?"*

"What do you mean?" Deshawna said, feigning innocence.

"Deshawna, you went over to their house with blueprints and drawings for the nursery in your hands. And Rosa Livingston wasn't any better."

"Well, after three sons, I was hoping for at least one granddaughter at the time."

"Well, you got your wish. Now we have two, plus three grandsons."

Deshawna sighed, putting the last of the dishes in the dishwasher before filling the detergent dispenser. "I'm not that bad, if, my dear husband, you'll remember how Daddy was when he..."

Her reminiscing was cut short by the ringtone of her cell phone. She picked it up from the counter, answering, "Hello? Hello, Trevell... Trevell, what's wrong?... Oh, no... Oh, my God..."

Linda Berry Delaney Edwards

When Mama and Daddy started reproducing, they did it with gusto. I guess that three-year wait until Daddy graduated from law school must have filled them with extra energy. Where the Edwards family ran to boys, ours went in the opposite direction. Further confirmation of that fact came when, during a thunderstorm on July 15, 1954, I came into the world, Linda Marie Berry. There is no doubt that they love us all unconditionally. Even when Carter was born, Daddy didn't show partiality. He was, however, typical of men of his generation when it came to his daughters—after we reached a certain age, any impropriety by boys was grounds for capital punishment.

The Edwards family must have been on the same track—stairsteps. Melvin Edwards II is only a couple of months older than I am. Most people called him Mel to distinguish him from his grandfather. I've known him all my life, since our parents are so close. I have to admit, our mothers seemed to get pregnant at the same time with their first three kids. Was it something in the water? In any case, Daddy and Mama, from the old stories they shared with us, wanted a whole houseful of kids. Their wish was granted.

Daddy, with the backing and the connections of Melvin Edwards, was on a fast track as an attorney. Even with that, he put his trust in Mama when it came to the books. Her experience as an office manager definitely made him look better, even as she was keeping up the home front with us. He was doing well as a defense attorney, not to mention wills, trusts, and contract law. All that changed around the time I was six, but I was too young to understand why. The only clues to this change were the attitudes of the adults around us and being told that Uncle Eldon had gone to heaven.

84

As for Mel, he was molded in his father's image, just like his older brother John; the total package of an Edwards man. From the way girls acted around him by the time we hit high school he could have easily had a swelled head, but he didn't. In a way, he was the kind of man every straight woman with a pulse wanted and every straight man wanted to be. From what I observed in the interactions between his parents and his grandparents, Mel would grow up to be totally faithful and true to one woman—a huge plus in his favor. I liked him, and by the time we were at Central we had become friends in that way children of parents who are best friends are. Classmates and adults around us thought we were more than that, and I wouldn't have minded at all if we were.

Mel, however, kept sending me all these mixed signals. One day we could be enjoying a deep conversation and hanging out, the next day he could be ready to tell me something and then back away or suddenly remember something he had to do. I was puzzled. He wasn't dating anyone else, in spite of the girls at school who threw themselves at him. I even asked his cousin, Wayne Hendricks, if Mel was into guys. His answer was, "Honey hush. Linda, if Mel liked men, I'd know it in a heartbeat." No, the only girl he was spending any length of time with was me. What in the world was going on?

During our senior year, Mel and I were crowned the Sno Daze King and Queen, and we actually went to the dance as a couple. Daddy even gave us his blessings. Everything was fine as long as the songs were fast jams. Slow songs, however, were another story. I could have sworn Mel lived up to that down-home saying, "nervous as a long-tailed cat in a room full of rocking chairs." He may not have been shaking, but I could sense it. And after he took me home, he left me at the door with a peck on the cheek. I thought he would redeem himself at the senior prom, but he acted as though someone had put a gun to his head before he asked me. At the prom, he was the consummate gentleman, and he was somewhat better than he was at the Sno Daze dance. At the end of the night, he gave me a real kiss. However, he went missing the next week—out of sight, no calls, nothing. When he finally did talk to me with some lame excuse, I had had it. As it happened, I'd heard from two of the colleges I had applied to, and I made my choice.

When I went off to Marquette University in the fall of 1972 I was ready academically, but Mel had confused the hell out of me. I just wanted to forget him—well, forget the possibility that we could ever be together as more than friends. Men were crawling out of the woodwork of nearly every dorm on campus to take me out at the time, but I stayed focused on my studies and kept them at a polite distance, protecting myself with a pack of girlfriends. As far as my schoolwork went, it worked—I finished my freshman year with a 3.7 GPA. Yes, I felt good about myself, and Daddy and Mama were quite proud of me and my accomplishments.

I was taking a walk past the Milwaukee County Courthouse at the start of my sophomore year when I first noticed him. He was coming down the steps in a professional but celebratory way, as though he'd just won a case. I'd been around Daddy long enough to recognize that look, the one that said he no longer had to play his cards close to his vest. His navy blue, three-piece suit and briefcase spoke of success with confidence. His 6'2" body wasn't that of a professional athlete, but it was powerful, and his clothes complimented it well. His looks—suave, handsome. I found myself thinking of a young Duke Ellington with a modified Afro. I even wondered how many languages he could say "I love you madly" in, the aura was that strong. After I watched him get into a new Chrysler Imperial with his colleague and drive off, I kept on walking until I reached the lot where my five-year-old Dodge Dart convertible was parked, appreciating the eye candy but firmly convinced a man like that had to have a wife and children somewhere.

A month later I had taken my usual seat in political science class, ready to participate and take copious notes for one of the many papers I had to write. Our professor, Mr. Hammond, also taught Black studies, and I was inspired by the way he mixed the two in his lectures. He walked to the front of the classroom, dressed as usual in a dashiki and black bell-bottom slacks, his big mixed-grey Afro glistening with Afro-Sheen spray. I sat up straight, alert and ready for a meaty lecture, when he said, "Students, today we are going to have a guest speaker, one who is not only knowledgeable about politics and our heritage, but also its ramifications when it comes to law. He is a graduate of Harvard Law School, and he has had a highly successful career as an attorney in criminal law. In addition, he is currently up for an appointment to a judgeship in our federal district court here in Milwaukee. Without further adieu, I present to you Mr. Prentice Delaney."

Our speaker strode into the classroom. *Oh, my.* It was him, the man I saw at the courthouse. When he spoke, he spoke from confidence rather than arrogance. He spoke to us as students with intelligence. His presence dominated the room, and I found him fascinating.

I took notes like crazy, and during question-and-answer time I asked questions that only an attorney's daughter would ask. When class ended, I was still at my desk wrapping up my notes; I didn't want to miss anything from the lecture. I happened to look up and saw Mr. Delaney surrounded by a crowd of admirers. The brothas in class wanted to pick his brains, and the sistahs, well…in any case, Mr. Hammond saved him from that fate with, "I know you have a lot of questions, but Mr. Delaney is a man about business, and he made the time to be here to share his experience and knowledge with us. So, let's respect his time."

My classmates protested mildly, but they respected Mr. Hammond's directive and left. I had finished my notes just after they had gone and I attempted to quietly leave the classroom when I heard, "Miss Berry, do you have a moment?"

I turned to face our guest and said politely, "Certainly, Mr. Delaney."

"I have to commend you for your knowledgeable questions. Do you have a legal background?"

"Not me per se, but my father was an assistant district attorney. He became a judge this year."

"Where?"

"Hennepin County, Minnesota."

"It figures." He looked over at Mr. Hammond and said, "Njeri, it was a pleasure to speak to your class. You have very bright students, and Miss Berry is a prime example. Miss Berry, I have another appointment, but if you'd do me the honor of walking with me, I'd like to ask you some more questions...and answer any other questions you have of me."

I had to admit, I was flattered. "I'd be happy to."

"Excellent."

I don't think I even noticed anyone around us as we walked across campus to his car. We were quite engaged in the topics of law and politics, from *Brown vs. Board of Education* to the Angela Davis trial. His conversation alone spoke of his level of maturity. One didn't jump straight out of law school into an appointment on the federal bench, so he had to be at least 35. At the time of his birth, William Henry Hastie had become the first Black federal judge, and now Mr. Delaney was following in his illustrious footsteps. That, however, was more of a plus, in addition to the way we communicated. Before we knew it, we had reached the lot where his Imperial was parked.

"I would like to talk more with you, Miss Berry. Would you have dinner with me on Friday?"

"Well, I wouldn't want to take time away from your family, Mr. Delaney," I demurred.

"Call me Prentice. And you wouldn't be, because I'm a bachelor."

"Oh," I said, appreciating his directness. "Well, in that case, certainly. And you can call me Linda."

"I'll look forward to Friday, Linda."

I noted the friendliness in his voice that didn't translate into a come-on and smiled. "Likewise...Prentice."

After he left with my phone number in his day planner, I walked back to my dorm room to study before dinner. I had to give him his props; he knew how to treat a woman. In the short time I'd been with him, Prentice had shown me nothing but respect; Mama would say that he had "good home training."

When Friday came, I was more than ready for my date—I was almost certain this was a date. Prentice would never know how much midnight oil I burned to complete all my assignments and studying that week to leave my weekend open. And though he showed up on time, I forced myself to make him wait for five minutes before making my entrance to the dorm lobby. I was glad that I took a page from Mama for formal dinner dress attire, because Prentice was dressed in a tuxedo and boutonniere. "Linda, you look exquisite," he said as he took my arm. "Shall we?"

"Yes. And thank you," I said as we went to the car and he opened the door for me. I did my best not to look back at my dorm mates, knowing they hadn't taken their eyes off Prentice since he stepped into the dorm. Knowing some of them, the custodian would have to clean up the puddles of drool on the floor.

Even though Milwaukee is known for beer, Prentice knew where the best restaurants were, and Fox and Hounds was no exception. I loved our dinner choices, from the prime rib to the key lime pie. Our conversation just flowed so easily. His interest in me was sincere. Over the course of the evening, if I had any doubts about what a man like Prentice saw in me other than the obvious, they were dispelled.

Even so, one date does not a courtship make. Sure, Prentice made an excellent first impression with his car, his intelligence, and his choice of restaurants, but after growing up with Daddy and being around the Edwardses I was not a woman who was easily impressed by trappings—something that Mama reinforced when I finally told her about Prentice. After a beautiful evening of dinner and dancing, he dropped me off at my dorm. "Thank you for a wonderful evening, Linda. I look forward to calling on you again soon."

"I'd like that, Prentice," was my answer, just before he smoothly captured my lips in a kiss, one that lingered long after he left and I found myself sitting on my bed, reminding myself to breathe.

Prentice's position may have kept him busy, but he made sure he made the time for me from the beginning. He was interested in my studies and encouraged me in my ambitions while I got to know the man behind the career, the last member of a very socially and politically prominent family in Milwaukee. He also introduced me to his friends. Unlike Mel, Prentice was crystal clear when it came to his interest in me. When I invited him to meet my family over Christmas, his reply was, "I'd love to."

Daddy was skeptical at first when I introduced him to Prentice. I'm sure he was wondering what a successful man of 36 saw in a 19-year-old girl—*his* 19-year-old girl. Even though I was a legal adult, Daddy still possessed that mindset. However, when they came out of the study, Daddy was treating Prentice like a new son-in-law and he hadn't even proposed to me yet. I half suspected that Daddy had run a background check on him, which I kept to myself. Mama resigned herself to the fact that a Berry-Edwards connection wasn't in the cards for me, so her advice was, "Marry well." I knew exactly what she meant--the total package of love, security, romance, and faith. What Mama didn't know was that I had already fallen for Prentice in a big way.

We saw the Edwardses over the holidays with the exception of Mel, who somehow managed to be out whenever we came by. I didn't understand Mel. That simply wasn't the way someone treated a friend, and it bothered me. Fortunately, the time with my family and Prentice more than kept me occupied. Meanwhile, my sisters had plenty to say about my new boyfriend. Sylvia and Deshawna, in fact, grabbed me and pulled me into the nearest bathroom for their appraisal: "I don't know how a man like *that* managed to stay single for so long, but now that you've got him don't you dare let him go! Mel Edwards may be fine as wine, but Prentice Delaney is marriage material with a capital M!" Sylvia insisted.

"And make no mistake, Linda, that man is totally in love with you," Deshawna added for emphasis. "You're a Berry, and for him there's no turning back!"

New Year's Eve found us at the ballroom in the Marquette Inn, at the time one of the newest hotels in Minneapolis by virtue of its connection to the IDS Center. Record-setting subzero cold dominated the previous few days, and New Year's Day would set a record of -30, but the ballroom was full of celebrants—any party that was hosted by Melvin and Lillian Edwards guaranteed that. The Edwards family was working the room, along with my parents, to ensure that their special guests, Ruby Dee and Ossie Davis, felt warmly welcomed and comfortable. Mr. and Mrs. Gray were also present and definitely having a good time, from the animated way Mrs. Gray was carrying on. Sylvia and Clint were almost joined at the hip, but that was to be expected for newlyweds. We chatted with my sisters and their dates, and touched base with Carter, who as usual was talking to Julian Edwards about something.

As the party progressed and there was time for dancing, Prentice whispered, "Let's step out for a moment." I nodded, curious as to his reasons but welcoming the opportunity for a little privacy. We found a relatively quiet corner outside the ballroom, where we took a seat.

"So, my handsome prince," I said, teasingly. "What's the big secret?"

"Well, my princess, it's like this." He reached into his pocket. When he went down on one knee, my hands went to my mouth and my heart skipped a beat.

"I never thought I'd meet a woman like you, Linda," he admitted. "I've been satisfied with my career and the success that's come with it, ever since my parents died. But you have shown me that there's so much more to life for me—better yet, for us. You're the woman I want to cherish, honor, and value. You challenge me in a good way. You bring out the best in me. I believe that together we have what it takes for a full, abundant life. I love you, Linda, and I want to keep on loving you for as long as I live. Will you marry me? Will you be my wife?"

When I looked into his eyes, seeing the sincerity—and more important, the love—there, I knew in my heart Prentice meant everything he said. I heard the Stylistics "Betcha By Golly Wow" in my head, and my answer was, "Yes, Prentice. I love you, and I will marry you."

A few seconds after he placed the beautiful engagement ring on my finger, I heard the crowd in the ballroom doing the countdown. When 1974 rolled in with cheers and celebration, Prentice's arms were wrapped around me, and his lips met mine in a deep kiss of desire and profound happiness. Several minutes later, we went back to the ballroom to rejoin the party. We must have looked suspicious because Mama approached me and asked, "All right, you two. What's going on?"

"Well, Mrs. Berry, a few minutes ago Linda agreed to be my wife," Prentice declared with a big smile. When I flashed my engagement ring in confirmation, Mama grabbed me and gave me a huge hug. Daddy shook Prentice's hand profusely and clapped him on the back. He wasted no time telling Mr. Edwards who stopped the party, grabbing a microphone to make the announcement. I could tell where each of my sisters were in the room by the shrieks that went up just before the general cheers and well wishes of the guests. They swooped down on me in nothing flat, wanting every juicy detail they could get out of me while Prentice was whisked off by Daddy, Eli Edwards, Grandpa Berry, Grandpa Langston, Melvin Edwards, and their circle.

Later that day, Prentice and I sat down and found a reasonable compromise for a wedding date, marking September 21, 1974 on the calendar. The very next day Mama, Grandma Berry, Grandma Langston, Auntie Elaine, and my sisters descended upon me to start the wedding plans—with all the grace of a bulldozer. Of course, the Edwards women were firmly in the loop with an abundance of support. How I managed to maintain my studies and plan a wedding I'll never know, but it happened.

Prentice never wavered in his attentiveness during this process, even as he served on cases and endured the "trial by fire" of his appointment process. Unlike Daddy's appointment to the state bench, the federal process involved more politics, senatorial and presidential approval, not to mention a monstrous FBI background check. Everyone who ever knew him, everything he ever did, was up for microscopic review. I could hardly believe that the government could run through his life like a 10-lane freeway and then prohibit him from seeing the report. In my nightly prayers, I prayed that God would move in that process for Prentice as we patiently waited for the results.

May 25 found me at Prentice's home on the North Shore in River Hills, packing my things in preparation for the Memorial Day weekend with my family.

"Baby, I have some news to share with you."

His expression was unreadable, and I sat down in a chair with concern. "All right. What is it?"

"It's about the appointment."

"Oh. I see."

"Well…can you be here for my swearing-in ceremony next month?" His face broke into a smile.

I leaped up from the chair, shouted and covered his face with kisses. "You bet I'll be there, Your Honor," I said playfully, even as I sent up praises in my spirit.

We could have easily jumped on a plane from Mitchell Field and flown to Minneapolis, but over the course of our courtship I'd learned that Prentice loved to drive and get out on the open road when opportunities presented themselves. In those days and even later on, we often had our best talks, shared our dreams, visions, and ideas on those drives. This particular weekend, we knew that our time together would change. I still had two years of undergraduate work left plus student teaching in my senior year, and though Prentice's hours would be closer to a nine-to-five, who knew what else he would be required to do in relation to his new duties? Needless to say, Prentice's appointment and our upcoming wedding dominated the conversation during those seven hours on I-94, back in the days when the speed limit was 55.

"Congratulations, Judge Delaney," Daddy beamed, giving Prentice a hearty handshake and a brotha hug when we arrived.

"Thank you, Judge Berry," Prentice beamed back. "So how was your week in court?"

"Some of it was good, and some of it wasn't. You'll find out soon enough."

"OK, Daddy," I broke in. "For now, let's celebrate and have fun this weekend."

"Certainly, Linda," he said, "but not until Prentice gives me the date he gets sworn in."

From the looks that passed between Prentice and Daddy, I knew they were going to talk shop at different times over the weekend, regardless of what I said. But Prentice happily complied with Daddy's request and asked, "Are you free on June 17?"

"I'll be free, and the family will be there. There's no way that we'd miss it," was Daddy's emphatic reply.

Our wedding at St. Matthew's was everything I ever wanted, even with LaVera acting like she was the star of a Broadway show rather than my maid of honor. All my family was there, as well as the Edwardses, Mr. and Mrs. Christopher, other family friends and neighbors I'd grown up with. I really felt for Prentice, who had no immediate family; his father died in combat in 1944, his mother from cancer in 1958. I could only imagine what that was like for him. Still, I was glad his friends and colleagues flew in from Milwaukee to support him, and he now had a family with us. Daddy shed a few tears before he walked me down the aisle, but that was Daddy, and I loved him for it. The church was full, and seeing my handsome, wonderful man waiting for me at the altar filled my heart to overflowing.

For the people who say that the wedding night is overrated, I would call them liars or just plain inept. Prentice, as I soon learned, was a lovemaking wizard, and he knew exactly how to handle the inexperience I brought to the bedroom. Granted, we'd had more than our share of steamy make-out sessions during our engagement, but they only went so far. On our wedding night, it was "Take Me to the Next Phase." When the Isley Brothers produced that song four years later, all Prentice and I could do was eye each other and grin, ready to race to the bedroom.

Prentice worked me into a sexual frenzy. My lips were swollen from his kisses, my nipples were erect, and I already had two orgasms from his oral technique—and he hadn't put that hot, throbbing manhood of his inside me yet! "Please, please," I begged him. "I want you inside me—now."

That had to have been a huge turn-on for him, having his virgin bride begging him to take her. I was beyond wet and ready. When Prentice pushed in with a confident thrust and slowly worked his magic, his eyes on me, I was a goner. The pleasure—the deep, surging pleasure of this physical intimacy—was enough to sweep me away. To further enhance the mood, he played Barry White albums, and we fell into the rhythms.

His stamina was incredible. The tension built and built until I exploded and screamed my ecstasy in starbursts of pleasure. Seconds later, I heard Prentice buck and roar as his release filled me with his seed.

With a man like Prentice, I certainly wasn't a woman who would just lay there in bed. I learned a few tricks of my own during our newlywed days. One of my favorite things to do was to dip my husband's spellbinding penis into chocolate syrup, and then lick and suck it all off just before I lowered myself onto him and rode him. It drove him wild! Yes, there was so much mutually satisfying fun, thinking of new and different ways to arouse each other.

Prentice and I wanted children—I would never have married a man who didn't—but we also wanted some time for ourselves before that happened, unlike Mama and Daddy's motivation for waiting. When I became pregnant during my senior year, Prentice felt like—and was—sitting on top of the world. I remember sitting there with my graduating class, about to receive my bachelor's degree in elementary education, seven months along and proud of my husband as he spoke to us on Commencement Day. Sure, some of my classmates could look, pant, drool, and get wet, but he was mine.

I half expected him to host his own fireworks show when, on July 4, 1976, I gave birth to our daughter, Sierra Linda Delaney. There was no question whatsoever that Sierra took after the Berry side of the family. Prentice doted on her. When he took her to his chambers in the Federal Building on one of his days off, Sierra captured the attention of the entire staff. *What,* I wondered, *would it be like when she became a young woman?* The answer came quickly. Daddy and

Prentice would guard her virtue with threats of life imprisonment or the death penalty.

I had learned firsthand what was required when you're the spouse of a judge, courtesy of Mama and Daddy. Daddy's appointment to the bench in 1973 brought changes to our family, and Mama sat me down for a talk about it prior to my wedding. "No one knows better than I that being a judge's spouse holds you to a higher standard. What you wear, what you say, how you conduct yourself, all these things come into play whenever you step outside your home. Prentice may be the judge in the family, Linda, but what you do and how you do it can either make him or break him."

Raising Sierra kept me busy in the early years, but as she got older and started school, I became more and more involved in community affairs, issues that were near and dear to our hearts in Milwaukee. Education was at the top of the list, and I often visited schools or spoke to Board of Education officials about the quality of education our children were getting. They knew they weren't talking to some empty-headed woman when dealing with me, so they had to, as younger people might say, "come correct."

Julian and Carter's wedding in the summer of 1983 was beautiful, and since I won the lottery it was an honor to be Carter's matron of honor. Once they married, Mr. and Mrs. Edwards became Uncle Eli and Auntie Donna; later, she became Madear. With the blessing and authority of Lillian Christopher Edwards, she also became the new society queen. We in turn brought more good news to the family at the rehearsal dinner; I was pregnant again, which Daddy proudly announced to everyone. Prentice and I were thrilled about having an addition to our family, and Sierra went on and on about having a new brother or a sister. I could have had an ultrasound done, like Deshawna did when she was pregnant with Linc, but we wanted to be surprised.

We certainly were when, on January 19, 1984, I gave birth to an eight-pound, three-ounce boy. Prior to his birth, we had discussed the Berry family tradition of grandsons. That, however, was before I saw the look on Prentice's face when he held our son for the first time. "Linda, I know about your family's tradition and I understand it, but there's no one on my side of the family left but me. Would you mind if we named him Prentice George Delaney, Jr.?"

There was no way I could refuse the man who'd given me so much love, devotion, commitment, and now a second child. My heart was full of love for him when I answered, "No, honey. I wouldn't mind at all. So shall it be."

Prentice, for all he was born into, wanted as normal a family life as possible under the circumstances, and I loved him for that. When Sierra and Junior grew from tots to grade school and then high school, we found through trial and error the balance between letting them be kids and instilling in them the values that with wealth and privilege came responsibility. Daddy, Mama, and the Edwardses were a strong support system in that area, given the way they raised us. From time to time, Daddy would tell me about cases he presided over in family and criminal court of trust fund brats who thought the law didn't apply to them until the sentences Daddy gave them for their crimes yanked them harshly into the world of reality. No, state prisons didn't care about your pedigree or the size of your bank account—do the crime, do the time.

I had heard about the "gift" Uncle Eli had that was passed down to his grandchildren, but I took it with a grain of salt. That is, until my niece Donna Jo zoned out on me while we were celebrating Sierra's 25th birthday on a trip to Minneapolis in 2001. "Sierra's getting married next year," she said in a strange voice, strange for an eight-year-old girl.

"What did you say?"

"She's gonna bring him to meet you on Labor Day." A few seconds later she seemed to come back from wherever she'd been and went off to play with her cousins, leaving me bewildered. I went over to Carter immediately, who was keeping an eye on my other niece Lilly while eating some barbecue. When I told him what happened, he treated it as though it was no big deal.

"Well, it looks like you'll have a son-in-law in your future," he stated.

"But I thought all that stuff about Uncle Eli's visions was just a family story."

"No, Linda. It's the real deal, and Donna Jo has inherited his gift."

"But why haven't I seen it before now?"

"You live in Milwaukee. You don't see her that often. Besides, it's random, something that happens once in a while. However, when it does happen, the visions always come to pass, just like they do with her grandpa."

"Can she see things that will happen to her?"

"No, she can't."

"It all sounds so unbelievable," I sighed, still having difficulty grasping the concept.

"We don't talk about it much. We try to keep things simple, mainly when she asks questions. A couple of her cousins have it, too, and it's treated as a private family matter. We want to keep this from getting out to the wrong people."

"I understand that, but still…"

"Just wait, Linda. You'll find out soon enough." Carter gave me a knowing smirk.

When Labor Day weekend rolled around, Prentice, Junior, and I were out at the park back home enjoying a holiday picnic with our neighbors, some of Prentice's colleagues, and their families. We were preparing to play volleyball when I spotted Sierra entering the park with a young man. He reminded me of Clarence Williams III of *Mod Squad* fame, and they were holding hands. I recognized the warm smile on her face immediately; I wore that same smile when Prentice and I were dating.

"Hi, Mom, Dad," my daughter said when they reached our picnic table. "You said I could bring a guest, so I brought Rashid. Rashid Hines, these are my parents. Mom, Dad, this is Rashid. Oh—the one over there that spiked the volleyball is my brother, Junior."

Rashid shook our hands. "Pleasure to meet you.".

"You play volleyball?" Prentice asked him.

"Well enough to keep up."

"Good. Let's go down and work up an appetite."

As my husband and Rashid went off to join the game, Donna Jo's vision smacked me in the face, figuratively if not literally. Even though Sierra was grown and living on her own, I was determined to get all the background information on my future son-in-law, and I gestured for her to take a seat at the table. "All right, Sierra. I know what I saw. Start talking."

The smile Sierra gave me was her *I've-been-busted* smile. "OK, Mom. Rashid is more than a guest. We've been seeing each other for a while now."

"And you didn't tell us?"

"I just wanted to be sure. You know how that is. Didn't you wait a while before you brought Dad around to meet the family?"

I hated it when she was right, but I wasn't about to get sidetracked. "Well, we're not talking about me, we're talking about you. So, tell me more."

"OK. He's from Kenosha, but he's living in Chicago. He graduated from Northwestern, and now he has his own business as an IT specialist."

"What about his family?"

"His parents still live in Kenosha, and he has two sisters and two brothers. His father is on the city council, and his mother is a store manager at Wal-Mart. And before you ask, we're not living together—at least, not yet. Right now, he comes up here or I go down to Chicago when we want to see each other."

I wonder if Rashid knows Allan Beckley Christopher, I thought as Sierra continued to share. Then again, who doesn't at least know of him—especially in that field?

On June 29, 2002, three days after Mama and Daddy's 54th wedding anniversary, Sierra and Rashid had a beautiful outdoor wedding on the grounds of our estate. The Berrys, of course, were well represented. Mama and Daddy had their front-row seats for the occasion, as did Rashid's parents and Uncle Eli and Madear; apparently Julian told his father about Donna Jo's vision, because he looked at me and gave me a secret nod. Mr. and Mrs. Christopher, who came up from Evanston, were also VIP guests. Junior brought his best friend Shayla, and although guests who didn't know our family well thought they made a cute couple, we knew better.

All eyes were on our daughter when Prentice walked her to the altar where our pastor and Rashid were waiting. Her Vera Wang wedding gown only enhanced her natural beauty, and I couldn't help but notice how spellbound Rashid was by her. As they said their vows, I thought about what Mama and my sisters told me long ago. *He has fallen hard for you, and there's no turning back, Sierra. No turning back...*

I wasn't surprised that my daughter was in no rush to have children. I didn't mind having her when I did, but I appreciated her desire to wait until she was a little older and had more time under her belt as an elementary school teacher. And so it was that Daddy, Mama, Prentice, Junior, Rashid's parents, and I were all gathered in the waiting room at the hospital while Rashid was doing his duty as a labor coach on December 29, 2004. Daddy was in absolute glory when Rashid came out of the delivery room looking a little awestruck and announced they had a son, who they named Earl Berry Hines. Rashid's father David was equally proud since, as it turned out, his middle name is Earl. He and Daddy avidly speculated on Little Earl's future in law or politics.

When I married Prentice, I dreamed of how we would spend the rest of our lives together, I loved him so much. When he wasn't in court and we had family time, he was active in what I considered robust health—swimming, cycling, racquetball, always up for a good volleyball game or touch football. Even when he hit his 60s, he was in better shape than a lot of men in their mid-30s; the way he held his own with Junior was amazing. That made it difficult to comprehend when 2005 rolled around, and I began to notice changes in him. Things he did with ease in the past now left him more winded, more fatigued. Occasionally he had difficulty concentrating, but not to the point where it interfered with his duties.

"Prentice, I think you need to take it easy. Maybe you've been under too much stress," I told him one day. "Frankly, I'm a little concerned about you, and I really think you should see your doctor."

"Linda, I know you mean well, but this just comes with the territory. You deal with it and you move on."

"No, dear. You've had tougher challenges than you have now, and they didn't have these effects on you. Something else is happening in you, and I will not let this rest until you see your doctor."

Gradually, it seemed, my husband was growing weaker, and the reports from his doctor weren't encouraging. He had been experiencing transient ischemic attacks, also known as "mini-strokes." In the past, he loved to drive up to Green Bay on the weekends when the Packers were playing. We still went, but the driving was largely done by me, Junior, Sierra, or Rashid because Prentice tired so easily. As fall turned to winter, not long after Junior met Trevell Ross, Prentice's health went downhill faster, to the point where he was forced to retire from the bench. That was a major blow for him, giving up something he loved.

I knew my husband was losing ground, but it was still hard when he suffered a major stroke and had to be rushed to the hospital on January 30, 2006. The waiting was excruciating. When his doctor came out to see us, I steeled myself for whatever news he had. "It's only a matter of time now—hours, days, maybe a week or so," he said. "I'm very sorry, Mrs. Delaney."

I did my best not to cry, but a few tears escaped anyway. "I want to see my husband. How soon can that be arranged?"

"Once we transfer him from ER."

"Sierra, I need a change of clothes and my overnight bag. Can you get it for me?" I asked. "Bailey will be there to help you."

"Yes, Mom. Anything you need."

"Junior, can you make some calls to the family? I need to be here for your father."

"Sure, Mom."

Those final days felt like a lifetime. To be more accurate, it felt more like attempting to fill a lifetime into a few days. Prentice was a man who believed that when it was his time to go, he had to face it head on. I don't think I left the hospital, except to change and freshen up. I was in daily contact with Mama and Daddy, as well as my siblings. I knew how hard it was for Sierra and Junior to see him in that condition, but their love for their father wouldn't keep them away. I had to listen carefully to understand what my husband was saying to me when he was conscious, and we shared all the special times of our life together. Whenever he said, "I love you, Linda," it was all I could do to keep from breaking down, but I was strong as I professed to him with conviction, "I love you, too, honey. Very much."

Sierra, Rashid, Junior, Trevell, and I were gathered around Prentice's bedside when he breathed his last on February 6, 2006. I loved him so much. He had been the kind of husband a woman dreams of having, and he kept right on showing me that for 31 years. As we were preparing for his funeral, memories of our life together dominated my thoughts like a flood. It didn't seem real. I kept thinking of him in the present, even when I talked to my family over the phone. Over the next few days, as family members came in from Minneapolis for support, I promised myself that his service would be beautiful.

So many of Prentice's colleagues and friends we made in Milwaukee were in attendance, as well as my family, the Rosses, and most of the Edwardses. In the city, Prentice had been highly respected, which was reflected in the remarks of the mayor, leaders in the African American community, and news commentary, not to mention Daddy's beautiful and eloquent remarks about my husband. Uncle Eli and Mr. Christopher also gave heartfelt testimony to Prentice's life, their words a soothing balm in my grief. In the legal community, he had become the standard by which others were measured. Five years later, my family returned to Milwaukee for the dedication ceremonies of a new middle school named in his honor.

Prentice also believed in having his affairs in order, as well as making sure I knew what needed to be done as his wife. He had left us well provided for, plus bequests to different nonprofit organizations in the community.

June of 2007 came around, and I managed to keep busy with my work in community affairs and helping Sierra now that she and Rashid had another crumb cruncher, my beautiful granddaughter

Destiny Grace Hines, who was then three months old. I hadn't been up to seeing anyone. There were plenty of men ready to put in their application for the position of husband, though. Some I could let off with a polite, "I'm just not ready." Others were more oblivious to that, to the point where I had to give them a firm, "No."

Glendon Price, however, was a different animal altogether. Sure, he traveled in the same circles as Prentice and I, and we had a nodding acquaintance. He was handsome and polished in his way, and he could say all the right things. The only thing was, whenever I was in his presence, I couldn't shake the feeling that something about him wasn't quite right. When Prentice was alive, I always made sure that I was never alone with Glendon. The power and influence Prentice had as a federal judge had held Glendon at bay, but when I became a widow, he was more determined than the rest to make me his.

He didn't come after me right away. It was when I started attending community functions again that he made it a point to be at every one. He was like a dog marking his territory, warning off other men when I had never given him any such signals. He called me at home so frequently that I had my home number changed and unpublished. I could even be out having lunch or dinner with friends and I could sense his presence in the restaurant before I saw him.

I'd had enough. My children had had enough. Glendon wasn't just a nuisance; this whole situation was becoming creepy. This was obsession. This was stalking behavior. I finally spoke to Daddy about it on one of his visits to Milwaukee.

"I've already arranged to have a security detail, Daddy. This man is going too far."

Daddy went into protective mode—no one messed with his children. "Good. And while you're at it, Linda, I would suggest that you apply for a harassment restraining order. You know that if he violates it, you have grounds to have him arrested and press charges."

"I will, Daddy. I still have Prentice's contacts."

"And you have Madear on your side as well."

I wondered what Daddy meant for a moment, then I remembered. Things had a way of happening when Donna Gray Edwards was involved.

"Would you like me to take care of it? I know people here. I can also have a talk with him."

"He may not listen to you, Daddy. He may blow you off. He certainly hasn't taken no for an answer when I told him."

"Linda, perhaps we need to give him the right persuasion." I opened my mouth to protest, but Daddy cut me off. "No, I don't mean beating the living daylights out of him, even though I think he richly deserves it. But there are other ways."

Daddy did have that talk with Glendon, warning him in his strongest judicial tone to stay away from me or else. From what Daddy told me, Glendon looked down his nose at him as if to say, "What can an old man like you do to me?" Shortly thereafter, my husband's contacts guaranteed a speedy granting of the restraining order I requested. Meanwhile, a conference between Daddy and Madear brought a few skeletons out of Glendon's closet, and he was hit with orders of back child support from four women.

That was only the beginning. They dug deeper, and they found enough on Glendon to keep him tied up in litigation for years on other criminal charges. *That fortune-hunting slime,* I thought when the news hit. Although I had protection and Glendon had more than his share of legal problems—thanks to Daddy—something about him when I saw him in court told me this situation was far from over.

Unknown to me, something else had already been set into motion. In late September, I was on the telephone with Sierra when the doorbell rang.

"Mrs. Delaney, there is a Mr. Edwards to see you," my houseman Bailey announced.

"Mr. Edwards? Which Mr. Edwards?"

"Mr. Melvin Edwards."

I was floored. What was Mel doing here? "Sierra, I have to call you back," I said before I hung up.

He's just like his father—he definitely got better as he got older. His curly hair was graying at the temples, and his body wore his earth-toned turtleneck, sport coat and slacks well. "Hi, Linda," he said, and I could tell there was something different about his demeanor.

"Mel. I must say, this is a surprise." I felt awkward—I didn't know whether to give him a hug or shake his hand, so I did neither. "Come in and have a seat." I sat down in my favorite chair in the sitting room while he took a spot on the love seat. "Would you like something to drink?"

"Sure. Cranberry juice works for me."

"Bailey, would you bring some cranberry juice for Mr. Edwards and mineral water for me?"

"Yes, Mrs. Delaney."

When Bailey left the room, I asked Mel, "So, how has life been treating you? And what brings you to Milwaukee?"

"Well, I'm sure you know all about the bridge collapse last month."

"I know. It was awful news. How's your father?"

"He has a long way to go towards recovery, especially with a broken hip, but I'm just...so grateful he's alive." We paused while Bailey brought in the refreshments and left again. "I know things haven't been easy for you since Prentice passed away."

I stared at my glass for a few seconds before I looked into Mel's eyes. "The hurt doesn't just go away. There are so many memories of him. There have been times where I woke up in the middle of the night and thought I heard his voice. It was a long time before I stopped having the table set for two. Still, I have to go on, one day at a time."

"I understand that. I know I haven't been the greatest friend to you—not the way we used to be. I messed up. For that, I ask you to forgive me. Linda, I can't turn back the clock, but..."

"What?"

"I'd like to be that kind of friend again. Someone you can talk to when you need to, someone you can call in those midnight hours." He took a sip of his drink and I saw something different in his hazel eyes. Was it pain, or regret? "Maybe these things have happened to us to remind us not to take so much for granted, I don't know. All I do know is that while I'm here, I'd like to spend some time with you…if that's all right."

The confused teenager I used to be whispered, "Mel left you hanging. Don't let him back in. He may be Julian's brother, but leave him in the brother-in-law zone." However, I had forgiven him long ago. If he came here just to see me, my adult mind told me he had to be sincere. Besides, all things considered, Mel was nothing like the suitors I had been forced to keep at arm's length. The question was, would he open up to me? I had to know. I nodded and said, "Tell me more, Mel."

By the time he left early that evening, Mel and I had shared things we'd never shared before, and it was a beginning of a renewed friendship. I had a far better understanding of the depth of his ex-wife's betrayal; I could have strangled the whore myself. He, in turn, listened attentively as I shared my feelings during Prentice's last days. During his stay, we went out to lunch, attended a dinner theater, and hung out as old friends do. Sierra and Junior showed up at the house from time to time, and they treated him as they always had.

I'm not sure just when friendship changed to something more over the next year. Maybe it was the gradually increasing frequency of Mel's visits to Milwaukee. Maybe it was the phone calls he made "just to check in" that I found myself looking forward to. Maybe it was the times we spent together enjoying our respective grandchildren. It could have been the long weekend when we went away to Nevis. Maybe it was the first serious kiss he gave me, after he finally told me how he really felt about me back in high school. Whatever the case, Mel was winning my heart. When he said, "I love you, Linda," it was from the depths of his heart—at last!

My family was back in Minneapolis, a few days before Barack Obama was first elected president, when Mel proposed to me. It was quiet that day in Minnehaha Park, sitting there by the river, hearing only the sounds of birds and the wind through the trees as the leaves fell. There was no trace of the shy, waffling teenager when he said

106

the words, "Marry me, Linda," and his eyes only confirmed what he wanted.

I didn't answer right away; a memory of a conversation with Prentice during his last days flashed before me. He had told me, "Linda, my love, I hope that at some point you do marry again. I can't bear the thought of you going through the rest of your life alone." I couldn't accept it at the time, but now I understood what he meant.

I was able to look at Mel and tell him "Yes."

Mel can never replace Prentice, and we can't make up for lost time, but together we can create new memories and a love that stands on its own merits. These were thoughts that went through my mind when we stood before Pastor Andrews on May 2, 2009, surrounded by our families and friends at St. Matthew's. At the reception, Mama and Madear greeted us with unadulterated glee, and it didn't take a rocket scientist to figure out why. When we saw similar expressions on our children, I pulled Mel off into a corner.

"Do you suppose there's been a conspiracy going on?" I wondered.

"Such as?"

"Look over there."

Mel followed my line of vision to where our mothers and our children had gathered together in celebration. "They look as thick as thieves."

"I have the feeling they've been working behind the scenes to bring us together for a while."

"Well, if they were, it worked. We're married," Mel said with a smile.

What could I say to that? "That's true," I sighed flirtatiously as Mel gave me a kiss. "Maybe they knew something we didn't."

"Maybe. Meantime, honey, let's let them have their moment." The amorous look in Mel's eyes turned on the heat in me. "We have a honeymoon to enjoy."

Aruba was breathtaking, and the three weeks we spent there for our honeymoon were beautiful and memorable. When we weren't seeing the sights and enjoying the hospitality of the country, our nights in bed were steamy. There was something about passion mixed with the experience that comes with maturity that made our lovemaking even more potent, a constant, slow-burning flame that left us more than satisfied. I loved to straddle him, feeling his hands on me as I worked my feminine walls on his diamond-hard manhood—ooh, Mel knew what to do with his hands! After all that time of doing without, I felt hot, sexy, and desired again in all the right ways.

We returned home rejuvenated and ready to settle into married life in our new home on Dean Parkway, the neighborhood nestled between Lake of the Isles, Lake Calhoun, and Cedar Lake. A few days later, we received a visit from Prentice and Trevell, just before the Memorial Day weekend.

"Hi Mama, Uncle Mel," my son said as they greeted us with hugs.

"Prentice. Trevell. Good to see you," Mel said. "Come on in."

We took seats in the family room while Bailey brought us refreshments and Ms. Sullivan prepared a light snack. We talked about the sights we saw on our honeymoon and showed them the albums we made up. They were very interested, but I sensed they were doing their best to conceal a big reveal.

Mel must have sensed it as well, because he went right to the point. "All right, you two. What's going on?"

"What are you talking about?" Trevell said, trying to play innocent.

"Don't play me, Trevell. Jerome had that same look when he..."

I saw Mel sitting there with his mouth open when I considered what he said. I soon noticed they had been taking great pains to conceal their hands. "Prentice, Trevell, is there something you want to tell us?"

"Mama, you know all those stories Grandma and Grandpa have shared with us," Prentice began.

"Yes..."

"Well, while you were on your honeymoon, Trevell and I went to King Park….and like Grandpa did to Grandma, I proposed to him." He turned to Trevell, who lifted his hand to reveal an engagement ring.

I melted. Romance had struck again. "Awwww. I should have known. Congratulations!" I beamed as Mel and I went to hug the newly engaged couple.

Over snacks I wanted to know everything about their wedding plans, while Mel asked the practical questions, such as where they were going to marry. After they left, I couldn't wait to get on the phone with Trevell's mother Darcelle to share the joy and indulge in some wedding brainstorming on behalf of our sons.

Getting grandchildren from Jerome and Ariel—as well as Prentice and Trevell—was a source of great joy for us, and that went double for our parents. Still, sometime after 2011 rolled around—with a higher than normal snowfall—I felt something weird in my spirit. I couldn't put my finger on it, because it came and went. As time went on, at times when I was out and about town, the feeling grew stronger. I shared my feelings with Mel, who asked me, "How would you describe it?"

I walked over to the bedroom window, looked out for a few seconds and walked back to my husband. "It's like…you know those cameras you see on some traffic lights?"

"Yeah."

I found myself pacing back and forth as I searched for the best way to describe what I was feeling. "It's like looking into one of them and sensing you're being watched. But how is that possible?"

"I don't know. But if it persists, we should investigate."

I didn't like the train my thoughts were taking as winter turned into spring, and shortly after our family gathered outside of church on Palm Sunday, Jerome was talking about the sermon when I saw that look on his face. He let go of his daughter Jennifer's little hand, which I grabbed as he said, "Auntie Linda, he's here in Minneapolis. He'll make himself known to you when you least expect it—unless you locate him first."

I didn't even need to ask who as my heart filled with a mixture of anger and dread. I turned to Mel. "I thought that restraining order would make him leave me alone. Apparently, he violated parole despite his legal difficulties."

Jerome came back to himself, his eyes now filled with concern. "What are you going to do?"

"Well, we certainly aren't going to run," Mel vowed. "But we are going to get protection and the legal balls rolling. That delusional creep is not going to wreck our lives."

After a quick conversation with Daddy, Madear, and Uncle Eli, two phone calls were made. A restraining order was issued in Minneapolis against Glendon Price, followed by a call to the Milwaukee County sheriff's office as notification. Daddy may have been retired, but his reputation and influence were such that people knew he didn't take no for an answer on certain things. Sure, Glendon may have been smart and slick but we were blessed by the fact he didn't know we were on to him, thanks to my stepson's "gift."

With help from my brother-in-law, Jarvis, a plan was set into motion. Glendon was found living under an assumed name in an apartment in the Whittier neighborhood, and surveillance was set up. I had no desire to be present when he was apprehended and taken back to Milwaukee, but Daddy insisted on being there when everything went down. It only took three days before Glendon made his move, and the police were there to slap him in handcuffs and take him into custody. According to Daddy, he had an air about him that shouted *nut job,* but he was on his way back to Wisconsin to face the charges against him. But would he get prison time? Would all of this finally be over?

"This has truly been a day of victory, on all counts," Linda stated as she and Mel curled up watching television, listening to the "talking heads" reviewing President Obama's re-election.

"I hear you, honey." Mel leaned over to give his wife a kiss. "Didn't Dad say something about his needing another term to do what needed to be done?"

"And he got it. I'll bet they're still celebrating over at campaign headquarters."

"Do you think Prentice and Trevell are still there?"

"Probably. But they know that Barack is fine spending the night here." At that moment, Linda found herself sitting up straight.

"What is it?"

"I don't know. I just want to check on him. I'll only be a moment." She rose from the sofa and headed for one of the guest bedrooms.

Linda walked softly into the bedroom, resting her eyes upon her sleeping grandson. She remembered how she loved watching her children sleep when they were little, and now she appreciated reliving those moments with her grandchildren on the occasions when they spent the night. Normally she felt more relaxed after checking on him, but not tonight. Something else was going on...

LaVera Berry St. James

Thanksgiving Day, before it was taken over by football games and the Christmas shopping season, is considered a holiday to take stock of all that we're grateful for. I can imagine my parents were doing just that as they, Sylvia, Deshawna, Linda, my grandparents, my Uncle Eldon, and Auntie Elaine were gathered around the table for dinner. The adults were probably hoping they could at least make it through dinner without any imminent signs of my arrival.

As luck would have it, the women in the family had finished putting away the food and done the dishes when Mama went into labor—just as it was starting to snow. So, a coin was tossed to see who would stay with my sisters and another trip was made to Fairview Hospital to herald the birth of me, the one and only LaVera Marchelle Berry, early in the morning of November 25, 1955.

With four sisters and a brother in the house, peace and quiet was something that only happened when everyone was either out of the house or sound asleep. By the time we hit our teens, Daddy and Mama finally put a second phone line in the house because we kept the first one busy. They didn't fully understand that since we were the most popular young women at Bryant and Central—not to mention the most beautiful—we had to be up on whatever was happening. I for one didn't agree with Daddy's rules about a time limit on calls; I deserved all the phone time I got. However, when he said, "You either respect the rules or I pull the plug on this phone," I was forced to concede. You didn't argue with Daddy when he gave you that "pronouncing sentence" look, even though I did grumble behind his back.

I'll be the first to say that Daddy had that look down pat, since he was well into his position as an assistant district attorney. I was only four when Uncle Eldon was killed. The only thing I remember about that time is a sense of how bad everyone felt. The fact that his murderer got off scot free only made it worse, because of the rules of double jeopardy. Once Daddy became a prosecutor, we didn't hear much about the cases he tried, but we could tell when a case wasn't going well by the way he acted when he came home. On those days, his jaws would be tight and he'd go straight to the den for however long it took for "down time" to kick in. Whatever he did in court, it was noticed by the governor and other VIPs, which earned him a seat on the bench during my junior year at Central High.

It was bad enough when Daddy was an ADA, but after he became a judge, my dating life really suffered. I loved having the brothas flock around me at school to give me the attention and appreciation I so richly deserved. However, only a handful ever got up the nerve to ask me out, shaking in their platform shoes after Daddy took them into his den.

It was liberation time on November 25, 1973, the day I turned 18 and became a legal adult. Thanks to the powers that be in state government back in June, I had been looking forward to that day—counting the days, in fact. The fact that I was still a senior in high school was a slight glitch, but that Friday my date and I could go out to the disco without being turned away at the door. The other glitch was my parents' curfew—I was required to be in by midnight so long as I lived under their roof. That was the part I didn't like; I argued about the unfairness of it all, but Daddy shut me down real quick. Graduation and college, though, would change that.

In the fall of 1976, I started my junior year at the U of M with acceptable grades—in my family, acceptable meant a B average or better. Chauntice and I found an upstairs duplex in southeast Minneapolis, a few blocks from Marshall-University High School. It had hardwood floors, off-street parking for our cars, and ready access to Dinkytown, the U of M, and Hamline University where Chauntice was taking her pre-law courses.

I don't know why Sylvia and Deshawna dragged me to a concert on campus at Northrop Auditorium that particular evening, October 16. Sure, I loved music—we all did. I loved R&B, jazz, disco, funk! Classical music wasn't my thing; that was something Mama and Daddy would go out for. When I pressed my sisters for details, all they would say was, "You really have to hear this orchestra. They will blow your mind."

I breezed through the program, noting the different selections and the names of the soloists, deciding I would humor my big sisters and endure this one night. I politely half-listened to the selections, and from what I heard, I had to admit the orchestra did well. However, my mind simply couldn't put "mind-blowing" and "classical" in the same sentence, no matter how well the musicians performed.

I hadn't expected to see the man who approached the podium onstage with his violin after intermission. Even in a tuxedo, I could see the powerfully built yet elegant physique he carried so well. His height was somewhere around 5'11", with silky dark brown hair hanging below shoulder length and soft brown skin that pulsated, vibrated, with health and vitality. There was no doubt in my mind that one of his parents was Native American, the other African American. His eyes had an intensity and purpose as he began his solo.

The music—oh, the music! The more I heard, the more I was drawn in. I felt as though he was giving the audience a glimpse of who he was, and something stirred in me, causing me to rethink my earlier opinion. My sisters were quite taken with his performance as well, and I was certain they would go home and rave to their men about the amazing violinist they heard.

I wanted to stand up and cheer with applause when he finished, but Deshawna grabbed my arm before I could move. "Shhhhh," she said. "You don't applaud until the end of the concert." I frowned at her briefly, and I then sought to make out the name on the program in the dim light. *Derrick St. James, Soloist*—so much for my preconceived notions about violinists. But notions or no notions, I would make sure he knew who I was, one way or another.

The first thing I needed to do was find out his itinerary. When I went home, I reread the program for any additional information on Derrick, pleased when I read the brief bio on him. From being raised in a suburb of Cleveland, he had become a virtuoso on the violin, a field one rarely saw Black musicians in. He had received many awards in state and regional music competitions. Different orchestras across the country had their eyes on him, and he was just starting his senior year in college. Small wonder—if he could stir *me* with his music, how many concert halls had he brought down? I read further. He was going to be in Minneapolis for a few more days before the next city on his tour, which meant I didn't have much time.

Undoubtedly that fine man didn't reach that level of excellence without hours and hours of practice, and that body of his didn't get that hot without some sort of regular workout. I certainly wasn't going to stand at the stage door like some groupie—a Berry woman simply didn't do that. But where could I position myself so that 1) he could see me and 2) think he was pursuing me? *Think. You're Judge Berry's daughter. Get more information to substantiate your case.*

Virtuoso or not, a man like Derrick would still want to hang out somewhere on campus during his free time. With some discreet research I not only discovered where he was staying, but his favorite restaurant in Dinkytown. In casual daytime wear, he looked like almost any other college student, his hair pulled back into a ponytail and strolling into the restaurant for lunch. I chose my attire carefully—a dressed down, casual look for fall with just a hint of the provocative, my medium-length hair styled with sassiness. As far as I was concerned, Samson was about to meet his Delilah—only I had no intentions of cutting any of that beautiful hair.

I was careful to ignore him as I walked in, but I made sure I was seated at a table where I could be seen. I ate my lunch at a leisurely pace, enjoying my food even as I sensed I was being watched. Intuition told me he had noticed me and, of course, he liked what he saw. I continued to eat, not even giving as much as a glance in his direction, patiently waiting for the moment that he would approach my table.

A coed who had seen his performance went over to his table and asked for his autograph, which he politely signed. He then rose from his seat to excuse himself before she could fall at his feet and kiss them. *Show some class, girl,* I scoffed, taking a sip of my apple juice as he went off to the men's room. Meanwhile, the server came with my favorite dessert—key lime pie. I had just taken a mouth-watering bite when I heard, "Excuse me, miss. Do you mind if I join you?"

I looked up into the drop-dead-gorgeous face of Derrick standing over me. I felt a strange but pleasant heat in me as I gave him a little smile. "Well, we should be introduced first, don't you think?"

"Certainly. I'm Derrick St. James," he said with a smile that enhanced the keen features of his face.

"LaVera Berry."

"It's a pleasure to meet you, LaVera. So, does that mean I can join you?"

"By all means, Derrick. By all means."

I appreciated the fact that Derrick asked me about my studies in business and economics while we chatted. He talked about his music here and there, but not to the point where it dominated the conversation. Of course, I asked the right questions at the right time, and when we went our separate ways—me to class and him to rehearsal—he had my phone number in his pocket and a look in his deep, dark brown eyes that informed me my mission was successful. It was no longer a matter of if he would see me, but when. Oh, I'm so good I amaze myself.

That manager of his was worse than Daddy when it came to Derrick spending late nights out on the town, even though he was 21. Instead, we went to see Gil Scott-Heron's performance on our first evening. The week that followed was the most intense week of dating I'd ever had. If he wasn't at the gym, rehearsing, or doing a concert Derrick would find some way to see me. By the end of that week he was comfortable enough to rest his head in my lap as we sat under a tree near the water tower in Prospect Park, with me running my fingers through his luxurious locks while we talked; he liked that. And his kisses…those days of fall may have been crisp, but I felt summer heat in his arms. When I was away from him, however, one thing was tops on my list of concerns: the time crunch.

Getting his attention was one thing, but how could I get him back here or keep him here a little longer? It was driving me crazy. I paced back and forth in the duplex Chauntice and I shared, peering out the living room windows from time to time at the falling leaves and begging for a solution to my problem.

I stopped in my tracks. Of course! On my own strength I could never rearrange Derrick's tour, but there was one person in town who could. If it took getting down on my knees and groveling to do it, I would do it gladly. I remembered all the fun I had and the celebrities I met at the senior prom Mrs. Edwards arranged for Carter and Julian earlier in the spring. That event was the talk of the town! If she could pull something like that off, surely a word from Julian to her could get Derrick a spot on the guest list at her fall party next Saturday. Yes, things happened when Lillian Christopher Edwards was involved; I was counting on it.

When Derrick invited me to sit in on his rehearsal, I came prepared. I was entranced by his playing, but not to the extent that I forgot to turn on the small tape recorder in my purse. When rehearsal ended, I was more than happy to accept his dinner invitation. "I have to go and get ready now, but I'll see you at 6:30," I said saucily, sashaying calmly out of the rehearsal hall and then hurrying to my Chevy Camaro to deliver the goods.

"Here it is, Julian," I told him in front of his parents' house after I handed him the envelope. "Thank you, thank you, thank you. I owe you bigtime for this."

Julian arched an eyebrow. "And you know I will collect, LaVera. Is all the other info in there?"

"It's all written down on those pages with the cassette."

"And the program?"

"It's in there, too."

"He'd better be great. Grandma believes in supporting young artists, and you know she has high expectations."

"Cross my heart, he is. And you can ask Sylvia and Deshawna, too."

"OK. Carter and I are going over to visit her on Friday. I'll talk to her about Derrick then."

I was dying to tell Julian to do it sooner—like yesterday. However, I, like everyone else in town, knew that Mrs. Edwards was not a woman to be pushed or rushed into doing anything. Not unless you wanted to be on the receiving end of The Look and have doors permanently shut in your face.

I would never admit this to anyone, but I thought I'd died and gone to heaven when I went to the party on Derrick's arm, dressed in a classically chic halter-top evening gown and my hair pulled back into a tight bun like Diana Ross in those days. As for Derrick, he wore his tux—it didn't wear him. Later, when he played, the guests couldn't take their eyes off him, listening attentively to his performance. I noted Mr. and Mrs. Edwards nodding, hoping it meant opportunities for Derrick and a way to bring him to Minneapolis for a long tour of engagement—with me. Meanwhile, the rousing round of applause when he took a bow was encouraging.

"You don't waste time, do you?" Sylvia asked as she and I partook of the appetizers set out for the guests.

I watched Derrick engaged in conversation with Mr. and Mrs. Edwards and then faced my sister. "Would you? It seems to me you snatched up Clint rather quickly."

"Probably not. With talent like that, Derrick St. James is going places." She gave me a suspicious glint. "But I find it most interesting that he wound up as a guest artist for Mrs. Edwards' party. What did you do to bring that about?"

"Me? Do? You must be kidding." I gave her a nervous smile.

Sylvia's eyes locked into a piercing stare. "Don't try it, LaVera. You've been hot for that man since you saw him at Northrop. It was written all over your face. Now what did you do?"

I waited for a few guests to move out of earshot. "If you must know, I taped him during a rehearsal, and I asked Julian for a favor."

"Hmmm. I take it Derrick doesn't know about this?"

"Of course not. A woman has to have some secrets. Besides, getting him back here was a way we'd have time together."

My sister rolled her eyes. "I have to say, I've never seen you like this with any other man. You must be serious."

"As a heart attack, Sylvia. As a heart attack. So, promise me you won't say anything?"

"If he's that important to you, I promise," she said as Derrick finished his conversation and approached us, whereupon I gave him a brilliant smile. He'd earned it, of course; when he wasn't working the room, his eyes were locked on me.

The following Monday I had finished my classes and went home for a snack before I hit the books. I happened to see a message by the phone from Chauntice saying, "Call Derrick." I dialed the number, soaking in the sound of his voice when he said, "Hello."

"Hello, Derrick."

"LaVera. How did classes go?"

"Hard, but good. I got your message."

"LaVera, I've got some news to share with you."

"Really?" I crossed my fingers.

"Yeah. I can hardly believe it."

"What? What?"

"My manager told me I've been booked to play Orchestra Hall next month."

"Wow! That is wonderful," I replied with a huge grin on my face. "Tell me more."

"Sure. Why don't we grab a bite to eat before you start studying so I can give you the details?"

"Sounds like a plan."

"I'll pick you up in an hour."

"An hour's fine. See you then."

The moment he hung up, I jumped up and down with glee. Mrs. Edwards had done it—he was coming back! With Minneapolis being a center for the fine arts, the new Orchestra Hall on the Nicollet Mall was *the* top venue for a young musician like Derrick. All I had to do now was give him more incentives to stay here without his knowing I was giving them to him. I had many weapons in my arsenal, and short of jumping into bed with him, I would use them. *Who knows? He could become part of the Minnesota Orchestra and be based here!*

While I was deciding on what outfit to wear for my impromptu date, the phone rang. "Hello?" I answered with a voice that was practically giddy.

"Well. Sounds like somebody's in a good mood."

"Hi, Mama. What's happenin'?"

"I should be asking you that question, LaVera, but I'm sure it has something to do with that violinist you came with to the Edwards' party on Saturday. Now, we expect to formally meet him, and soon."

I stopped in my tracks. "Mama, he's only going to be here for a couple more days."

"Then you make sure you bring Mr. St. James to see us tomorrow for dinner. Your father and I have spoken."

"But—"

"We'll see you then. Goodbye."

I knew that tone. On the one hand, they had to have been impressed with Derrick's talent. On the other, if I didn't produce Derrick tomorrow and Daddy didn't talk to him, he'd be treated like new prey. Sure, Clint, Prentice, and Jason came through Daddy's "trial by fire" unscathed, and Julian was practically family, but that didn't hold any guarantees for Derrick. What was I going to do?

I looked at the dress I had planned to wear for our date and hung it back in the closet. I pulled out a different dress. *Hmmm.* It gave just the right hint of promise without being whorish. Chic. Classy. Between that dress, the right set of heels and my natural Berry charm, Derrick would be begging to meet my parents by the time the evening was over. I was counting on it.

Seeing familiar cars parked in front of my parents' house the next evening was enough to convince me this was going to be a family inspection. When I walked into the house with Derrick, my suspicions were confirmed. With the exception of Linda's family, everyone else was there, including my grandparents.

Although they had been introduced to Derrick and heard his performance at Mrs. Edwards' party, sitting him down and talking to him at length was different. To pave the way with my family, I showed him off and sang his praises—I only hoped I didn't sound like a salesperson in an auto showroom. Derrick's graciousness and manners won my female relatives over. Daddy was cordial during dinner, and after dinner he took Derrick into the study. I did my best not to clench my teeth. Yes, I was nearly 21 and if Derrick and I took our relationship further, that was our business. However, it would still be a plus to have Daddy on our side.

When the door to the study finally opened, Daddy and Derrick were still talking. "So, Derrick, is your Shawnee blood on your mother's side or your father's?"

"Mom's. Her name is Aiyana, which means 'endless beauty.' She's done research on the Native American tribes that were in Ohio, as well as how the removal affected them."

"There's no excuse for the way this country treated Native Americans and slaves," Daddy said with bitterness.

"Tell me about it. Now, Judge Berry, which tribe are your ancestors from?"

"Cherokee, on my father's side. But I wouldn't be recognized as such by the Cherokee Nation because it wasn't documented, what with the intermarriage of Cherokee people and African slaves back in that time. Not to mention that travesty known as the Trail of Tears. In short, I have the blood, but not the credentials."

They grabbed some sparkling water and went off into a corner, where they took seats and continued to discuss the First Nation as though I wasn't even in the vicinity. I stood there with my mouth open, wondering what happened, when Mama approached me. "You can relax and close your mouth, LaVera. Look at the way they're communicating. Your father has already given his verdict, and it is in your favor."

A month after commencement exercises—June 24, 1977, to be exact—Derrick played another recital in Orchestra Hall. He always gave an outstanding performance, but this time he outdid himself. The audience was mesmerized, and my heart was full. He had them eating out of his hand, and I loved it. The skill, the passion, the drive he brought that evening—it was like a force of nature which drew you in and all you could do was fasten your seat belts and enjoy the experience.

At the end of his performance, after bowing to cheers, thunderous applause and taking two curtain calls, Derrick went over to the nearest microphone and motioned for the audience to quiet down. "Thank you, thank you for coming this evening. I couldn't have become the violinist I am without the support of the people closest to me, such as my parents and my teachers. That also includes someone who has become my inspiration. LaVera, would you come up, please?"

I wasn't expecting that, but I was thrilled for the acknowledgment. I rose from my seat and came onto the stage to applause, looking absolutely stunning in my black sequined evening gown. My hair, now almost shoulder length, was styled in a big, curly mane inspired by Beverly Johnson. After all, a Berry woman always represents well.

My man was so handsome, so desirable, and he had the audience's undivided attention. His eyes, however, were fixed on me, and they were filled with love as he professed, "LaVera, you inspire my music and my life in so many ways, more than I ever dreamed of. I love you with all my heart. That being said, I have a very important question to ask you."

My heart was pounding as he reached into his pocket. My mouth dropped when I saw what was in his hand as he went down on one knee. His mouth opened, I heard that sexy voice of his ask, "Will you marry me?"

For one of the few times in my life, I was speechless. All I could do was nod in reply. The smile on his face as he placed that exquisite—and I mean Cartier's exquisite—diamond ring on my finger said it all for me. The audience went up in renewed cheers and I thought I would levitate off the ground, but the kiss he planted on my lips stopped me from doing that. This was real. Derrick St. James was going to become my husband. This was a proposal a woman in love dreamt of.

The very next day I flashed my ring at Chauntice, who gave me an enthusiastic hug even as she let out a whistle at the diamond settings. Deshawna, who was getting married next month, was happy for me as well, even when she teased, "You chased him until he caught you, didn't you?" Telling my grandparents meant one thing: my grandfathers were ready to welcome another grandson-in-law, while my grandmothers gave me that predatory smile that said, "baby carriage."

Just who said planning a wedding would be fun? Everyone got on my nerves, even Chauntice, who was my maid of honor. Could she not understand the simple concept of total perfection? There were plenty of times I couldn't stand to be around Derrick or put up with all the rehearsal time he had to put in. I had to change the color schemes six times because they weren't right. I wanted a perfect wedding, and things and people kept coming up short. Finding the right caterer was a dismal chore. I wasn't about to use somebody's cousin I'd never heard of for a photographer, and even the photography studios around town had tired products and layouts. As for wedding gowns, I went through dozens and dozens of them, and I only found a suitable one after I went off to New York. And Daddy...he may have been paying for the wedding, but he needed to come off the money and spend more! I wanted to scream, and I did. *I* was the bride, and it was my absolute privilege to change my mind as often as I pleased. This was *my* wedding, and they were all working for *me!*

April 1, 1978—my wedding day—was fast approaching. Chauntice, as it turned out, had just about had it with me. A week before my big event, she literally sat me down and gave me a mutinous look. "Listen, Bridezilla," she growled, "this may be your wedding, but you are not—I repeat, *not*—going to drive everyone around you into the loony bin. It's a miracle that Derrick is putting up with you at this point. If I were him, I'd be ready to call off the wedding now!"

"Look, Chauntice! You're my maid of honor. This is *my* day! I want my wedding to be absolutely *perfect!* If I say 'Jump' you're here to say, 'How high?' If I want you to prance through hoops, you lift up your hooves and *prance!* That's what you, the bridesmaids, the caterers, and everyone else are here for!"

Chauntice's voice got low and deadly. "One more crack, LaVera, and not only will I smack that makeup off your face, but the rest of us will come in here and beat the crap out of you. By the time we're done with you, no amount of makeup will cover that up."

Slowly, my sisters filed into the room and gave me the same deadly expression as Chauntice, ready and willing to carry out her threat. I knew at that moment I'd said too much. "By the way, don't think for a minute that Daddy doesn't know about the way you've treated everyone." Linda's voice was frosty. "He's probably ready to cite you for contempt of court and have you locked up. As for Derrick, if this wedding is any indication of what your marriage is going to be like, I hope he dumps you before it's too late."

I was ready to give Linda a quick retort, but it stopped in my throat as I scanned the room, with the murderous looks still cast in my direction. Deshawna took a step towards me. "Now get this straight, LaVera. Either you pull it together and clean up your act, or we are going to walk out on you and leave you hanging. Is that clear?"

I nodded quickly, especially when I noticed that Mama had entered the room and was giving me The Look. My sisters exchanged glances, pondering my acquiescence before Deshawna continued. "Chauntice, since you're the maid of honor, is there anything you want to add?"

Chauntice stared at me like a hungry hawk ready to swoop down on a rabbit. "As a matter of fact, there is. You're going to go to Derrick and apologize to him for your behavior and your drama. You're going to do it today, and it had better be sincere."

I have never been one to grovel, but after a healthy serving of humble pie, when he came home from rehearsal that evening, I did just that. It was no surprise Derrick didn't let me off the hook easily. For the next five days, he watched my interactions with everyone involved in the planning to make sure my actions matched my words. That, added with my Berry charm, finally convinced him Bridezilla was dead and the fabulous LaVera Berry was back. Inwardly, I breathed an immense sigh of relief at dodging the firing squad.

I wouldn't have believed it, but things went smoother after that "intervention." The rehearsal dinner was lovely, and Derrick's parents, Wardell and Aiyana St. James, could witness the love between us and the warm hospitality of my parents. On my wedding day, I felt positively beautiful in my strapless, modified A-line wedding gown as Daddy walked me down the aisle, seeing my very handsome husband-to-be standing at the altar and the wedding party at their respective places. My sisters were smiling, but there was no mistaking the cautionary look in their eyes that said, "LaVera, don't you dare screw this up."

I wanted to savor every moment of the day, especially the ceremony itself. When I looked into Derrick's eyes I very nearly melted, I was so full of love for him when we said our vows. When we kissed, the promise of our future was very bright, indeed.

I may have been a virgin on my wedding night, but white lingerie didn't suit my personality. For me, hot pink satin was the ticket. When I came out of the bathroom of our suite, Derrick was lying on the bed, his hair flowing down to the middle of his back, wearing black linen drawstring pants—and no underwear. During our engagement, I learned that my husband was very much into scents when it came to women, scents that were enticing but not overpowering. I, being the resourceful woman that I am, experimented with different perfumes to gauge his response, and for tonight I found the one that was guaranteed to bring out his most passionate responses to me.

I loved seeing his shirtless torso, the play of his sculpted muscles, the richness of his skin, sleek and supple from the daily applications of cocoa butter to his body. I was mesmerized by the intensity of his gaze as he got up and walked slowly toward me, his manhood steadily rising to the occasion until it tented his pants. I let out a low whistle, feeling my panties growing wet from my feminine juices, enjoying his body's powerful response to me and the scent I carried.

"I'll say it again, LaVera…you looked like a goddess when you came down the aisle," he said in a husky voice. "And now…"

"Now?" I asked, eating this up.

125

I saw his chest rise and fall as he took in my scent, running his hands through my hair and caressing my neck. "Don't be surprised if I can't keep my hands off you…tonight or ever."

The song wasn't out at the time of my wedding, but Derrick's lovemaking was on point with the Pointer Sisters' "Slow Hand." His easy, teasing touches over every inch of my hot, luscious body had me climaxing three times before he finally entered me. After they were speaking to me again, my sisters filled me in on the paradise of the marriage bed, and they were absolutely right. Did my wits fly out of my head when that pole of Derrick's stroked my insides? I'm not sure. Did I give as good as I got? Yes. Were my womanly folds begging for more? Oh, yes. Did he send me crashing over a waterfall with yet another orgasm? *Yyyyyyyessss!!* Did Derrick give me encores of his sexual concerto throughout our honeymoon? *Yes!! Yes!!! Yes!!!!*

It wasn't long after our honeymoon that I found out I was pregnant. Derrick was on tour; waiting until he came back to give him the news almost drove me crazy. I finally broke down and told my siblings, swearing them to secrecy. When he returned from his tour he was on a high and, of course, happy to see me. I subtly suggested he show his appreciation by taking me to dinner at Lord Fletcher's. The scenic drive along Lake Minnetonka and the wonderful cuisine provided the perfect setting for me to deliver my news. Derrick appeared to be in shock at first. After that he kept saying, "You're kidding me. You're kidding me." When I finally convinced him that I was on the level, he got up from the table, walked around it, and gave me a huge kiss right there in the restaurant.

Sure, I was thankful that I was pregnant, but Mama and my sisters said I had the temperament of an opera diva onstage. That Derrick tolerated me during that time was nothing short of amazing. My hormones were all over the map. The least little thing would set me off. I was positively irritable when he was in my presence, but when he walked away, I shouted things like, "Where are you going? Why are you leaving me like this?" When he was away doing concerts, I felt so guilty about the way I acted that I vowed to do better when he returned.

I found myself driving over to see Sylvia and calling Linda and Deshawna while he was away, swallowing my pride and desperately seeking advice on how to control myself. On one such trip during Kwanzaa, I found myself wailing and crying at the top of my voice, "He doesn't care about me. He doesn't love me. How can he leave me alone?"

"Get a grip, LaVera, or you're out of here," Sylvia said firmly. "OK, so you're pregnant. You're moody. But that is no excuse to take it out on everyone else. You can't stand it when he's there, and you can't stand it when he's gone. Suck it up! You're not the first woman to be pregnant, and you sure won't be the last. You give new meaning to the phrase 'high maintenance.'"

At that moment the baby decided to kick me. "Why do babies have to kick so much?"

My sister looked at me like I'd gone bonkers. "That's what babies do. Deal with it."

"But it keeps me up when I want to sleep, and I hate having to run to the bathroom every fifteen minutes! *And I feel fat all the time!*"

"You know something? I'm beginning to wonder if you really want this baby at all. Is that what you're telling me?"

Wow—that was hitting below the belt. How could she even ask me that? I got quiet fast. Sylvia had this dead serious look in her eyes while she said, "Listen to me, and listen well. Once this baby is born, *everything* changes. Things are no longer all about you. It's about what's best for your son or daughter. Frankly, I think Derrick is more prepared to be a parent than you are."

I was ready to go off on my sister for making that remark, but I stopped myself while she continued, "He's going through this with you, but you have to find a way to calm yourself and let him in. He can't support you if you're treating him this way. He deserves better than this. And another thing: if your behavior is stressing him out, he can't give a good performance at concerts, and that affects your livelihood."

Swallowing my pride, two days later, after work I went home, dressed up in one of my new maternity outfits, and prepared a sumptuous meal for my husband, during which I shared all my anxieties and concerns, topped by a humble apology. One of the signs that Derrick is stressed is the way he frowns with his eyebrows; if I'd been honest with myself, he'd been doing that frequently. It felt good to see that frown go away, and during that evening as we both opened up to each other, we grew closer as a couple. When he placed his hand on my stomach and the baby kicked, this time I could appreciate it.

And so it was on the afternoon of February 27, 1979, Derrick and I became parents to our first child, a beautiful little charmer we named Ashley Winona St. James. Not that the hours before her arrival were charming—I felt like I was living the movie *House on Haunted Hill* and I was Nora Manning, screaming my head off through the entire ordeal. When I held her for the first time, though, it seemed like all of that went away, and with my husband's arms protectively around us we were a family.

Derrick's career was on a steady upward curve as he continued to hone his craft. Whenever he played at Orchestra Hall, I would get Sylvia, Chauntice, or Mama to babysit for me to make sure I made it to every opening night. I still do that to this day, only this time all my family is with me in the audience to enjoy the artistry of his gift.

1982 was a most fruitful year in the Berry family. Chauntice, Sylvia, and I were in various stages of pregnancy, to the delight of Mama, Grandma Berry, and Grandma Langston. Aiyana and Wardell, of course, insisted upon regular visits to see Ashley and check in on me. With the good living Derrick provided, I was able to be a fashion plate during my pregnancy, and Derrick made sure not to schedule any out-of-town engagements during my last two months. Ashley, in the meantime, was almost at the preschool age, and had her daddy well wrapped around her little finger. What father wouldn't be?

At the time of the Edwards fall party, my due date was imminent. Nine months pregnant or not, there was no way on earth I was going to miss it. When I showed up on Derrick's arm, Mama thought I'd lost my mind. "What were you thinking, LaVera?" she chided. "Didn't your doctor say you were due any time?" When Daddy saw me there, he had a frown on his face, too.

OK, so I was defiant, but everybody who was anybody was going to be in attendance, including some VIPs in the world of classical music—Lillian Edwards had seen to that. I would make sure Derrick met them, and at the same time prevent any unattached women from getting ideas about my husband.

Things seemed to be going well until the party was in full swing. Derrick was talking to the right people, and other women knew to keep their filthy paws off him if they wanted to leave the place in one piece. When Daddy finally got me alone, lecturing me about me coming in the first place, I went into labor. I groaned through a contraction while Mama and Sylvia talked me through it, hoping my water wouldn't break and cause me further embarrassment.

Despite my protests, Derrick took me straight to the hospital where, after untold hours of pain, I gave birth to Devon Berry St. James sometime in the late morning of September 26, 1982. About a week later, Derrick's parents came to Minneapolis to visit. While Aiyana held Devon, she softly chanted something to him. When she finished, she looked up at us and said, "He has two spirits."

Derrick and Wardell nodded in understanding and acceptance, but I was confused. "Two spirits? What are you talking about?"

"Devon is like your brother," Derrick explained. "In Native American culture, he would be called a *berdache,* or 'two-spirited person.' A two-spirited person was highly respected and revered in a tribe. Many times, they were spiritual leaders and healers. Whatever his gift is, we'll know in time, and one day he will fall in love and take a husband."

"Oh," was all I could say, even though I wondered how in the world my mother-in-law knew this. "Well, I just hope they decide to give me grandchildren when the time comes."

As my sisters steadily had babies—which pleased Mama and my grandmothers to no end—I actually thought I could close up shop. I was safely on the pill since I already had two children, and I had earned the right to be smug. When we had the opportunity, Derrick and I could make love to our hearts' content, so the family gathering on Christmas Day of 1987 seemed like any other holiday. Wrong. One moment I was telling Linda and Chauntice about how Mama outdid herself with her Christmas cookies, and the next I was puking my guts out in the nearest bathroom. They were waiting for me when I staggered out, with those suspicious knowing looks on their faces.

"Well, well, well," Chauntice gloated. "Looks like Mama's going to get another grandchild."

"It can't be—it can't be," I moaned in misery. "I'm on the pill. I can't possibly get pregnant."

Linda looked at me incredulously and shook her head. "LaVera, aren't you forgetting something? The Pill isn't 100% guaranteed. Do you remember when you got sick around Halloween and you couldn't take your kids out with Derrick?"

"Yes, but what does that have to do with this?"

"What did your doctor prescribe?"

I thought for a moment. "Antibiotics."

"Well, certain medications nullify or weaken the effects of contraceptives. Antibiotics are in that group."

That bit of news was more than I cared to deal with on top of being pregnant. "Please, please don't tell anyone until I've had a chance to tell Derrick," I pleaded on my empty but still nauseous stomach.

"Well...all right," Chauntice said in a cautionary tone. "But we know you. Don't wait too long, or we'll tell Derrick ourselves."

Once I got over the shock, I resigned myself to my fate and told Derrick and then the kids on New Year's Day. During this pregnancy, my sisters couldn't resist rubbing it in after the way I'd bragged about being on the pill like it was ironclad insurance. Grandma Berry, once she found out, couldn't wait to tell half of Minneapolis. Daddy smiled and said, "I hope it's a boy."

Derrick endured my drama, but the smile on his face told me he was already looking forward to the possibility of another musician in the family, since Devon had already shown signs of musical talent. Personally, I felt God had an odd sense of humor when Linden

Berry St. James made his debut on July 31, 1988, the hottest day in Minneapolis since 1936 with a sweltering 105 degrees.

Seeing Ashley grow up convinced Derrick and I that we had our work cut out for us. I wasn't surprised when the boys started flocking around her. She was, after all, her mother's daughter in that respect. Between her parents' respective genes, she wound up looking like an African American version of Kim Kardashian, something that became even more apparent as she grew into a young woman. My Langston and Berry grandparents had since passed away. However, Daddy, Derrick, and my father-in-law Wardell had already picked up the torch. I was also a bit wiser, to the point where I could sit my daughter down and advise her, "Ashley, you've inherited some amazing looks, and those looks are a gift. However, your looks will only take you so far, and they will change."

"Well, what about you, Mom? You still look awesome."

"Thank you for the compliment, but sooner or later that will change. You have to be smart. Oprah has said that many times over and look what she's done with her life."

At 17, I wasn't surprised that Ashley thought she knew everything, but she asked, "You mean like going to college, a career, that stuff?"

"Yes. Perhaps even starting your own business."

I had half expected Ashley to go into the world of fashion, be it modeling or design, especially since she had the flair for it. Instead, she followed in Auntie Elaine's footsteps when she graduated from Spelman College and became a court reporter for Hennepin County. She was quite pleased with herself, looking so professional and businesslike, focused to the max on every case and committed to excellence. Her decision even surprised Daddy, but he had only high marks of praise for her skills. Auntie Elaine, of course, was quite satisfied that she was able to pass on her skills and abilities to a new generation.

I had to wonder if like attracts like when Ashley brought home Shawn Yang to meet us. A pleasing combination of Hmong and African American, Shawn was a court clerk for Ramsey County. "What is this thing about law and order?" I questioned Derrick when we had a moment in the kitchen of our beautiful home off Mississippi River Boulevard and Summit Avenue in St. Paul.

"Well, it gives them common interests. Besides, think about the members of your family who are in the legal arena. Now, you know I'm going to smoke him out, so just be patient, honey."

"Well, look for the most important thing—that he loves her," I emphasized.

"Of course, he loves her. I don't know what it is about you Berry women, but Shawn has been practically eating out of her hand all evening."

I turned my eyes on him and gave him a sultry smile. "Like you, dear?"

"You know it," he said as he took me in his arms for a simmering kiss. "Now let's get back in there before they think we got lost."

I was "mother of the bride" to the nth degree when Ashley married Shawn on April 29, 2006, walked down the aisle by my proud husband and positively stunning in a Pnina Tornai mermaid-style wedding gown. Unlike me, Ashley was the epitome of grace, appreciation, and consideration during her engagement and the wedding plans, something my sisters and Carter would not let me forget. Still, some facets of my daughter the apple didn't fall far from me the tree when Ashley announced that she was pregnant less than two months after the wedding.

As a result, my granddaughter, Brooklyn Houa Yang, was born on February 5, 2007, the coldest day of that year with a -17 degree air temperature and a -35 wind chill factor. When Derrick and I saw her, my first thought was, *If she ever decides to become a model, Brooklyn will be unforgettable! She'll be able to write her own ticket, but she'll be smart and exceedingly wise about it.*

On August 31, 2010, Ashley and Shawn were blessed with a son. He has my complexion, but otherwise he's the spitting image of his great-grandmother Aiyana. To honor her and keep the Berry tradition, he was named Tecumseh Berry Yang. Needless to say, my mother-in-law was over the moon.

As for Devon, he inherited his father's hair, complexion, smile, temperament, and his musical ability, but the rest was from me. That was probably a good thing; otherwise he would have scared off Dominic Robertson after their first date six years ago. When Derrick and I first met Dominic, I could have sworn I was looking at a youthful reincarnation of the late actor Howard Rollins—until he opened his mouth and sang. Paul Robeson would have been proud to hear a voice like that.

It was fascinating, to say the least, to have Derrick on violin, Devon on cello, and Dominic adding vocals to form what I considered an unusual trio. I could only imagine the challenges they would face in having time together, what with Devon being part of the Minnesota Orchestra with his father and Dominic performing with the Sounds of Blackness. *Oh well, if they're meant to be together, they'll work it out.*

And they did. Three years later we all went to D.C. to attend their wedding on April 18. It was a place I remembered well, since Devon and Derrick had performed at the Kennedy Center two years earlier, happily attended by my parents and my in-laws. I also had my wish granted from years ago when, on August 11, 2011, Devon and Dominic presented me with a granddaughter, Delores St. James-Robertson...

"Now what?" Derrick said as LaVera hung up the phone.

"That was Linden. He had another fight with Daria," she sighed in frustration. "You'd think he'd get the hint by now. That girl is nothing but drama. She can take a teaspoon of water and turn it into Lake Superior."

Derrick rolled his eyes as his wife walked off to the kitchen. 34 years of marriage—along with his in-laws as enforcers—had mellowed LaVera, but she still had her moments. In those moments, it usually took her a while to recognize the drama queen in herself when she took Daria apart. Still, he admitted to himself that Linden had attracted a woman who was high-maintenance—approaching toxic levels—and the sooner he broke free of her the better. His son deserved better than that, especially in the context of having his older children who married well. Though he chose to stay out of his children's love lives, his task at hand consisted of quietly steering LaVera away from those turbulent waters.

Normally LaVera would put all the dishes in the dishwasher and call it a day. She only washed dishes in the sink when she was upset, and this was one of those times. "What were you thinking, Linden, taking up with that piece of work?" she muttered as she attacked a dish. She could count the times when her youngest son smiled since he met Daria on one hand. The girl looked like a music video vixen, and everything was all about her. The nerve of her! While she washed the steak knives, she contemplated what it would be like to throw them at Daria the next time she walked through their door.

No, if Linden won't get some sense and dump her, I'll have to get rid of her myself. Or maybe Linden should switch teams and find some nice guy with Derrick's temperament and live happily ever after. That would really break her face. Hmmm. Perhaps Aiyana missed something when he was a baby…

Having taken her frustrations out on the dishes, LaVera turned off the kitchen lights and went to the den, where Derrick was watching the commentary on the election results. At least there's some good news tonight. *She took a seat next to her husband and witnessed the First Family greeting thousands of well-wishers in Chicago.*

"Well, we did it," Derrick beamed. "The Obamas will be in the White House for another four years."

"Yes, they will," LaVera concurred, taking his hand. "These past four years were a challenge, given what he was left with when he started."

"And yet he has been doing what he said he would do. That speaks volumes."

LaVera nodded in agreement. "And Michelle…she's the kind of role model young women can aspire to be."

They continued to listen to the news commentary, absorbing the celebration, the Daria drama forgotten for the time being. LaVera took a moment to check out her husband while he was focused on the television, noting the laugh lines on his face, the long hair now streaked with silver, and his fit, mature body while thinking about how much she loved him. Maybe she was something of a drama queen when she was young, and yet he loved her, warts and all. For some reason, her parents came to mind, followed by the ringing of her cell phone...

Chauntice Berry Varnell

These days, the staff at Fairview's maternity ward would probably be thinking, *Here she comes again.* However, on February 28, 1957 nobody batted an eye when Mama was checked in and Daddy took up his post in the waiting room. After all, this was during the height of the Baby Boom. LaVera had broken the string of "dark and stormy night" births in the Berry family, but I, along with my cousin Ellen, had ushered in a new one—snowy day births. Our family track record was such that boys' names were an afterthought. Daddy, however, was ever proud of his daughters, including his newest one, Chauntice Laverne Berry.

With so much law and order running through our family, it was inevitable that it would rub off on at least one of us, and I was the lucky candidate. Shortly after Daddy was appointed to the bench, during my sophomore year at Central High, I did a class project about him. He had made history in Minnesota by becoming one of its first African American state court judges. Prior to that, he had been a prosecutor who racked up a 98% conviction rate. I did extensive research on his career, and I interviewed him like a teenage version of Oprah. It was there that I tapped into his deep passion for justice, and the seeds of a future attorney took root in me.

Mama and Mrs. Edwards never gave up hope for a Berry-Edwards love match. Even Mrs. Hendricks signed onto the campaign, since her son Kevin and I were both in Central High's Class of '75. Sure, we liked each other, and we were friendly, but that was as far as it went. I'm happy, though, that they finally got their wish through my brother Carter and Mrs. Edwards' youngest son Julian. Of course, I saw that romance coming miles away. Carter was doing everything in his power to get Julian to notice him. It was Kevin's brother Wayne, however, that told me how Julian really felt about Carter, after he had given him a good shove in the right direction.

As for my own love life, being a Berry woman, I was never dateless unless by choice. One by one I watched my older sisters falling like bowling pins to matrimony. At LaVera and Derrick's wedding in 1978—during which LaVera got on my *last* nerves—I caught her bridal bouquet because I couldn't get out of the way in time. Mama happened to see that and gave me a glittering Pepsodent smile. Carter also saw Mama's smile and said with a teasing smirk, "I believe that means you're next."

"What do you mean, 'I'm next'? She might have been looking at you and Julian."

"Maybe, but I'm not the one that caught the bouquet."

"Carter, don't even joke about that. Who knows what Mama might have up her sleeve, now that we're the only two who aren't married yet? And then there's Grandma Berry and Grandma Langston to deal with. Grandma Langston isn't as obvious about it, but Grandma Berry..."

Carter's laugh faded. "Oh. I forgot about them."

"Exactly. They are not going to rest until we're off the market, and for them that means *marriage*. Although, dear brother, you've been off the market ever since you laid eyes on Julian, so it's only a matter of time."

"I notice you didn't mention Daddy in all this."

"Do I really have to? What does Daddy always say to us besides, 'Don't sacrifice your family at the altar of your career?'"

"'When you really love someone, and he loves you back, marry him.' OK, Chauntice, you win. But I'm only 19," Carter protested.

I sized him up as he stood there in his tux, ready with my comeback. "Mama was 19 when she married Daddy. Daddy's friend Mr. Christopher got married when he was 19. You'd better hope Mama & Co. don't remember that. Trust me, Carter, 21 will get here before you know it, and then they'll really have you in their sights."

With LaVera now married off I had the duplex to myself, but I preferred having someone there with me. Fortunately, my cousin Ellen agreed to be my roommate, which brought certain benefits. Ellen has a placid temperament which translated into an easy living arrangement, in contrast to LaVera, who tips the scales as a drama queen.

Given what had happened to Uncle Eldon, it's a wonder Ellen wasn't bitter about losing her father to that horrible scumbag. Ellen, however, has always had a strong prayer life, which only enhanced the outer beauty that Berry women are gifted with. As far as I was concerned, justice was finally served when the son-of-a-bitch died a long, slow, painful death from untreated cancer on—of all days—August 19, 1978. The irony was lost on no one.

The work I put into my pre-law studies paid off with my graduating summa cum laude from Hamline University in 1979, poised for law school at the U of M with an LSAT score in the top five per cent. Ellen had an equally strong suit in economics, with our parents having prime seats for the commencement exercises. At the graduation party I noticed that Ellen had brought her boyfriend of six months, a handsome brotha and promising new hire at Edwards Enterprises named Kenneth Grayson. The look on his face said it all—another man had fallen like a pine tree for our charms and intelligence. Auntie Elaine and Mama were watching them with smiles that said, "He's going to pop The Question—soon." Daddy, on the other hand, was filled with fatherly advice for me about law school, lavish in his praise for my grades. Because of the rotation of judges, I would come and sit in the gallery when he was presiding over civil cases, usually when I was ahead on my studies and had time off from classes. I may not have been pursuing criminal law, but his experience with the basics of law school was invaluable.

It was a ladies' night at Pudge's in 1980, and I needed a serious break from the books and the law library. With Doris Hendricks, LaVera, Ellen, and Elizabeth, we tipped on in there. The DJ was playing Linda Clifford's hit "Red Light," and we teased Ellen about how hard she worked to "get" Kenneth, even though it only took zero effort on her part. Yes, the engagement ring was firmly on her finger and the wedding was less than six months away. Doris' nuptials were even closer, with four weeks to go. LaVera, the only married woman in the bunch, had left Derrick home with their daughter so she could have some "down time." Elizabeth needed some "down time" as well, since she was studying to take over Grandpa Berry's dental practice in the future. Looking out at the dance floor, I realized I wasn't the only one who needed a study break; Carter and Julian were out there dancing under the disco ball as though they were on *Soul Train.*

Ellen didn't drink, which made her a perfect designated driver, but the rest of us had our beverages of choice; mine was a Tom Collins. We laughed, we "let our hair down," the music was great, and my brother and Julian were obliging as dance partners when they were available. At one point, the DJ played Kool and the Gang's "Ladies' Night," which got everyone up and on the dance floor.

Normally one drink is my limit, after which I switch to club soda, but for some reason I don't remember I had two—and most of a third. For me, that was enough to feel tipsy. The number of people in there that evening had increased, to the point where I felt sticky sitting at our table. While everyone else was still on the dance floor, partying to Teena Marie's "Behind the Groove," I weaved my way outside for air.

I had forgotten my coat, and the fact it was an early spring night in March. All I knew was that my head was woozy. Taking a few breaths of air, I staggered to what I thought was LaVera's car. I didn't remember it being parked so far away, and I thought my eyes were playing tricks on me; we certainly didn't bring any men with us to Pudge's. Once I reached it, my inebriated state took over and I collapsed on the hood. Why, oh why, did I have those drinks on an empty stomach?

I came to at home, on the living room sofa with an aching head and drool running down a corner of my mouth, with Ellen and a strange man hovering over me. "Chauntice, you have no idea how worried we were about you." Oh, I wished she would speak softer.

"We didn't know where you'd gone. If Jarvis hadn't brought you home, we were ready to call the police."

"Jarvis?" I muttered. "Who's Jarvis?"

In a sober moment, the man's voice could melt cheese, but my head was unable to fully appreciate that fact at the time. "I'm Jarvis. Jarvis Varnell. You fell out on my car."

"I...what?"

"You'd had a bit to drink. You were talking kind of crazy. I didn't know if you were with anyone, but I had to get you out of there."

Still fumbling for words, I managed to utter, "But...how did I... did anything..."

"When you left the club, you left your coat, but you took your purse and your keys," Ellen said. "Jarvis brought you home, and he was here when I got here. Nothing happened, Chauntice. We've been waiting for you to wake up. He told me why he had to get you away from the club."

"W...why?"

Jarvis pulled out his wallet, reached inside, and pulled out what looked like identification. "I'm a private detective, and I was on a stakeout for a client. You were starting to carry on a little too much."

"Oh, no," I moaned, mortification compounding my disheveled appearance and the bass drums pounding in my head.

"I think she'll be all right now," Ellen got up and walked Jarvis to the door. "Again, I want to thank you for looking out for my cousin."

"Any time, Ms. Berry," he said. "And if you two ever need anything, here's my card."

When I woke up in a sober state late the next morning, I felt chastened because I had almost blown Jarvis' stakeout. Wanting to make amends, I called the number on his business card. We sat down and had coffee at a little diner on the St. Anthony side of the river, off East Hennepin Avenue, a few days later. He struck me as a cross between Billy Dee Williams and Richard Roundtree. Standing 6'0" to my 5'8", he was well put together, able to more than take care of himself, and extremely easy on a woman's eye.

I had grown up watching private eyes like Paul Drake on *Perry Mason*. As such, I had to give him respect when he smoothly reminded me, "Private detective work isn't always what it's made out to be on TV or the movies. There are many times when it can seem boring and you have to do a lot of legwork, but you still must do your best to satisfy your client."

"True. The same goes with lawyers, if you're really worth your salt. Me, I'm a first-year law student."

Jarvis studied me for a minute. "You know, Chauntice, there's something familiar about you. Wait...your last name is Berry. Are you..."

"Yes. Judge Berry is my father."

"Hmmm. I thought so. I've done work for some defense attorneys who had him as a trial judge. The man doesn't play."

"That is also true. So, Jarvis...can you promise me your discretion about the way we met?"

"You have my word, Chauntice. Now, tell me more about the life of a law student."

Inwardly, I felt relief and gratitude as I shared my passion for law with Jarvis, along with those getting-to-know-you questions in the hour we spent together. With the promise of a date as soon as his current case was over, we went our separate ways. I thought about him off and on while I pored through books in the law library, making dinner at home, or helping Ellen with some of her wedding plans. Jarvis Varnell came across as a man I wanted to get to know better, possibly introducing him to Mama and Daddy.

Yes, I, Chauntice Berry, the one who was determined to stay single, had found someone with the potential to be more than just a Friday night date. Of course, the last thing I wanted was for Daddy to find out about my drunken performance on the hood of Jarvis' car. On that note, I had both sworn Ellen to secrecy and sworn off alcohol for good.

I thought it would be somewhat dicey for Jarvis to be a defense witness in a trial a month later, particularly one that Daddy was presiding over. I found myself with tense shoulders, holding my breath as I sat in the gallery, watching Jarvis be examined and then cross-examined, looking for signs of body language that would indicate Daddy's displeasure. All I got was Daddy's poker face, coupled with his impartial interpretations of the law as he overruled and sustained objections from both sides. It wasn't unusual for me to sit in on a trial given that I was his daughter and now a law student—I'd been doing that since I was in high school. I only hoped he didn't make the personal connection between Jarvis and me—at least, not yet.

Late in June I decided it was time for Jarvis to formally meet the rest of my family. Ellen and Carter already knew everything and had been gently nudging me in that direction, so the 4th of July weekend seemed like the best opportunity. Deshawna, Linda, and their families would be in town, and a picnic was planned at Minnehaha Park. Jarvis promised to clear his schedule while I prayed that Daddy, given his own past as a prosecutor, wouldn't be biased by Jarvis' testimony as a defense witness. Maybe Daddy wouldn't remember Jarvis even being in his courtroom. Yeah, right.

The picnic was in full swing when I arrived at the park on Jarvis' arm. Ellen and Auntie Elaine were the first to see us, greeting us with hugs and an appreciative eye for Jarvis. Kenneth was helping with the grill, and my stomach rumbled at the smell of barbecued ribs, chicken, and hamburgers.

"So, this is the private eye Ellen's been telling me about," Auntie Elaine said with a lovely but knowing smile as Mama approached us. "Juanita, I do believe Chauntice has some introductions to make."

"Mama, I'd like you to meet Jarvis Varnell. Jarvis, this is my mother, and this is my auntie, Elaine Berry."

"It's a pleasure to meet you, Mrs. Berry, Mrs. Berry." Jarvis bestowed Mama with a charismatic smile. "Did anyone ever tell you that you could be related to Marilyn McCoo from the Fifth Dimension?" He then turned to Auntie Elaine. "And didn't I see you on *Star Trek,* as one of the bridge officers on the USS Enterprise?"

"Why, thank you, Jarvis," Mama said, clearly eating this up while Auntie Elaine looked upon him as her new best friend. "Now, you must tell me more about you. How did you and my daughter meet?"

My stomach did an unpleasant flip-flop at her question. Jarvis, however, smoothly replied, "Actually, we met while I was on a stakeout."

"A stakeout?"

"Yes. I'm a private detective. We really couldn't talk because it would have blown my cover, so we agreed to meet at a later date."

I breathed an inward sigh of deep relief at dodging that bullet. I figured I would be ready for what was to come, and I wasn't disappointed. Mama was clearly sizing him up as husband material for me, and my bringing him to the picnic was evidence beyond a reasonable doubt. Auntie Elaine was no help in that area, for she joined Mama in smoothly grilling him as they walked him to a picnic table, insisting that I get "my man" a plate so they could intensify the process.

By the time I returned to the table, Mama and Auntie Elaine had been joined by Grandma Langston and Grandma Berry. Jarvis, I must admit, had charmed them, and my concerns fluctuated between Daddy's potential response to him and my female relatives hauling us off to a justice of the peace as soon as the picnic was over. "I trust everything's OK?" I asked my relatives as I put a full plate and a plastic cup of lemonade in front of Jarvis.

"Couldn't be better," Grandma Langston assured me with a certain gleam in her eye. "I don't know why you kept this delightful young man under wraps for so long. Now you know we love you, and we don't bite."

I fought the urge to roll my eyes. "All right, Grandma. Mama, where's Daddy?"

"He took some of the grandbabies to look at Minnehaha Falls. He should be back soon."

Jarvis was in the middle of regaling them with details of some of his more interesting cases when I spotted Daddy heading toward our table. He was holding my three-year-old nephew Ricky by the hand and they were engaged in a conversation. He happened to look up and see me sitting next to Jarvis, and his eyes scrutinized him in an effort to figure out where he'd seen my boyfriend's face. By the time they reached the table, praying my female relatives would have my back, I went on the offensive. "Hi, Daddy. I'd like you to meet my boyfriend, Jarvis Varnell. Jarvis, this is my father."

Jarvis stood up and greeted Daddy with a firm handshake. "Great to meet you, sir. You have a beautiful family."

"Thank you." Daddy took a seat at the table and sent Ricky off to his father. "So, tell me about yourself."

"That's just what this fine young man has been doing," Grandma Berry beamed. "The stories he told us about some of his cases… fascinating. Simply fascinating. Reminds me of Paul Drake on that TV show *Perry Mason.*"

"Oh. Then you're a private investigator."

"That's right, sir. I also do the best by my clients and respect the law. That's helped me build my business and my reputation."

"That's good. A man's reputation is everything. Where are you from?" Daddy was now in judge mode.

"Oakland, California. I moved here six years ago."

Daddy was about to ask another question when I saw recognition in his eyes. "Wait a minute, I remember you. You were a witness in a trial I…" He paused and looked around the table. Mama, Auntie Elaine, and my grandmothers were giving him The Look, daring him to open his mouth.

"Yes, I was, sir. And I acknowledge you for being a tough but fair judge," Jarvis replied.

Under the burning glares of my matrimony-minded elders, Daddy sighed and chose the path of least resistance. "Thank you, Jarvis, for your candor. I want to know more about you. Have you had enough to eat?"

"Well…"

"Don't worry about that, Earl. We'll take care of it," Grandma Langston interrupted. "Juanita, Chauntice, take care of your men."

While Mama and I went to make up more plates, I breathed freely again and thanked Mama for her support. "Any time, Chauntice," she said sweetly. "As they say, first comes love, then comes marriage, then comes…"

"I know, Mama, I know. Just give us some time and it will happen." As I finished with Jarvis' second plate, I noticed that Grandpa Berry and Grandpa Langston had joined in with Daddy on interviewing Jarvis. Or were they grilling him like a steakburger?

"Jarvis is doing just fine," Mama said, in answer to my unspoken question. "They're merely smoking him out. It's no different for you than it was with your sisters."

When Ellen and Kenneth married two months later, under Auntie Elaine's ecstatic grin, I was in attendance as one of her bridesmaids, with Elizabeth as maid of honor. The fact Jarvis was there as my date was high-octane fuel for my grandmothers' expectations as they gave me smug looks and nods of encouragement whenever they saw us together at the reception. *Let them enjoy the circumstantial evidence. When the time is right, we'll tie the knot. But until then....*

Halloween found Jarvis and I out partying at Pudge's, where we enjoyed a break from our respective work schedules. Jarvis was smoothly dressed as *Blacula,* while I took a page from Princess Ananka in the Universal *Mummy* series. Shirley Temples and virgin daiquiris were much more my speed at that point, and I found I had more energy to dance. We knew going in that we'd spend a good share of our time on the dance floor, and dance we did. At one point, Kool and the Gang broke out with "Celebration," followed by Brass Construction's "How Do You Do (What You Do to Me)." Jarvis had na-na-naaahed his way to me, close enough for me to feel his rising manhood through his slacks. He even enveloped us in his cape, and I took the hint and ground my hips against him in response. As crowded as the floor was, no one would have really noticed what we were doing, or even cared. I did know this, however: I was ready for anything with Jarvis that night.

The ride back to his house in the Bryn Mawr neighborhood of Minneapolis was filled with the music on KMOJ and anticipation of the release of the sexual tension that had been dogging us to the point where holding out was futile. Yes, we had our share of scintillating kissing sessions and other forms of making out. Still, I am a Berry woman. I knew he wanted me, but I have a high respect for myself, enough to say no to a fling. At this point, we were exclusive. The previous night, he said the three magic words I had been waiting to hear, and I knew he meant them.

Once we were inside his house, it was on. Jarvis pulled the false fangs from his mouth and gave me a deep, deep, sizzling kiss, running his hands through my hair and squeezing my backside. I moaned and ground myself against him, relishing the feel of his body against mine and the insistent throbbing at his groin. I don't remember how we made it up the stairs to his bedroom, but we probably left a trail of clothes along the way. Sucking my earlobes and my neck, I felt myself growing wet, juicy. I knew he was marking me as his, and I didn't care if anyone saw those marks in the morning. I was, in retrospect, thankful that I was on the pill.

Mmmmm, mmmmmm, mmmmmm...that night, Jarvis and I were like wild animals in heat. Yes, I pushed him to the brink of orgasm and pulled him back, leaving his manhood harder, thicker and leaking. And yes, he licked and squeezed my sensuous body everywhere, and worked my clit into a frenzy. Just when I thought I reached my limits, he entered my vaginal tunnel in one slick, swift, heated thrust. As we danced the horizontal tango, his desire-laden eyes told me, without a doubt, that he was mine. And he didn't just thrust. He rocked to the left, to the right, up, down, corkscrew, in enough positions that made me wonder, in a rational moment much later, if he had the Kama Sutra in his personal library.

I remember screaming my head off and creaming all over his hot, hot penis with my first orgasm that night, followed by Jarvis yelling my name as he let loose and filled me with his seed. Legend has it that Donna Summer had three orgasms while recording "Love to Love You Baby." As for me, I lost count as we made love over and over and over until just before dawn. When I finally fell asleep in his strong arms, a satisfied smile on my face, I couldn't stop thinking about how much I loved this man.

Valentine's Day 1981 saw Mama glowing with the satisfaction that all her children were coupled up. Four of us were married and showering her with grandchildren, Carter and Julian had been a couple since high school, and I had a boyfriend in Jarvis. And of course, Daddy could still bring out a girlish giggle from Mama with just the right words. I had to admit, seeing them still going strong after 32 years was highly encouraging to me about a future with Jarvis. Little did I know that on that day, Jarvis would ask me a life-changing question...

On September 12, 1981, with my niece Zora preceding me as my flower girl and Ellen as my very pregnant matron of honor, Daddy walked me down the aisle at St. Matthew's. My wedding was nowhere near the extravaganza Doris Hendricks Kennedy had the previous year, yet it was beautiful in its own right. I went for elegant simplicity in every area, including my mermaid-style wedding gown, and I got it. The look of love and unabashed appreciation on Jarvis' face when he laid eyes on me was all I needed. Love and desire radiated from him like the sun on that clear, warm day of late summer. While Rev. Dalton was speaking, I knew only that I loved him, and I looked forward to growing old with him, like Grandma and Grandpa Berry, Grandma and Grandpa Langston, Mr. and Mrs. Varnell, Mama and Daddy...

The next thing I knew, Jarvis was on the floor, out cold. I had heard of this phenomenon of grooms fainting at the altar, and there was the hard—strike that, unconscious—evidence spread out in front of me. Mild pandemonium reigned as I wondered if this was an omen of things to come. The church mothers, however, were prepared for everything. After Jarvis was carried into a room off the sanctuary, they put smelling salts under his nose to revive him.

"Where...where..." he groaned.

"You're at church, honey. You fainted while we were standing at the altar."

He managed to sit up and shake his head. "Oh. Right. You know...I think this is some sort of payback."

"Payback? What are you..." At that moment I realized what he meant and started to laugh, which started him laughing.

"What's so funny?" Daddy wondered.

"Just a private joke, Daddy. You can tell Rev. Dalton we'll be ready in a few minutes—unless Ellen decides to go into labor."

I told myself I wouldn't cry, but a tear managed to slip down my cheek when we finished exchanging our vows and exchanged rings. I looked up and saw Jarvis' loving smile, hearing our pastor say, "I now pronounce you husband and wife. You may kiss your bride."

I was sure I felt my feet leave the floor when he kissed me, knowing that we were now on the beginning of our adventure as Mr. and Mrs. Jarvis Varnell. We had a great wedding reception, and I couldn't help but notice Mama and Mrs. Edwards looking at Carter and Julian like velociraptors stalking their next meal. Now that I was a married woman and my brother was 22, I knew they would not rest until they completed their mission. Come to think of it, Auntie Elaine was giving Elizabeth that same look, only Elizabeth was pretending not to notice. I wondered if she, like me, would attempt to get out of the way when I tossed my bridal bouquet?

There were times during our first year of marriage where a case would take Jarvis out of town. I wasn't always happy about that, but as long as he was a one-man shop, I had to deal with it. Not that being in law school was a picnic, either, with mock trials, moot court, and endless studying at the law library. I had days when I would find myself complaining to Daddy about the process, getting his usual reply of, "Chauntice, it comes with the territory." How could I argue with that? *Just suck it up and buckle down,* I told myself, imagining that Daddy probably said something similar when he was my age.

Daddy and Mama had front row seats when I received my Juris Doctor from the U of M law school in the spring of 1982. I had chosen business and corporate law, and while I was gearing up for the bar exam, I was blessed with an internship at the law firm that represented a subsidiary of Christopher Electronics. Daddy and I could "talk shop," even though he had been on the bench for several years. It brought us closer in a certain way, because I had followed in his footsteps career-wise. Eli Edwards, Jr., Kevin Hendricks, and Vickie Christopher Mitchell also had that kind of bond with their fathers, and from time to time we'd get together and share the various ways our dads groomed us.

At the same time, Jarvis' PI firm took off. He had taken on two operatives due to the volume of cases coming in. He had listings in the Yellow Pages, but the vast majority of his new business came by referral. Though I was pleased for his success, I was also concerned about him taking on cases that were too dangerous at the time and told him so.

"All right, Chauntice, I'm listening. Why?" he said one day over dinner.

"Because of something I found out," I said, feeling a little nervous.

"And what did you find out? Is it something related to any of my cases?"

"No, Jarvis. Actually, I went to see my doctor the other day. I'm… pregnant."

The initial shock on his face changed to tenderness as my words sunk in. He left his seat and took me in his arms, his eyes locked on mine. "Baby, some things come with the territory, but I would never purposely put myself in a position that would place me or our family in danger. I love you. I want to grow old with you, and I want to see our family grow," he said with all the sincerity in his heart before he gave me a long, lingering kiss.

Jarvis had his own concerns about me as well. I'm passionate about law, just like Daddy, and during my internship I put in a lot of hours. "Baby, I know how you feel about your career, but you're carrying our child as well. I'm concerned that you'll overdo things at work, and that's not good for either of you." I assured my husband that I wouldn't, and for a while things were OK. However, the firm became involved in a class action suit, and everyone was called upon to put in extra hours. I came home tired, stressed, and worn around the edges. Jarvis did his best to take care of me at home, but despite my husband's admonitions to cut back my hours and work I kept on going. This was too important a case and I needed to prove myself.

On an early afternoon in late October, near the end of my second trimester, I was in the middle of a deposition when I felt sharp pains. The witness called our legal assistant, Marguerite, into the conference room, where she found me almost doubled over in pain.

"Chauntice, what's the matter? Is it the baby?"

I looked up at her and nodded in agony. "Call the hospital," I managed to get out. "And call my husband. Something's wrong."

Marguerite immediately called in our receptionist and had her take the numbers from my Rolodex to make the calls. The office seemed to fill up with curious onlookers as the paramedics took me out on a gurney and rushed me to Fairview Hospital. I don't remember much about my time in the ER, but when I recovered in a hospital bed in the maternity ward, Jarvis was there holding my hand. Instinctively I put my other hand to my stomach, and the fear in me subsided when I felt a still rounded shape.

"What...happened?"

"You were having contractions. They were able to stop them, but you almost lost the baby." Jarvis squeezed my hand. "When you're released, you have to be on total bed rest for the next three weeks, and I will be there to make sure that you are."

"But your business—"

"I can do some work from home. I can delegate. I'll be there for whatever you need. Nothing is more important than you and our child."

I was wracked with guilt. I hated seeing the worry on Jarvis' face, knowing I had put it there. How could I have done this? How could I have been so driven that I would put our baby's life in jeopardy? What was I thinking? It was then that I remembered one of the cardinal lessons Daddy taught me: "Never sacrifice your family on the altar of your career." In the weeks that I was at home on bed rest, I prayed and made a solemn vow that I never would.

During my third trimester I went on a reduced work schedule, faithfully seeing my obstetrician every week. Both he and I were encouraged by my reports that the scare was over, and my new regimen helped keep it that way. The proof came on the morning of January 29, 1983, when I was delivered of a healthy baby girl, Antonia Janise Varnell. Jarvis was my labor coach—I was so glad he didn't faint. Flowers and well wishes poured in from my colleagues, my friends, and my family. When I was alone in my hospital bed, though, I couldn't help thinking about what might have happened, and I cried tears of gratitude.

When I was pregnant with our second child, Jarvis would give me a sharp look if he even suspected I was coming close to overdoing things or taking on too much stress at work. That was usually enough to make me stop. Fortunately, this pregnancy was easier than the first one, and James Berry Varnell arrived on schedule on February 15, 1985. If there's one thing Jarvis is, it's potent, and before I knew it, I was pregnant again. This time around, I didn't just have morning sickness. I had morning sickness, afternoon sickness, and evening sickness to the point that I was on my knees at the toilet begging for my second trimester to kick in and give me relief. I took it as easy as I could, considering we already had two preschool children. However, Kira Suzanne Varnell took it upon herself to make her debut five weeks ahead of schedule on April 19, 1987.

Even with the way judges were rotated and my specialty in corporate law, every so often I would represent a client in a civil suit, and off I would go to the twin towers of the Hennepin County Government Center. Part of me wanted to go ahead with a case where Daddy was the presiding judge, yet I knew when that happened that he would have to recuse himself from the case. That didn't stop me from sitting in the gallery when he was the trial judge in a criminal case. *Heaven help that guilty defendant,* I often thought when it came time for the sentencing portion of the trial and said defendant had to stand in front of Daddy.

As for Jarvis, his agency was a well-run operation that continued to flourish over the years. With the country becoming more and more litigious, cheating spouses, spouses in the throes of divorce, light-fingered corporate execs, and occasional requests from select defense attorneys, there was no shortage of work for him and his operatives. Still, he knew the importance of delegating to maintain our family life—maybe he took a page from Daddy. He also added family connections to his staff, engaging the IT services of Rashid Hines, my niece Sierra's husband, after they married in 2002.

In the fall of 2001, with Antonia off at college at the U of M-Duluth and James and Kira still in high school, I now had my own law firm. I was in my office on Mainstreet in downtown Hopkins, reviewing paperwork for some investors when Daddy dropped by.

I got up and gave him a hug. "Hi, Daddy. What's up?"

"I just thought I'd like to see my daughter in action again. How's business?"

"Mostly contract litigation these days," I replied, catching something in his eyes. "But I don't think that's the only reason you're here."

"Touché," he said half-heartedly, taking a seat. "That's what I get for having a daughter in the profession."

"Well, there is some truth in that saying about the apple not falling far from the tree." I put down my work and gave him my full attention. "So, what's going on?"

"I wish I didn't have to tell you this, Chauntice, but it involves a number of your clients."

My stomach sank, but I put on my best lawyer game face. "Which clients?"

"There's a man out there who's bilking investors. He calls himself Wilbert Morris, but he has a rap sheet in other states—for embezzlement, grand larceny, you know what I mean."

I did not need this—not that day. "Not good. Not good at all. Now you said this involves my clients. How do you know about this?"

Daddy gave me a solemn expression. "Eli."

Now Daddy definitely had my attention. "Oh. His gift."

"Exactly. This character has covered his tracks fairly well, until now. I also gained some information from someone he swindled out of millions of dollars in Missouri, who recognized him at a fundraiser here in town. Fortunately for my source, he wasn't seen by our con man. I suspect this Wilbert Morris is running a Ponzi scheme, and several of your clients are being fleeced by him."

"We have to report him. Is this person who told you a credible witness?"

"Impeccable."

"What is Mr. Morris' real name?"

"Benjamin Maddox. He's gone under many aliases."

I took a deep breath. "So, we have to come up with enough evidence to convict him, and we're going to need help. Jarvis has operatives who can help us with that."

"We're going to need a forensic accountant as well."

"Hmmm. Ellen's husband Kenneth has those skill sets. I'll call Darius and see if he can spare him to help us. Do you think Mr. Maddox is computer savvy?"

"He could be. He's been pretty slick."

"Well, Jarvis has one of the tops in the field when it comes to computer technology. In fact, she was trained by Uncle Eli." I quickly made notes on what we needed, ready to make the necessary phone calls after Daddy and I finished brainstorming. "What about the police? Do you think they'll take it seriously?"

"They'll listen if I bring it to them," Daddy said without batting an eye. "But discretion is imperative in this investigation, otherwise Maddox will bolt."

Even with Darius Edwards' loan of Kenneth and the help from my husband's staff, it wasn't an easy investigation for us. The hardest part was telling my clients what this sleazy con man had done, and at the same time stressing the importance of not tipping him off. It took all the finesse of a sting operation to trap him. At the trial, Benjamin Maddox's defense was so glib that he almost got off. When Daddy took the stand as a witness, however, Maddox's true colors came out; it was the look in my father's eyes that cracked the defendant's veneer of smug self-confidence.

In the end, he was sentenced to a term of 15 years for each count of larceny—10 counts in all, to be served consecutively. Most of the money he had stolen had been found in offshore accounts, so my clients had received some compensation. Before he was taken from the courtroom, Maddox looked around until he saw Daddy and mouthed the words, "You're dead."

Sure, Benjamin Maddox was cooling his heels in the slammer, and the threat he made to Daddy was the kind that could fill packing crates, given Daddy's career. So many criminals never believed they were guilty. Then again, there was that cold, dead look in his eyes. Of course, I'd seen that in convicted criminals as well. Only time would tell.

I was only too happy to conspire with Willona Hendricks to bring Keith and Kira together. My youngest daughter, as far I was concerned, was a far better love match for him than Terri Peterson. This was confirmed when we went over to Robbinsdale Armstrong High School and spied on Terri from a distance during a lunch period in 2003.

"I tell you, Chauntice, every time I've seen her, my intuition tells me she'll only ruin my son," Willona said grimly. "She'll latch onto him like a leech."

I observed the teenaged hussy in question and nodded. "Now that I see her away from Keith, it's even more obvious. That's what Xenobia must have been like at that age. What does Kevin say about it?"

Willona gave me an incredulous look. "Are you kidding? As soon as I said that Terri reminded me of Aunt Xenobia, I thought I saw a thousand new grey hairs appear on his head. He wants her out of the picture once and for all. And I *know* that Kira is the right girl for Keith."

"Well, before we bring them together, the first thing to do is to arouse Kira's interest, especially since they attend different high schools. Do you have a wallet-sized photo of Keith? A recent one?"

"Certainly. We can go by my house and get it before the kids get home from school."

"Good."

"Next, we set up a little dinner party on Saturday."

"Who have you planned on inviting—besides us, of course?"

"Let's see—besides you and Jarvis, I invited Julian and Carter, their daughters Donna Jo and Lilly, Doris and Gene and their youngest, Wood."

"Perfect. A gathering of family and friends shouldn't arouse any suspicions from the kids. Is everyone else on board?"

"Trust me, they're on board. And our men are solidly behind us—all I had to do was mention Aunt Xenobia's name." I saw Willona cringe at the utterance of said name. "The thought of another like her in the family is unthinkable."

"Excellent. Now, let's go to your house and get that photo. I know exactly what to do with it. Saturday should prove most interesting."

We looked at each other and smiled in agreement as I started up my Infiniti. "In the meantime, let's pray that Terri is kept away from the party. Better yet, that Keith hasn't gotten up the nerve to invite her to the house yet," Willona said with glee as we took off.

I am so happy I married a private detective. Jarvis had one of his operatives run a full background check and surveillance on Terri and her family in the days preceding our dinner party, information we immediately shared with Kevin and Willona. In the meantime, when she didn't think anyone was watching, I observed Kira's response to the strategically placed photograph of Keith. The secret smile on her face, the eyes filled with curiosity, the call on her cell phone to her best friend. She was hooked.

"Ah, the things we do for our children," I commiserated in a phone call to Willona the night before the party.

"Don't I know it."

"How did you handle things with Keith?"

"He'll find out tomorrow afternoon. Hopefully, that's too late for him to invite Terri. Then again, he still hasn't breathed a word about her, so that could work in our favor."

"I hear you. See you tomorrow."

The drive on U.S. Highway 169 from our house in Hopkins to Kevin and Willona's house in New Hope was a typical one. Jarvis and I enjoyed a jazz CD, while Kira was talking on her cell phone with her friend. We made plausible reasons for her attendance at the dinner party; fortunately for us, she didn't question them. She did ask, "Why isn't James coming?"

"James and Jonathan are up at Gull Lake with Jerome and Ariel for the weekend," was Jarvis' matter-of-fact answer.

"Oh. Well, I hope they clean the fish before they come back instead of leaving it to Mama and me," she said before getting back to her phone call.

Greetings were given upon our arrival, with Jarvis and I discussing our week with Willona and Kevin. A few moments later, Keith happened to appear in the hallway. Kira was talking to my niece Donna Jo, seemingly unaware of his presence. I, on the other hand, gently nudged Willona. The look on his face was one of those Kodak moments—he was absolutely mesmerized. Willona and I smiled and nodded; the Berry charm had struck again. Kevin and Jarvis glanced at Keith out of the corners of their eyes. They didn't let on to Keith that they were watching, but later our men high-fived each other in what they considered a done deal.

At dinner Keith insisted on sitting next to Kira. For a young man with a hearty appetite, it was a wonder he even ate half the food on his plate. On her part, Kira tried to play nonchalant, but from time to time she would look over at him and give him little smiles of encouragement.

A week after our dinner party, Antonia drove down from Duluth for a visit. Kira practically dragged her big sister off to her room and shut the door. Of course, a Berry woman appreciates the art of eavesdropping, and I walked down the hall in stealth mode, putting my ear to Kira's door. The conversation between my daughters was "old school" music to my ears. Kira was raving about Keith as though he was, as Mama would put it, "the best thing since sliced bread," while Antonia was pumping her for every detail. Pleased with the results, I tiptoed back to the kitchen, grabbed the cordless phone, and hurried to the porch, making a call to someone I knew would be dying to hear the news.

"Mama, guess what?"

156

She was chomping at the bit. "I know that tone, Chauntice. What is it?"

"If we continue to play our cards right, you'll have another Berry-Edwards love match in the family."

"Who? Who?"

"Kira. With Keith Hendricks," I said smugly, knowing Mama would be on the phone to Madear the second I got off the line—providing, of course, that Willona hadn't told her first. After I allowed a minute for Mama's screams of happiness and exultation, she settled in to grill me.

"All right, Chauntice. I want every detail on how this happened."

"Yes, Mama, but only if you promise not to call Willona to book her for wedding plans tomorrow. They are still in high school, you know."

I could almost hear Mama's brain cells working overtime in plot mode even as she conceded, "Oh, all right. I promise. Now talk."

I gave Mama the 411 on the planning and execution of our dinner party. She loved it. What I didn't tell her about was the follow-up visit Willona and I made to Robbinsdale Armstrong High to spy on Terri again. This time, the gleam in her eyes was gone. Her jaws were tighter than a bear trap. She was far from being a happy camper. As it happened, we saw Keith walk by her and they had words. When he finally walked away, Terri could be heard shouting obscenities at him. "You know something? I do believe Terri has all the earmarks of a young woman who's just been dumped," Willona declared as we shook hands in triumph.

"I do believe you're right," I beamed. "But let's keep this under our hats for now. I just want to relish this moment."

"Savor it!"

"Yes! A Xenobia-in-training has been locked out of the family."

Further confirmation of our success came when Keith formally brought Kira to Sunday dinner at the Hendrickses the following week, giving her the title of girlfriend. It was no surprise when Kira invited Keith to our house for Sunday dinner soon afterwards. Mama and Daddy "just happened to be in the neighborhood" that afternoon. They were so transparent, but we had more than enough food for everybody. As Keith and Kira exchanged besotted looks and compliments over dinner, we adults were gloating. Mama had to be reined in to keep from putting our prior conversation "on blast." We had even more to gloat about at the Edwards fall party, when Keith walked in with Kira on his arm.

"I knew it. I just knew it," Madear declared as she, Mama, Willona, and I watched the young couple on the dance floor. "There's going to be another wedding between our families. All we have to do is wait."

"And I will make sure my calendar is cleared for their big day." Willona's face, like mine, was filled with glee. "After all, they deserve the best."

At that moment, Daddy happened to walk by with Uncle Eli. Looking out over the dance floor and then back at us, he asked, "Are you ladies, by chance, plotting again?"

Mama gave him an incredulous look and replied, "Plotting? Us?"

Of course, they weren't buying it, but Uncle Eli let it pass. "Never mind. You prevented another Xenobia from getting into this family, and that is priceless." Just then we saw that certain look in his eyes, and we leaned in close, quietly waiting for him to come back and glad there were no outsiders in the vicinity. When he did, he said, "Keith and Kira have career plans they want to launch first. Keith will be joining Kevin at Hendricks Automotives. Make sure Kevin teaches him the way his father taught him. Chauntice, you will get a law partner in Kira, so groom her well. But they will also become Mr. and Mrs. Hendricks."

We were over the moon. Confirmation! Kool and the Gang's "Celebration" was music to our ears…

"I knew Madear and Mama were happy about Keith and Kira's wedding. Maybe happy is too mild a word, but I didn't realize how much until they sprung their gift on them," Chauntice said as they drove home. "Seven weeks, all-expense-paid honeymoon trip around the world—go figure."

"Where do you suppose they are now?"

"I think Dubai was their next stop."

Jarvis nodded, remembering the travel brochures of the country. "You know they're going to become travel bugs when they have time off from work."

"Maybe, maybe not. Right now, it's their honeymoon, and it'll be memorable."

"How much do you want to bet they're congratulating themselves again at the party?"

Chauntice rolled her eyes. "That's a no-brainer. That's like saying Uncle Eli's visions always come to pass."

"Like the one he had about Obama being re-elected?"

"There you go."

"Now, all Daddy Berry needs is for Uncle Eli to visualize one of his grandchildren..."

"Or great-grand..."

"...becoming a Supreme Court justice and he will buy up billboard space for it," Jarvis said, chuckling.

"Daddy wouldn't do something quite that obvious. No, he'd put in a call to the Star-Tribune and insist that it be placed on Page One."

"And let the church say, 'Amen.'"

They exited I-394 to southbound U.S. Highway 169, listening to the sounds of KMOJ and recounting the good fortune of Election Night. "Hey, that's your phone," Jarvis said at the sound of the ringtone.

"Hello...hello...oh, hi, Trevell. How are you tonight?" When she heard the answer, Chauntice grew still. "What did you say?"

Carter Woodson Berry-Edwards

After five daughters, I can only imagine that Daddy was in nirvana on a snowy January 25, 1959, when Dr. Bradford said, "It's a boy." Mama has a strong sense of the value and importance of African American history, which may be the reason she named me after Carter G. Woodson. I'm sure that Daddy agreed with her choice. Now that he had a son, he probably would have agreed to almost any name she came up with.

There is something to be said for having five big sisters. If I wanted to keep something secret, I learned early on not to confide in my sisters much. I love them, but while I was growing up, they considered it their sworn duty to stay in my business. The same went for my cousins, Ellen and Elizabeth, since they spent a lot of time after school at our house until Ellen turned fourteen. Douglass Edwards and Julian Edwards were closer to my age, but we went to different elementary schools, so we'd hang out at the park sometimes or whenever our parents got together.

I was only a toddler when Uncle Eldon was killed, but things changed for our family when that happened. Daddy became an assistant district attorney with a mission of putting the criminals away and getting justice for their victims. When I was older, he told me about how Uncle Eldon's murderer got off, and part of me hoped the dude would suffer the way my uncle did. "You keep putting the bad guys away, Daddy. For Uncle Eldon," was my reply. I could imagine him saying that to himself after each conviction that was upheld. Learning that the perp suffered the torture of death by cancer in 1978, a few months after LaVera and Derrick's wedding, was vindication of a sort and it gave our family closure, even though it didn't bring Uncle Eldon back.

Daddy's appointment to the bench in January of 1973 was the culmination of a dream for him, and I was quite proud of him; I told my teachers and classmates all about it. When we moved next door to the Edwardses in July, I thought my own dream would come true when Julian Edwards came over to help out. I was a grade behind him, so I guess I was "under the radar" as far as he was concerned.

He was, without a doubt, one gorgeous man, and he still is. Unlike his older brothers, he looked something like the singer Jackie Wilson in his prime. I couldn't help but notice him peeking out of his bedroom window as we were moving furniture into our house—Mama wanted everything in its proper place, what with Sylvia's wedding taking place at the end of the month. Sure, our families know each other, but Julian's parents had moved when I was in elementary school. Once we were both back at Bryant Jr. High, I was operating under the disadvantage of being a grade behind him and moving in different circles, all because he was seven months older than me. At the age of 14, though, I found myself looking at him in a very different way. I couldn't help but hear the way my sisters talked about this boy or that boy once they hit their teens. Now I understood what they meant. Mine happened to conveniently live next door.

I was struggling with a heavy mirror, attempting to get it out to the edge of the van so Daddy could help me with it, when I heard someone behind me say, "Need some help with that?"

I looked up from my task and—*wow!*—there he was. I took a moment to wipe some sweat from my brow; no way was I going to turn down that kind of help. "Sure. Thanks." He climbed up into the van to grab one end of the mirror, while I checked him out as nonchalantly as I could. "Julian?"

"Yeah. I'm your new neighbor."

"You went to Bryant."

"Right again. I start at Central this fall."

"I wish I was. I have to wait another year," I said wistfully.

161

"Trust me, it'll pass before you know it." We edged our way down the ramp, managing the mirror as best we could. "You know, my brothers know your sisters."

"Yeah, come to think of it. I remember Linda talked about your brother Mel a lot. What's he up to?"

"Just working a summer gig, then it's back to Northwestern."

"Linda's at Marquette. Careful, the steps are coming up."

"Thanks." He backed slowly up the steps, and I appreciated the way we fell into sync. "So, what's it like to have five big sisters these days?"

"OK, I guess—if they weren't always in my business."

"Still, Carter, you do have some fine sisters."

"That's just it, they know it. But they're cool. I feel sorry for the dudes who come around to date them. When Sylvia was living at home, Daddy would take her dates into the den and close the door. I don't know what he said, but they always came out of there looking like he'd held them at gunpoint. And he was the picture of cool and calm. Same with Deshawna and Linda."

"Dad was pretty strict with my brothers, too. John told me it took an act of Congress to get Dad to let him use the car for the homecoming dance. Of course, that was before John bought his own car." We chuckled as we reached the next set of steps. "But Ma...if they brought home a girl she didn't like, she'd give them The Look and it was all over but the shouting. So, which way do I go?"

"Uh....to the left and straight back."

We set the mirror down in the dining room and went back outside to get more furniture. As we went up the ramp, I heard a familiar voice calling, "Carter! You'd better be careful with my bed!"

"Relax, LaVera. Stop acting like it's a Brink's delivery," I said sarcastically. As we carried out a box spring mattress, my sister came outside. As far as looks go, she could give Beyonce some competition, but her attitude left something to be desired. "LaVera, you remember Julian Edwards? Julian, LaVera."

She regarded this introduction from her regal pose for a moment and said, "Oh, right, you're Mel's little brother. Hi."

162

"Hi, LaVera. Where does this go?"

"Upstairs, second door on the right," was her lofty reply, giving the attitude that only corroborated my character assessment.

As the afternoon wore on, we managed to get everything off the truck while putting up with LaVera's and Chauntice's orders. Mama and Daddy gave Julian compliments about his helpfulness, but I saw him as my dreamboat. The way he could be awkward and graceful at the same time, tall and gangly yet built, with buns to die for. The smile, had he known it then, that had me ready to melt while Mama prepared a meal to replenish our strength after our hard work.

After that day, we were nearly inseparable. We were at each other's houses so much that our parents took it for granted. I watched him grow taller until he hit 6'4" and filled out to desirable proportions. I had stopped at 5'8", built like a gymnast with a touch of bodybuilder. I hoped and hoped Julian would make a move or something, yet I didn't want to scare him off. It just seemed like forever; it wasn't until later that I learned Julian felt the same way as I did. He was just shy about approaching me, like that Pointer Sisters song that came out in the '80s. Even with that knowledge, it was still a waiting game. Man, how I wished that the Berry charm Daddy and Grandpa Berry bragged about would work for me when it came to Julian Edwards, preferably sooner than later.

One evening during spring break of my junior year at Central High, Julian invited me over to his house. Ordinarily it would be no big deal, because we spent so much time at each other's houses. This time, I sensed something different when I followed him up to his room; the house was so quiet. I started to ask him where his parents were, until I remembered that they went to a fundraiser with mine. Still…

"Where's Mrs. Banks?" I asked.

"Oh, she has the night off," he said with what looked like a nervous yet secretive smile.

We sat in his room as usual, talking about school or family stuff and listening to Donna Summer albums. I'd been around Julian long enough to tell when he was building up to something, and this had all the earmarks of it. On a hunch, I gave him my most encouraging look. *Please, Berry charm, go to work. Please, please, please……*

"You know, Carter…I like you. I like it when we spend time together." He moved closer to me.

"I know."

"I mean, I *really* like you. The way our classmates do when they're going together."

At last. "I know that, too, since I feel the same way about you."

"Maybe we've been dating and didn't know it. Well…I want to make it official." He took my hand. "Will you be my boyfriend?"

My face must have been a combination of megawatt smile, passion, and sheer happiness. I saw a major grin spread across his face in return. "Julian, I've been hoping you'd ask me. You have no idea how long I've wanted to hear that from you, man."

Julian got up and stood in the middle of the floor when I heard a familiar song play. I knew it was his favorite, and he had a very inviting look in his eye. "Wanna dance?"

"You've got it," was my heartfelt answer as I got up to join him, feeling like I had just won the Showcase Showdown on *The Price is Right*. Strike that—I was the Double Showcase winner.

That first time we danced together was so hot. "Love to Love You Baby" had a whole new meaning to me when Julian was in my arms, kissing him over and over and over while I was grinding my hard nightstick against his during that long slow drag. A young man can only endure so much, especially when he's finally gotten what he's been dreaming about for so long. Before the song was over, I heard a moan from Julian as I came in my jeans. It was a little embarrassing, but it wasn't so bad because Julian had a sticky mess in his pants, too. Our relationship had been taken to a new level.

When it came time for the senior prom, I didn't even consider going with anyone but Julian, but pulling it off seemed like an insurmountable task. I learned through that experience, however, that there were times when who you knew had unexpected benefits. Julian's grandparents, Lillian and Melvin Edwards, didn't force the school district to allow us to go to the prom as a couple. They did something even better and more far-reaching at the time: they put together a senior prom that upstaged every high school prom in the Twin Cities. Not only that, the school superintendent, our principal, the mayor, and assorted celebrities were there by invitation, in addition to the big names in music at the time for the entertainment. It was a senior bash that people talked about for a long time, and Julian and I were exceedingly grateful for everything they did for us and the other LGBT couples that were able to be part of that experience.

It's not easy to be 17 and filled with raging hormones when the object of your desire lives right next door. Knowing at last that he wanted me both fueled the fire and forced me to wait, especially after Julian turned 18. I was more than ready for our 4th of July trip up north and taking him in the way I had often dreamed of taking him. When he told me why we had to wait it was a bummer, but I loved him too much to get him into trouble.

When my 18th birthday rolled around, we went out dining and dancing. It was a lot of fun and I expected us to make love afterwards, but Julian had other ideas. "My parents are going out for Valentine's Day, and Mrs. Banks has that night off. My parents won't be home until late."

"How do you know that?"

"They always are on Valentine's Day. That means I have the house to myself, and you'll have a Valentine's Day treat you'll never forget," he said.

"You know I'm going to hold you to that, Julian," I replied, just before he gave me a passionate kiss while we were parked.

Wow, was he ever worth the wait. Finally, finally, we went all the way on that Valentine's Day. Julian went to a lot of effort to make that evening memorable, from the dinner, the romantic setting in his room and our favorite music. Apparently, he had taken some pointers from his cousin Wayne, for he was more than prepared and ready for me. When I pumped inside of him, kissing him and nuzzling his neck, I was ready to do it for hours, and the 18-minute version of "Love to Love You Baby" fanned the flames. By most men's standards, I'm a very well-endowed little guy (I suspect I inherited that asset from

Daddy), and Julian wanted me to stay inside him as long as possible. All I had to do was see his own large, generous tool throbbing with his sexy moans, and was that ever a turn-on. Even more so was the sensuality in his eyes between kisses.

It took every ounce of willpower not to climax too soon; recuperative powers or not, I wanted the lovemaking to last the first time out. My breathing was heavy, and I couldn't stop saying, "Julian." We were heated and sweaty, reaching that point of no return. I heaved and bucked and finally yelled, just before I deep kissed him again and came like I'd never done before. Not 10 seconds later, I felt the splashes of Julian's passion juice generously coating us as we rode that wave.

Now you know I wanted to spend the night curled up with Julian in his bed in the worst way. Forcing myself to get dressed and leave before his parents came home took superhuman effort. Valentine's Day or not, it was still a school night for me, and Julian had a full day of classes at Augsburg College. Even so, I'm not even sure my feet touched the snowy ground when I went home. What I was sure of was that I had another erection, and I vowed to see Julian again for some more of that mind-blowing passion as soon as possible. *Thank you, Donna Summer, for a night I'll always remember,* going to sleep to her rendition of "I Love You."

Several months later during the summer, Julian and I were apartment-sitting for Wayne and Theo while they vacationed in New Orleans. We engaged in a nude wrestling match, and I reveled in the excitement I felt from Julian's rod rubbing at the entrance to my love tunnel. I had to admit, I liked it and I was curious, to the extent that I wanted to feel him inside me. Once I gave my honey the green light, in he went, and I found myself hard as a rock and begging for more. It wasn't long before he hit my P-spot, and ecstasy was taken to a whole new dimension for me. My wits took a vacation. I forgot how strong he was, for he picked me up and kept on stroking into me while he was standing up. Wrapping my legs around his waist, I held on for the toe-curling ride of my life before I exploded in pleasure, my love juice shooting all over us, while his release shot deep inside me. Hours and several orgasms later, my mind was coherent enough to entertain the thought, *So, this is how Julian feels when I make love to him. Wow! I wonder what it would be like to do this outdoors?*

For so long, I had hoped the Berry charm and looks I inherited from Daddy would work for me. Once I made love to Julian, they came out in full force. I never thought so many men and women would be "feeling me," as the kids put it these days. However, I made it very clear as we worked our way through college that I was in love with Julian, and nobody could hold a candle to him. Some folks even tried every trick in the book to break us up—that is, until we had a chat with his Grandma Edwards. When one by one those same people suddenly left town, the scheming soon came to a halt.

We moved into a spacious two-bedroom apartment in the Cedar-Riverside complex after I graduated from Augsburg College in 1981 with a degree in sociology. Setting up housekeeping was probably the biggest test for us. Even though we'd known each other since we were kids, you never really know somebody until you live with them. We had so many disagreements about decorating the place. I was a night owl; he was an early bird. I liked detective and cop shows, he liked sitcoms, and so on, and so on, and so on. We could agree on major decisions, but those little things that can be annoying really took time to either adjust to or live with. When I brought them up to Daddy, his reply was, "Carter, you're not the first one to deal with it, and you're far from the last. This is just a normal part of learning how to live with someone."

One day after Thanksgiving in 1982, while Julian was at work, I went over to Daddy's chambers for a conference. At the time he had just pronounced sentence upon a slimeball defendant, and he was between trials.

"Hi, son," he said as he took a seat. "Just give me a moment." I waited patiently as he took off his black robe and hung it up; that was his way of shifting gears from judge to father. He joined me on the leather sofa, giving me his undivided attention. "Now, what did you want to see me about?"

"Well, it's about Julian."

"All right. Is there anything specific you want to talk about in regard to him?"

"You know we've been going together since high school."

"True. And he is a fine young man."

"I know," I agreed wholeheartedly, smiling and blushing a little. "I really love him, Daddy. I want to spend the rest of my life with him. And that's why I'm going to ask him to marry me."

Daddy's face broke out into a grin and he gave me a big hug. "Well, well, well. After the trial I just had, you have made my day. Congratulations, son! When are you going to 'pop the question'?"

"At Christmas. And Daddy…could we just keep this between us for now? Mama has been praying for a wedding between our families for the longest time. If I tell her or my sisters, there's no way on earth they'll be able to keep it a secret."

He gave me a conspiratorial smile. "I'll be the sole of discretion, son. Go ahead and do your planning for the big event. I just hope Julian doesn't beat you to the punch."

"So do I, Daddy. So do I. But if he does, it'll would still be OK."

Daddy nodded his head in agreement. "Remember, you're a Berry, and you deserve the best. I found that in your mama, and I'm glad you found it in Julian. But fasten your seat belts, Carter. Once you propose to him, your mama and your future mother-in-law are going to take you two for a ride to the altar—on a bulldozer."

I sighed and nodded, knowing that for a fact. "Anyway, I have another favor to ask."

"Anything."

"I'm going to buy his engagement ring in a few days. Can you recommend a good jeweler?"

"Of course." Daddy went to his desk, picked up his phone and made a call. "Hello, Aaron, Judge Berry here. My son needs an engagement ring. Can you take care of him? Great."

On Christmas Day, we were all gathered at Mama and Daddy's house. My sisters and my brothers-in-law were all there, along with my nephews and nieces. Sylvia and Chauntice were getting around as best they could, since both of them were pregnant at the time, and LaVera was still nursing three-month-old Devon. Yes, Mama was getting her wish for lots of grandchildren, but the best was yet to come.

Auntie Elaine arrived shortly after we did, along with my cousin Elizabeth, my cousin Ellen, her husband Kenneth and their toddler Krystle (OK, so my cousins were huge *Dynasty* fans). With all the family that was there, the holiday was most festive, and everyone was looking forward to Mama's famous Christmas cookies. Julian's family, we knew, would drop in at some point or we'd head over there—such was the convenience of having them as neighbors.

As people were unwrapping presents, I managed to slip mine in without anyone noticing, feeling both excited and nervous. Julian received a generous share of presents from the family. He loves clothes, sweaters, and cologne, and his face was warm with appreciation. I stole a glance at Daddy as I took a seat closer to Julian, and he gently nodded. There were still a lot of conversations going around as Julian opened the last gift. His pupils dilated when he opened the small box with the card attached to it.

I heard Deshawna blurt out, "Look! Look!" as I eased down onto the carpet on one knee. That's where I was when Julian looked up from reading the card. I never saw a room full of family members get quiet so fast. Mama, Auntie Elaine, my cousins, and my sisters surrounded the room, anxiously waiting to hear what I was going to say. My heart was full to capacity with love as my eyes locked on Julian's, seeing the tear run down his cheek as I told him, "I love you, Julian, in every way. I feel so blessed to have you in my life, and I want that to be now and forever. Will you marry me?"

Those moments that I waited for his answer were probably the longest ones of my life. Everyone was watching, and my female relatives were holding their breath. Julian was overwhelmed. Just when I thought I couldn't stand it anymore, Julian replied, "Well, as Barbara Lewis sang, baby, I'm yours."

Screams and cheers surrounded us while I placed the diamond engagement ring on Julian's finger, followed by a kiss that brought more cheers. Mama, Auntie Elaine, my sisters, and my cousins swooped down on us, drowning us in a sea of hugs.

"Now this is a Christmas present I've been waiting for!" Mama shouted. I wasn't surprised at that, not with the way she'd been steadfastly determined to see all her children married off. In the midst of the celebration, she flew to the telephone and called Mrs. Edwards. It didn't take long for the Edwards family to come over, between the wedding advice we received from my sisters and my cousins and the knowing looks from my brothers-in-law.

"Juanita," Mrs. Edwards said as she entered the living room, followed by Mr. Edwards, John and Helen, and Junior's family, "you were so excited over the phone. So, what's this big news?"

Mama looked in our direction with this huge, satisfied grin that would take months to come off. "Carter, Julian, you have the floor."

Mrs. Edwards put her hands on her hips and scrutinized us. "Well, son?"

Julian attempted to put on a poker face, but he failed miserably. Slowly, he took his hand out from behind his back and raised it for his mother's appraisal. Her pupils dilated, she put her hand to her chest, and her lips parted. My sisters ate it up. My honey was so happy when he announced, "Ma, a few minutes ago Carter asked me to marry him. I said yes."

"Finally!" she shouted. *"Finally! Finally! Finally!"* This, of course, set off another round of screaming and shouting women. She hugged us hard enough to nearly cut off our air supply, followed by Sandra and Helen. The Edwards men gave us brotha hugs and smiles, followed by Daddy and my brothers-in-law. Mama and Mrs. Edwards, I knew, were ecstatic for yet another reason; their long-standing dream was about to be realized.

"This news has just made my Christmas, Juanita," Mrs. Edwards gushed as she and Mama shared hugs and tears of joy. "I *always* knew those two were made for each other."

"Tell me about it, Donna," Mama agreed. "Now we have another wedding to plan!"

"Yessss!!" Mrs. Edwards said excitedly.

All the adults toasted our engagement with hot apple cider. We decided on July 2, 1983 for our wedding day, Julian's reasoning being that we could "start our honeymoon off with a bang." Mama and Mrs. Edwards wasted no time in setting us down to start wedding plans. Grandma Berry, like Linda, looked at us and said, "Took you long enough," before she gave us a hug, after which she added, "You *are* going to give me some great-grands, right?"

Leave it to her to be direct and to the point. "Yes, Grandma Berry," I confirmed as Julian and I wrote down names for the guest list under the watchful eyes of our mothers.

"Good. Because you know I'm going to stick around until I get them."

"That makes two of us," Grandma Langston added, as she and Grandma Berry exchanged a look, a high-five and then turned back to us as if it were already a done deal.

The best people in our wedding party were picked early in the planning stages. Mama reminded me of the wedding tradition amongst my sisters, and that when the time for me to marry rolled around my best people would be chosen by lottery. As it turned out, Linda and Prentice were the winners, but knowing my sisters, the remaining four would shoot me if they weren't included in the wedding party. As for Julian, his brother Junior and his sister-in-law Sandra had the honor of being his best people, with assorted relatives rounding out our wedding party.

Julian and I had originally planned for his family, my family, and some of our friends and classmates from Central High and Augsburg College on the guest list—about 75 people. By the time our mothers and our grandmothers were through with us, the guest list stood at 400 people—and this was before it included assorted people from Who's Who in Black America that Lillian Edwards insisted upon being there, like Allan Beckley Christopher and his wife. He may have been a multimillionaire at the time and the head of one of the largest Black-owned corporations in the country, but when his Auntie Lillian called, he knew it was in his best interest to honor her request.

Every day, our phone rang with something pertaining to the wedding. It was exciting on one hand to plan it, but on the other hand the women in our families had our heads spinning. So many details to take into account—invitations, color schemes, catering, the officiant, photographers, videographer, music for the wedding and the reception, the cake, flowers, decorating the church, formal wear for the wedding party. I found myself looking at Julian and saying, "I'm just glad we don't have to be dragged down to a salon to look at wedding gowns."

"Maybe not, but your sisters—and your future sisters-in-law—are already going there. And LaVera is leading the pack."

"Oh, no," I groaned, collapsing onto the couch.

"Well, look at it this way—at least she isn't a matron of honor."

It reached the point where Julian and I went away for a long weekend in April just to get away from all the ideas that were thrown at us about the wedding. Sure, it's great to have such supportive families. However, our wedding was starting to resemble a runaway train, with Mama and Ma Edwards as the engineers. The Edwards family cabin, on Gull Lake up in Beltrami County, was always a great place to get away, to breathe and regroup. By the time we were on the highway back to Minneapolis, we knew we had to do something about the situation—but not without some help.

"I know you're wondering why we asked you all to be here," Daddy said, sounding as though he was presiding over a trial. Julian and I were seated together in the living room at my parents' house, flanked by Daddy and Dad Edwards. Facing us were Mama, Ma Edwards, Grandma Berry, Grandma Langston, Grandma Edwards, Grandma Gray, Auntie Aurelia, Auntie Elaine, Linda, and Sandra. "Carter and Julian came to us because they have some concerns about the wedding."

I heard murmuring from our female relatives, but Dad Edwards raised his hand. "As we said, they have some concerns about the direction this wedding is headed, and they want to share those concerns." Gradually the murmuring ceased, and he looked over at us. "You have the floor."

"Mama, Ma Edwards, everybody," I began, "first, I want to say thank you for all your support, and that we love you very much. We know this is a huge event for you, uniting our families and all, and that you all want to be part of it in some way. It's a special day...but somewhere along the way I think you forgot that it's *our* special day."

"We wanted a relatively intimate wedding, but now we have four hundred guests," Julian added, doing his best to muster up enough calm and reason in the estrogen-filled room. "The invitations are already out, so that's a moot point. The thing is, it seems as though the whole thing is getting out of hand."

"We like some of your ideas, but we also want something that's uniquely us in the mix." I scanned the room, noting the listening ears. "For example, the idea of the carriage ride from the church to the hotel. That's fine—for Charles and Diana. We'd rather have a white stretch limo with 'Just Hitched' on the back."

Julian looked at Grandma Edwards. "It's not like we don't want something with a certain style and class about it. We do. We're only getting married once. We just want our wedding to show more of who we are as a couple."

The voices were low as the women talked among themselves. Daddy gave me a nudge and a look that said, "Be patient." Finally, Mama and Ma Edwards left their seats and took us by the hand.

"We love you, too. And you're right—this is your wedding," Ma Edwards conceded.

"I guess we did get carried away with all the excitement of a Berry-Edwards love match—at last," Mama admitted.

"We understand that, Mama. That's been a dream of yours for goodness knows how long," I said with gratitude.

"So, do you forgive us?" Ma Edwards asked.

"Of course, Ma. Of course." Julian took a moment to hug her.

"Now, if we get too far afield of your wishes, just say so. There's still time to make whatever changes need to be made," Mama added.

"Thank you," I said, looking at Daddy and Dad Edwards and breathing a sigh of relief. After they left with the satisfaction of a mission accomplished, Julian and I turned to face our female relatives. "Since you're all here, we do have some changes we want to make. And we have a favor to ask."

"Name it."

"We need someone to rein in LaVera. Her color and dress choices for our attendants are…well, a bit too revealing."

"We'll have a talk with her," Grandma Edwards, the queen of Twin Cities society, said in a tone that guaranteed resolution of the problem as we sat down for the planning session and updates.

Things seemed to calm down after that talk, along with a stress level reduction. Our wedding was shaping up to be the dream we wanted it to be. Three weeks before the big day, however, things took an unexpected turn; Julian got sick, that feverish, green-around-the-gills type of sick. When I wasn't home to look after him, Mama and Ma Edwards were like helicopters. Every known home remedy— chicken soup, castor oil, you name it—was poured down his throat. It was a miracle he got any rest. He drank so many fluids that there was a well-worn path in the carpet from the bedroom to the bathroom. Our grandmothers called for daily updates, taking on the mantle of prayer warriors. With Linda and Deshawna out of town and Sylvia and Chauntice nursing infants, LaVera and Helen were constant visitors, doing their share to vanquish the enemy of disease that dared to stand in the way of getting us to the altar on schedule. As overbearing as it all seemed at the time, it worked. After nine days, my fiancé was on the mend.

That wasn't the only thing that happened. Right about the time Julian got sick, Mama and Daddy were acting strange. They wouldn't talk about what was going on, but something had them distracted. When I came to church once or twice, I'd notice some people talking among themselves, and they'd suddenly shut up when I approached them. They'd speak to me as always and then ask about Julian, but I thought it was a little weird. Ma Edwards and Julian's Auntie Debbi seemed to be that same way, too. I asked Ma Edwards about it, and her reply was, "It's a business concern that has to be handled."

"What kind of business?"

"That's all you need to know. I'll handle it. And we'll be there to help you make sure Julian gets well quickly."

I knew from experience when to stop pushing for details and concentrated on the health of my fiancé. The funny thing was, just before Julian's condition improved, the odd tension in the air came to a halt. Everything seemed to go back to normal—well, as normal as they can be when you're planning a big wedding. Mama and Daddy had a relaxed air about them again, and Ma Edwards had the satisfied aura of someone who had successfully solved a problem.

On July 2, 1983, dressed in a flawless white tux, I was walking down one aisle with Daddy beside me, while Julian—in a matching white tux—and Dad Edwards were walking down the other aisle, to the tune of "One in a Million You." We were doing our best not to cry during our wedding ceremony, but Mama, my sisters, Grandma Berry, and Grandma Langston made that impossible. So did Wayne, when he sang Natalie Cole's "Inseparable." It was a good thing we didn't have to wear makeup, because it would have been ruined before we could walk back up the aisle as Carter and Julian Berry-Edwards. And fortunately for us, there wasn't a repeat of the ceremony-stopping event at Chauntice's wedding.

The reception was wonderful as well, although I did notice Grandma Edwards give Julian's Aunt Xenobia The Look when she passed by her. Given that nobody liked that snobby woman, it was typical. What was funny, when I think back on it, was the way Aunt Xenobia avoided some last-minute guests from Kansas that Ma Edwards invited for the entire time she was there. However, it was our wedding day and I let it pass, and Julian and I partied to the max. We even got to celebrate Linda and Prentice's pregnancy news.

Now, our families were united. My sisters had a new set of cousins, and for them, Mr. and Mrs. Edwards were now Uncle Eli and Auntie Donna; after her mother's death in 1993, we then called her Madear. She has been that ever since.

Grandma Berry was as good as her word. Even though, by her standards, we dragged our feet—OK, so we waited nine years—she was ecstatic when our first child, Donna Joycelyn Berry-Edwards, was born on October 3, 1992 by surrogate. With Madear's hearty blessing, she was soon nicknamed Donna Jo. She looked like Julian, and she had her Grandpa Edwards' hazel eyes. Grandma Langston hung in there as well; there was no mistaking the twinkle in their eyes when we would bring Donna Jo to see them. By the time our second child, Lillian Juanita Berry-Edwards, was born on January 25, 1998, both had gone on to heaven, and our mothers were well equipped to stand in the gap and fuss over our girls.

Julian and I had always been active in community affairs, especially those involving communities of color and LGBT concerns. Being a community liaison for many years was the motivation for me to start Ujima in 1996, a nonprofit organization created specifically to address those needs and service said communities. Sure, financially we wanted for nothing, but serving the community was something our fathers taught us from an early age. Not that the road was easy.

Finding qualified staff was the first hurdle; we needed the kind of staff that was in line with our vision and in it for the long haul. Daddy, my brother-in-law Prentice, the Edwardses, and the Christophers were our biggest contributors, yet it was important to get others from the community involved in order to limit our reliance upon state funding. Finally, there was the matter of clients. What kind of outreach could we do that would overcome fear, shame, and stigma, to speak in a way that encouraged people of color—including those who were also LGBT—to seek our services? We still have our struggles even now, especially in coming up with new ideas to keep present clients satisfied and encourage new clients.

Daddy retired from the bench that same year, but his last trial as a presiding judge gave me cause for concern. It involved a man named Jackson Trent, someone Julian and I knew of. Trent was on trial for murder, specifically the murder of another gay man we knew of, Chalmers Aldrich. Trent was a man on the DL, and Aldrich had grown tired of being a dirty little secret. He had murdered Aldrich to conceal that fact from public knowledge, including his wife. I despised him for his dishonesty while Julian and I sat there during the trial, seeing the pain of betrayal in his wife's eyes. I couldn't see any way he could justify killing Aldrich.

How are you keeping your cool, Daddy? I thought as I watched him and the grief-stricken expressions on Chalmers Aldrich's relatives. The jury subsequently found Trent guilty of second-degree murder, and Daddy gave him 25 years. Understandably, his wife divorced him. I had seen some self-hating men in my time, some of whom came through Ujima's doors as clients for our counseling services. Still, I had never experienced the degree that Trent displayed it, the way he blamed Daddy for his own actions and the resulting consequences. Not coming out when you aren't ready is one thing, but that's no excuse for murder. After the verdict, Mama, Julian, and I met Daddy in his chambers. I remember the look on his face when he confided in us, "Off the record, if the choice had been mine, he would have gotten life imprisonment."

Serving the community on a larger scale happened in 2005, when Donna Jo, Lilly, and I witnessed Julian take office as Hennepin County's first openly gay county commissioner, with Daddy and Dad Edwards looking on amidst a strong showing of Berrys and Edwardses. He had worked in the planning department for the city of Minneapolis during our marriage. The fact that he was also African American, as we saw it, was a plus. Politics in the family—who knew? Then again, it wasn't that much different from the times Daddy was up for re-election to the bench until mandatory retirement kicked in. We knew going in that we had to have a clear vision on how to best serve the county and yet not make Julian's orientation the defining issue in the campaign. It was by no means a slam-dunk, but Daddy's motto—"Never give up"—prevailed in those last hours, and we were excited when the final results were reported...

"We're on our way." Julian disconnected the call. He looked upon Carter's face, and what Carter saw on it gripped his heart in a highly unsettling way.

"What is it? What happened?"

177

"That was Sylvia. We need to get to the hospital."

"Why?"

"It's Daddy Berry. He's been shot."

As the Berry-Edwards family made the grim trip to Hennepin County Medical Center, Carter couldn't help but wonder about Daddy's last trial, and the fact that Jackson Trent had been released on parole two months ago...

Prentice George Delaney-Ross

Mom tells me that my aunties and Uncle Carter were either products of dark, stormy nights or snowy winter days. My big sister Sierra didn't follow that tradition since she was born on a hot, sunny 4th of July—Bicentennial Sunday, no less—but I did when I came into the world on the cold, snowy afternoon of January 19, 1984. Dad didn't care about the weather, from what I was told—he was too busy celebrating the birth of his only son after a seven-year wait. I can imagine he glowed even more than Mom did, after which I was promptly named Prentice George Delaney Jr. It wouldn't surprise me that Grandpa Berry probably felt the same way when Uncle Carter was born. Sure, the public knows him as Judge Berry, but to me he's always been Grandpa. He's always been special to me because Dad's parents died long before I was born—in fact, before Dad married Mom.

Sierra looks like Mom, but I look more like Dad in most respects. He actually saw Duke Ellington in concert back in the day, and people in the audience kept saying he looked enough like "Sir Duke" to be his son. Mom says I have Dad's ambitious streak, but I inherited Grandpa Berry's hair, his temperament, and his smoky gold eyes. Mom has those eyes, too.

By all standards, Mom and my aunties are among the most beautiful women on the planet, even now. It doesn't stop with looks, because Mom cares about making the world around her a better place, any way she can. It's easy to see how Dad fell in love with her and made her his queen. In spite of the demands of his position, Mom, Sierra, and I were the center of his world. I guess the apple really doesn't fall far from the tree, because Grandpa Berry treats Grandma

Berry the same way. Sierra requires it of my brother-in-law Rashid. Given my own feelings about Trevell, that makes it unanimous.

Dad was a graduate of North Division High School in Milwaukee, and he was given the title "Most Likely to Succeed" of the Class of '55. Milwaukee changed over the years since Dad graduated from high school, and there were more African Americans living along the North Shore of Lake Michigan by the time I graduated from Nicolet High School in 2002. Our home was in River Hills, and like they did for Sierra before me, Mom and Dad threw a great graduation party. Grandma and Grandpa, my aunties, and their families, all made the trip, as well as several of my closest classmates and friends.

I had dated different guys in college, but none of them clicked. Sure, they were handsome, and for the most part decent and ambitious. However, that certain chemistry or whatever wasn't there, that sense in my heart that I always thought would show me the right one, like the connection Uncle Carter and Uncle Julian have. My parents told me, "Give yourself time. It's all right to look for the qualities you want in a husband, but ask yourself if you possess those qualities as well."

Sierra threw in, "The clubs are all right if you want to have fun for an evening, but don't expect to find someone there—not someone worth having. Trust and believe, I've been there." I had to agree with her on that point, in part because of Dad's and Grandpa's prominence in their respective communities. In fact, I could not take a walk along Teutonia Avenue in the community without someone—especially the elders—saying, "You're Judge Delaney's son." High expectations, high standards.

I often wonder sometimes if there is an unspoken expectation in our family, since both Dad and Grandpa were judges, Auntie Chauntice is an attorney, and Auntie Elaine a court reporter. My cousin, Ashley St. James Yang, certainly followed it when she chose a career. Dad was subtler about it than Grandpa. When I was in elementary school and we'd visit Minneapolis, Grandpa would talk about Clarence Thomas. He didn't agree with his political views, but he'd say, "See, Prentice? That could be you on the Supreme Court."

In the fall of my senior year at Marquette University, the family packed into Dad's Cadillac Escalade and drove up to Green Bay to see a Packers game. Dad always made sure he purchased his season tickets well in advance, which guaranteed us good seats at Lambeau Field. Mom and Dad looked forward to those times; not only were they among our established family outings, but Dad could really "let his hair down" without being caught up in the propriety of a judge. My nephew Earl wasn't even a year old yet, but Sierra and Rashid had the little guy dressed down in Packers gear—cap, sweatshirt, the works. However, they were wise—with Grandpa being a Vikings fan, they kept a set of "purple people eater" clothes in Little Earl's wardrobe as well.

Green Bay was playing Chicago that Sunday, and Dad was in his glory, holding his grandson in his arms and telling him what was happening on the field as though Little Earl could understand everything he said. Dad had seemed tired lately, more than what we considered normal, and we were concerned about him. I was glad Little Earl picked up his spirits, and I knew whenever I became a father, my child would receive an abundance of love from his grandparents, not to mention his great-grandparents.

It had been a highly defensive game, and at halftime I volunteered to get refreshments for everyone to complement the food we brought along. I was standing in line for my order when my eyes fell on the 6'4" brotha standing in front of me. His dark brown hair was close cut but not shaved. His skin was a silky, deep brown, and he was built like a quarterback with a booty you could easily set a Pepsi can on. Something about him, the way he stood, the way he was built, and the way he carried himself, looked familiar but I didn't know why. He happened to look sideways, reaching for his cell phone.

Wait a minute. He reminded me so much of one of the team's former players. But who?

There must have been some law against a man looking that good, with the kind of lips that I could easily kiss for hours, and I found myself checking him out as I heard him saying, "Sure, Dad...no, I'm still in line...OK, extra relish on your hot dogs and extra mustard on

Mom's…see you in a bit." He put his phone back into the pocket of his cargo pants when I caught him checking me out. He turned toward me, hopefully for a better look. "Hey, what's up…besides the wait?"

"Just came up with the family to check out the game," I said, keeping my eyes on him. There was no denying the look in his dazzling brown eyes that spoke of more than casual interest, and I was equally interested. Besides, I could easily gaze into those eyes for days on end.

"From where?"

"Milwaukee."

"I thought so. I've never seen you around here before." He extended his hand. "I'm Trevell Ross."

"Prentice Delaney," I answered, accepting his hand in greetings. "So, you live here?"

"Yeah, born and raised here." Trevell was still holding my hand as I relished the energy that flowed between us.

"Trevell. That's an interesting name. Is there a story behind that?"

"Well, it's a combination of my parents' first names. Are you a Packers fan?"

"I get it from both sides. Dad was born in Milwaukee, so he's in the Packers camp, and Mom is from Minneapolis, so she's pro-Vikings. They agree to disagree on that subject." I looked him over again. "I hope that won't come between us getting to know each other."

"Oh, so it's like that, eh?" Trevell said, flirting with his eyes and a captivating smile.

I always felt that I could give as well as I got, so I flirted back. "Yeah. Definitely like that. What are you doing after the game?"

"Probably head back to campus or see the folks for a while."

"Which school?"

"UW Green Bay. What about you?"

"Marquette. Unfortunately, we have to leave as soon as the game's over. My dad hasn't been well."

"That has to be rough. You have your cell with you?"

"Sure," I replied, feeling encouraged. "Let's exchange digits. I'll call you as soon as I get in."

Our orders were ready shortly after we input each other's numbers into our phones, and we discussed school and the game as we walked back to our respective seats. I reached the family with their sodas, juices, and bottled water while Trevell went down to his seat near the fifty-yard line. While he handed his parents their snacks, I caught his father from an angle.

With Dad being such a fan, I can't believe I hadn't put it together before. Tremayne Ross had recently retired from the team, but he had made a name for himself as one of their best running backs in his prime. He was probably in his mid-40s, yet he was still one fine, fit man, and Trevell was definitely molded in his image. Dad and Grandpa, of course, had taught me to get to know someone on their own merits. One of Mom's lessons to me and Sierra was, "Take your time choosing a man and marry well." As I sat through the rest of the game, I hoped to find out as much as I could about Trevell—without making it look like I was cross-examining him on the witness stand.

To our great pleasure, Green Bay won the game, and that evening Trevell and I talked on the phone for hours getting acquainted. I loved hearing his voice. I loved sharing our plans, and the anticipation of seeing each other again. Even during that first phone call, Trevell sounded like the total package. I didn't let on that I knew who his father was; I wanted him to know that I wanted him for himself, not because of Tremayne Ross' celebrity status with the Packers. I was confident that when the time was right, Trevell would trust me enough to tell me. Sure, my father was prominent in Milwaukee, too. Fortunately, it wasn't in the same way—not unless a high-profile criminal case received media attention.

In those early days of dating, our cars burned up a lot of miles on I-43 over the weekends when classes ended and we could visit each other. Still, that two-hour drive was worth it. I made it a point to do all my studying for classes and exams during the week, along with writing my papers, so that Trevell and I could spend as much time together as possible on weekends. Occasionally we'd go to the clubs in Milwaukee and the one dance club on Main Street in Green Bay. Sometimes we'd even drive down to Chicago. However, we had better times hanging out at the lake, the zoo, the park, and the assorted laid-back things that people who are dating do when getting to know each other.

On homecoming weekend, Trevell was my date for the dance. Some of my classmates couldn't close their mouths when they met him. Others made comments like, "Mmm, mmm, mmm. Eye candy of the sweetest kind. You'd better make sure you keep all your dental appointments with him around." Still others, like my best friend Shayla Connelly, remarked, "Make sure you get your picture taken before you leave tonight, Prentice. You two make one drop-dead-gorgeous couple."

That, by far, was the best homecoming dance I'd ever attended. On Sunday afternoon, after Trevell left for Green Bay in his Ford Mustang, Mom, Dad and Sierra sat me down while Rashid played with Little Earl outside.

"So, have you met Trevell's family?" Dad asked.

My mind wandered back to the sensuous goodbye kiss we'd shared, one that had left me aching for more, before I realized what Dad had said. "Well, not yet."

Mom gave me a knowing smile. "You can come down from the clouds for at least a few minutes, son. How soon will you meet them?"

"We planned on doing it before Thanksgiving."

"It's not easy being in his position. You constantly have to screen out people who want to cozy up to you, so they can get something from the celebrity you're related to. Has he talked to you about his family? Or has he been circumspect about it?"

That was Dad, in his loving but lawyer mode. "He started talking to me about them a few weeks ago," I said thoughtfully. "We want to take it slow and get to know each other. You know, I can only imagine how hard it was for him growing up, when his dad was active in the NFL. Mr. Ross had to be away for training camp and the away games during football season. He did ask me what it was like to have judges in the family."

"Oh, he did, eh?" Dad said with a little chuckle. "Did you tell him that we keep you 'on lockdown'?"

"Prentice." Mom laughed as she chided him. "We don't want to scare the young man off."

"Besides," my sister threw in, "he's not the only one who gets in the spotlight. Remember what happened last year, when Dad was the presiding judge in that big RICO case?"

"Oh yeah, that," I sighed. "There was that reporter who saw me and thought he could get a story out of me about Dad. He actually thought you discussed every detail of the case over dinner. I didn't think he'd ever leave me alone."

On the weekend before Thanksgiving Trevell invited me to meet his parents. Mr. and Mrs. Ross seemed larger than life during the time Mr. Ross was active in professional football, if the interviews and commercial endorsements were any indication. However, that evening they were simply parents who were interested in the person their only son was involved with. They were really interested after he introduced me with, "This is my boyfriend, Prentice Delaney." I'd been around just long enough to know when a man gives you a title, he's serious about you regardless of your gender. He has bigger plans for you. I should know—I'd already begun referring to Trevell the same way around my family. Finally meeting his family and the other people he cared about only set more bricks in the foundation of our relationship.

"Trevell told us your father is a judge," Mr. Ross stated as we ate dinner.

"Yes, Mr. Ross. He's a federal judge in Milwaukee."

"He must have presided over some high-profile cases. I read about the RICO case last year."

"That's the thing about those cases," I said, inwardly pleased that Mr. Ross had taken an interest. "Dad can't talk about them while they're going on, not even to us. We only know what's televised or published until it's over."

"And your mother? I've seen her picture from time to time in the news," Mrs. Ross observed.

"Mom is very involved in civic and community affairs. For her, the quality of education for minority students is a major cause. I guess it's because her grandparents were teachers, so anything involving the Board of Education is going to get her attention, including lobbying at the State Capitol. Plus, my sister is a teacher."

During the course of the evening, it was inevitable that the conversation would soon turn to sports. Mr. Ross was pleased to hear that Dad was a dyed-in-the-wool Packers fan and that some of it rubbed off on me. I could picture him and Dad having many in-depth discussions about the team. Mrs. Ross was happy to see I not only had "good home training," but I had goals of my own, which included becoming an investment counselor. They could also see, before the evening was over, how much I cared about Trevell.

On Thanksgiving weekend, the family went to Minneapolis, and Trevell came with us to meet the extended Berry family. Normally we'd drive, but this time we flew up there because Dad tired more easily. He and Mom had already welcomed Trevell with open arms, and Sierra and Rashid teased him good-naturedly. When we arrived at Grandma and Grandpa's mansion, the holiday festivities were in full swing. Trevell got so many hugs from my aunties and cousins, while my uncles brought him into the fold as though he already belonged there. And of course, the women in my family, including Mrs. Bynum, made sure he was well fed.

"You know, Junior, this is what it was like when your dad first came up here to meet the family," Grandpa told me when we had a moment to ourselves.

"I don't think Trevell's ever been around such a big family, but he's really enjoying himself," I beamed. "And the verdict is?"

Grandpa stroked his chin in a mock serious way before he cracked a smile. "I'd say your young man fits into this family quite well, especially since your grandma is making sure he gets a box of her famous cookies to take home with him."

Even as Trevell and I grew closer—which was wonderful—it was hard for us to witness Dad's health gradually but steadily go downhill as fall turned to winter. According to his doctor, Dad had been suffering from TIAs, also known as mini-strokes. He was only 68, but he had taken on fewer and fewer cases, until he was forced to retire in early December.

Whenever we went to the mansion, Trevell never failed to find something he could do to help and support Dad, or to help Mom support Dad. We couldn't go up to Minneapolis for Christmas, so we invited the Rosses to come down from Green Bay and spend it with our family. We could see Dad was getting weaker and he couldn't get around the way he used to. That concerned us, but we were grateful to have him there for another Christmas. Having his family around meant so much to him.

At the end of January 2006, Dad had to be rushed to the hospital. He'd suffered a major stroke, and we were all there, keeping a vigil over him. Over the next few days, his condition continued to decline, and the doctor didn't hold out any hope of recovery. On February 4, Trevell came down for the weekend as we sat with Dad at the hospital. Sierra had taken Mom out for a break—she barely left his side, since she was committed to be there until the end.

Dad was lucid at different times, although we had to listen carefully to understand what he said. He experienced one of those times while Trevell and I sat with him that day. One of the last things he said before we left was, "Take good care of my son, Trevell."

"Yes, sir. I will, sir," Trevell vowed, doing his best to blink back the tears.

"Son, you've got yourself a keeper," Dad managed to get out. He looked at us, his hands holding ours, and I felt overwhelmed, knowing in my heart that Dad only had a matter of days, maybe hours, and he knew it.

On the morning of February 6, all of us were gathered around Dad when he passed away. Trevell never left my side, and his support as well as that of his parents was a great source of strength and comfort to me. It didn't seem real that Dad had died; we all thought he would have more time with us.

Dad's funeral, in addition to all the Berry family present, resembled a Who's Who of Milwaukee, and as such was considered newsworthy. Mr. Christopher, Grandpa Edwards, and Grandpa Berry made brief statements to the media about Dad. They were more eloquent about him at the funeral, and we protected Mom who mourned Dad with grace and dignity.

We wanted to be left in peace in the weeks and months afterward while we sorted things out in the grieving process. Grandpa and Auntie Elaine drew on their experiences from Uncle Eldon's death to help us, as did our pastor. Shayla, Trevell, and Sierra and Rashid's friends were also strong sources of support. Mom's position as a wealthy widow of a prominent public figure, however, made her the target of men who viewed her as a meal ticket. This was only aggravated by the fact that Mom inherited the looks and the charm of a Berry, her effect upon men still mesmerizing. In response, she spent those initial days and weeks after Dad's death in seclusion, only receiving family and close friends.

My graduation from Marquette three months later was bittersweet, largely because of Dad's absence. He was supportive of me even when I didn't choose to go for a law degree, encouraging me to do my best in the world of finance. On the other hand, because of Dad's legacy in the city and her influence with the Wisconsin Department of Education, Mom was asked to be the keynote speaker at the commencement exercises, and she did it with that strength and class she possessed. Man, I was so proud of her.

As for my personal life, I can only be grateful to Trevell for being so patient with me. That in itself was another reason I loved him, and we didn't hesitate to tell each other those three magic words. Dudes only looking for sex would have left long ago, but not Trevell. The fact he didn't mind waiting was merely confirmation of Dad's last words to us, not to mention Grandpa Berry's "verdict." It only made me love him that much more. When Trevell's spring break rolled around in 2007, I was given permission from Grandpa Edwards to use one of the cabins for the week. I was ready to take our relationship to the next level.

Fishing season hadn't begun yet, but that didn't dampen the anticipation of a week alone up in northern Minnesota. We took the scenic route by way of Duluth, stocking up on groceries and supplies when we reached Bemidji. "You know I'll be looking forward to one of your famous desserts tonight," Trevell said while we loaded up my Saturn Vue SUV. "What's on the menu?"

I gave him a look that screamed *desire* from every pore of my body. "You," I purred, drinking in the naughty smile that spread across his face.

Once we reached the cabin on Gull Lake and settled in, our clothes came off faster than you could say, "Turn off the lights." That old Teddy Pendergrass song had me going all right. After 18 months of waiting, I finally drank in Trevell's unclothed, fully aroused body. It was so hot I could feel the heat before I even touched him. I had the opportunity to check out his fine—and I mean *phyne*—physique when we went to the beach the previous summer, and it was Mr. Universe quality in a natural way.

Added to the mix this time was his erect manhood—something that was probably outlawed in several states. I felt myself rising to the occasion and my heart rate increased. "Man," I said quietly, staring at him for indeterminate moments before I realized Trevell couldn't seem to take his eyes off my crotch. I'm a couple of inches shorter than Trevell in that department, but I'm thick, and he licked his lips, slowly going down on his knees and taking me in his mouth.

He did things with his mouth and his throat that had me on the verge of exploding, and then he pulled me back from the brink, kissed me deeply and starting over again. The thing is, there is only so much a man can take. I begged, "I want you, babe, and I want to be inside you—now." Taking his mouth off my throbbing penis, he gazed up at me with misty eyes of deep desire and a smile that promised the best was yet to come.

He stood up, backing into me and letting out a lusty moan as I squeezed his muscular melons and fingered the buried treasure between them. I reached around and fondled his tool, a tool that only got harder with my touch. Gently pushing him down on the bed, I grabbed what I needed in preparation as he lay back and spread his cheeks. My eyes burned with passion at the sight of his love tunnel, which was winking with the need for me to take him without further delay.

Being inside Trevell was sheer ecstasy, but what took it to a higher level was how much he loved it. The way he moaned when I hit certain spots only encouraged me to prolong the pleasure as long as possible, knowing that I was the one causing those responses. Was the wait worth it? Yes, yes, and yes! A big, strong, powerful man who reveled in being taken has always been a turn-on for me. One who felt good about himself as Trevell did and was not ashamed of it made it even better. Our dates gave us time to really know each other, so not only was I making love to his body but his mind as well. He begged me not to stop, a request that was easy to grant because this was lovemaking with a capital L. His star-glazed eyes were so romantic, and it made me want him even more.

"Uh. Uh, yeah. Uh, yeah. More," he called out as I pumped deeper inside him, further aroused by the throbbing of his massive shaft and the erotic squeeze his inner walls gave me. As I grabbed his luscious, well-rounded backside and bent down to give him a buried-treasure kiss, I had reached the end of my endurance. Our screams were muffled by our kiss, and I felt jets and jets of seed shooting between us, which set off my own powerful release.

We made love two more times that night, waking up late Saturday morning in a tangle of arms and legs. I felt his aroused state against me, and I turned to behold his well-loved face, seeing a gleam in his eye I simply could not refuse if my wet, throbbing love tunnel was any indication. I applied the lube and straddled him, slowly lowering myself onto his hot, hard, and ready tool of immense delight. It was a morning to remember.

I had only been taken once before. It was okay, but nothing to write home about, so I chalked it up to my being a top and turned other dudes down who wanted some of my b-box. Trevell changed all that in one fell swoop. This man knew exactly what to do and how to do it to me, and I turned into passion unleashed once he hit that P-spot inside me. I was hard as a rock, and I did *not* want him to stop. This was the man I loved, and he was letting me know it in the most intimate way. Only with him had I ever been this responsive. I definitely worked my honey walls to satisfy him and me to the utmost. When I went over the cliff, shouting in extreme pleasure, I vowed that he would spend as much time inside me as I did in him—and he did.

Yes, my love life had gone through the roof, and Sierra was happily married to Rashid, who was certainly keeping her happy. However, the suitor situation was problematic for Mom. There was one dude in particular pursuing her, Glendon Price, whom I didn't like at all. His attentions were both unwanted and relentless. Sure, he was presentable, but I always came away from him wanting to take a bath or a shower. Mom's eyes told me that she wanted nothing more than to be rid of him. Glendon had a way of turning up wherever she went. It got to the point where she hired private security as protection. Sierra and I threw manners to the wind and told him point blank where he could go, but he remained oblivious to facts. Or he was just plain obstinate.

I confided in Shayla about the situation, to which she advised me, "Prentice, that man is trouble, and he will remain trouble until your family can find a way to put him on lockdown."

"Shayla, I'd like nothing more than to break every bone in his body. Don't forget, I've had Ninja training."

"That's fine for momentary satisfaction," she said in a serious tone, "but that's all it would be. Besides, that could come back on you. No, you need something more permanent than that."

I had to concede to Shayla's reasoning. But what could we do to get rid of him, not to mention the other men that circled Mom like vultures? This was the concern I shared with Sierra a week later while we had lunch at the Hilton Milwaukee City Center, just before the beginning of the new school year.

"You know, Junior," she said, "maybe we're going about this all wrong."

"What do you mean?"

"Well, Mom is still a gorgeous woman, and we can't stop men from flocking around her. But we can try a different approach."

"Like what?"

"Like find someone who truly has her best interests at heart."

I regarded my sister thoughtfully and conceded to her reasoning. "Well, you have a point there, but…wait a minute. You already have someone in mind, don't you?"

The smirk on her face told me she'd been busted. "Yeah. It may be a long shot, but I don't think so."

"All right, Sierra, you've got me. Who do you want to fix her up with?"

She paused to give me a meaningful look. "Mr. Edwards."

"Now you're confusing me. Which Mr. Edwards are you talking about?"

"Uncle Julian's brother, Mel."

Uncle Mel, the man who'd sworn off marriage? I was skeptical. "Yeah, right. And how do you know he's the one?"

"Jerome told me. He overheard Grandpa Edwards and Uncle Mel talking one day. He carried a major torch for Mom back in high school. He never got over her, even when he married Jerome's mother and later divorced her. That's why he never remarried. Mom was the one that got away."

I was intrigued. "Oh, really?"

"Really. Furthermore, I heard Mom talking to Auntie Deshawna on the phone the other day. They were reminiscing, and she mentioned how much she liked Uncle Mel back in high school. Of course, that was long before Dad stepped in and swept her off her feet."

"I have to give you high marks for eavesdropping. Why didn't Uncle Mel do anything about it back then?"

Sierra rolled her eyes. "I hate to say this about him, but some men just don't get it, especially when they have the chance."

"Of course, if he had at the time, Mom wouldn't have married Dad, and we wouldn't be here."

"True. But now Dad's gone. I'm married, and someday you'll marry Trevell, but Mom deserves to be happy, too. And I think Uncle Mel could be the one to do it."

We exchanged a conspiratorial smile as the server brought us dessert. "You think Jerome will help us?"

"All we have to do is say the word, and he's in."

"But we have to make Uncle Mel think it's his idea. If he even suspects we're playing matchmaker, he'll buck like a Denver Bronco."

"Got that right."

The more I thought about it, the more I liked the idea of Uncle Mel and Mom together. One thought, however, reminded me of my main concern. "What about Mr. Price?"

"Hmmm." Sierra frowned at the mention of that creep's name. "That means we'll have to work fast. I don't trust that man farther than I can throw City Hall. There has to be a way to keep him occupied and out of the picture."

We sat in silence for a couple of minutes while our table was cleared and the server brought us our desserts. At that moment a revelation came to me. "You know, there is someone who could help us with this problem."

Sierra caught the gleam in my eye, and I saw the lights go on in hers. "Of course. Madear! Mom told me how she and Grandma Berry were over the moon when Uncle Julian proposed to Uncle Carter. Just the thought of another Berry-Edwards connection...trust and believe, she'll pounce on this!"

As soon as we finished eating and tipped the server, Sierra and I hurried out to her car. She speed-dialed Madear's number and put us on speaker when she answered, filling her in on our dilemma with Mr. Price and our idea to get Mom and Uncle Mel together. We were delighted to hear the glee in her voice as she vowed, "Don't worry about Mr. Price. Your grandfather and I are taking care of that. In the meantime, children, we have plans to make. Now, let's bring Jerome in on conference call." By the time the four of us were done with the call, a plan had taken shape.

There was no way on earth that Uncle Mel couldn't have known about Dad's passing, but I was sure that the details and happenings since then largely remained a mystery to him. With that in mind, Sierra's family took a trip to Minneapolis, while Trevell and I came up with a plan to keep Mom busy until my sister completed her mission. I have to hand it to her; according to Madear, Sierra talked about Mom's status in such an indirect way that Uncle Mel perked up with interest. The real icing on the cake was her expression of concern for Mom's predicament with that slimeball Mr. Price. "He was still indecisive, until she told him that," Madear said during our conference call with Jerome. "After that, you could see the steam coming out of his ears. How is your mother doing, Prentice?"

"So far, so good. She's coming home from Hilton Head with Grandma Berry today," I beamed, pleased with Grandma Berry's idea to help us along with our efforts.

"Great. Now, we must continue to act as though nothing's going on. Let Melvin stew for a bit. It won't be long before he takes action." Madear paused and let out a somber sigh. "With everything that's happened as a result of the bridge collapse, he has to be seriously thinking about this. All we have to do is sit tight."

"Yeah," Jerome agreed. "Dad's been different since then. That was a wake-up call for a lot of people. He's not about to let history repeat itself."

Seeing Uncle Mel at the house with Mom was our first sign of success. Sierra and I treated him the usual way, so as not to make him suspicious. Learning that he spent quite a bit of time with her during his visit to Milwaukee was even more encouraging. Sometimes we'd catch Mom on the phone with Uncle Mel when they were apart. She insisted they were just friends and in-laws, but as time went on, it was obvious to us that something else was going on, something beyond friendship. He was courting her! Of course, Jerome, Sierra and I reported everything to Madear and Grandma Berry. We felt like secret agents on a mission, but oh, what a mission it was.

When Mom and Uncle Mel gathered Jerome, Sierra and I together to announce their engagement in the fall of 2008, we did our best not to look smug while smiling and congratulating them. Alone, however, we shouted with the thrill of victory. We remembered how Uncle Mel's feet hadn't touched the ground, and Mom had a familiar smile on her face when she looked at him. At their wedding reception the following May, we toasted our success with Grandma Berry and Madear. Even Grandpa Berry got in on the celebration, jokingly saying, "I hereby sentence the defendants, Melvin Edwards II and Linda Berry Delaney Edwards, to a lifetime of happiness."

Milwaukee had been our home for all of Sierra's and my lives, not to mention Dad. We knew Mom would never forget Dad, but at the same time we respected the fact that she wanted a new start with Uncle Mel, which included moving to Minneapolis. When Mom moved into the new home on Dean Parkway that he'd bought for them during their engagement, we followed suit. Moving during the winter had certain advantages because houses were slower to sell. Sierra and Rashid took advantage of that fact to get a good deal on a house, with the help of Auntie Deshawna. Trevell and I held out until we found an older home that suited us and the kids we wanted to have, and again Auntie Deshawna's expertise allowed us to close on it at the end of winter. And, of course, Grandpa and Grandma Berry were extremely happy now that, at last, the whole family was living in the Twin Cities metro area.

A week after Uncle Mel and Mom went off on their honeymoon in Aruba, Trevell and I took a stroll over to Martin Luther King Park after a satisfying meal at Curran's Restaurant. We were still getting settled in our new home off West 44th Street and Wentworth Avenue in the Kingfield neighborhood. Already we'd established the place as one of our favorite neighborhood dining spots. Unknown to us, Grandpa Berry would often take the family over there, back in the days when it was a drive-in restaurant as a treat. Having the park right across the street made it ideal as a place to walk off our meal. With May well under way, the park was greening up, the sun was bright, and temperatures were comfortable, and at some point we found a bench to sit on.

"You know, my family spent a lot of time at this park, even though they moved near Phelps Park later on," I told Trevell.

"I can see why," Trevell stretched out his legs. "There are a lot more trees over here, plus the tennis courts and all that stuff."

"A lot of this was renovated when they renamed it King Park back in the late '60s, from what Mom and my aunties tell me. But their history with this place goes further back."

"Like how?"

"It goes back to my grandparents."

"From the smile on your face, it must have been something pleasant." Trevell turned toward me with a curious look. "Well, are you going to tell me, or do I have to guess?"

I couldn't help but smile at the man who had shared my life for the past three years. He actually looked better now than he did when we met. Or was it, perhaps, the intimate knowledge we shared that enhanced his appeal? "Well, this is where my grandpa proposed to my grandma." I eased down to the ground on one knee as Trevell drew in a sharp breath. "I love you so much, and this is where I want to ask you a very important question."

Trevell's hand flew to his mouth, clearly overwhelmed. "Oh, man..."

"Will you marry me, Trevell? Will you spend the rest of your life with me? Love each other, raise kids together, be my husband?"

Trevell's eyes shifted from mine to the engagement ring I had pulled from the pocket of my sweatpants, which was now sparkling in the late afternoon sunlight. "I love you, too, baby. And yes, I will, to all of the above."

There were very few people around at that hour, but it didn't matter to me as I put the ring on his finger, and we sealed it with an embrace and a deep but tender kiss. We knew in our hearts that we were meant to be together—forever. And as we sat there in the park, basking in love and a new commitment, I felt that Dad was somewhere smiling down at us.

I knew my sister would never let me hear the end of it if she wasn't among the first to know, so shortly after the dinner hour we climbed into Trevell's Mustang and made the 20-minute drive north to Sierra and Rashid's house. It's located in one of the newer subdivisions of Brooklyn Park, where Sierra teaches in the Osseo school district. It was apparent that dinnertime was over, with Rashid supervising the kids while Sierra finished putting the dishes in the dishwasher.

"So, how's the house shaping up?" she asked us.

"Well, it's coming along. We're still working on ideas for some of the rooms," Trevell answered as we accepted glasses of lemonade. "But something else happened today, as a matter of fact."

"Really?" Sierra beamed the way women do when she saw the engagement ring on Trevell's finger, coupled by the grins we could no longer hide. "Let me guess. You liked it, so you went and put a ring on it, right?"

"Exactly. Rashid's not the only one who can do that," was my reply as they came and hugged us, followed by Little Earl and Destiny.

"Where are you going to tie the knot?" Rashid asked.

"We were going to go somewhere in New England. But now that Iowa's on board, Davenport looks good."

"Well, I know Mom and Uncle Mel will love to hear this news when they get back." Sierra went to the cupboard, grabbing four goblets while Rashid opened the fridge and pulled out a bottle of sparkling grape juice. "Have you told your parents, Trevell?"

"They're next on the list, and then your grandparents. We already booked the flight, so my folks are in for a big surprise."

After Rashid poured the grape juice, Sierra handed us our goblets in anticipation of a toast. "I was hoping you'd say that. This is definitely the kind of news that needs to be shared in person."

And so, the Berrys, the Edwardses, the Rosses and assorted Christophers flew to Davenport, Iowa on October 21, 2009 to witness our nuptials, with my best friend Shayla and my stepbrother Jerome serving as our best people. It was exciting having the family gathered around us as we stormed the Scott County Administration Building to get our marriage license; some of the employees recognized Mr. Ross and asked him for his autograph.

The rehearsal and the rehearsal dinner went by like a blur, but our wedding day—October 24—was something we'll always remember. The local MCC church was thrilled to perform the ceremony, all of which was recorded on video. We were both crying tears of love as we said our vows and exchanged rings. When the pastor pronounced us married and said, "You may kiss your husband," we heard the cheers in the sanctuary as we tenderly kissed.

We finally turned to face our guests and family, seeing all the smiles and teary eyes. I happened to lock eyes with Grandpa and Grandma Berry, and the abundance of warmth and love on their faces nearly had me ready to start the waterworks again. When we heard the words, "I now present to you Prentice and Trevell Delaney-Ross," Trevell and I exchanged a huge grin as we started the recessional, ready for a fantastic reception at the hotel. But not before we paid homage to our ancestors and jumped the broom.

During the reception all the guests around our age were out on the dance floor to the tune of Beyonce's "Single Ladies." Yes, every married and engaged couple—especially us—flashed our rings in the fun of the moment. Afterwards, on our way back to our table, we were met by our parents.

"Now you know your dads aren't getting any younger," Mama Ross teased, "so when can we expect some grandchildren from you two?"

Even though she already had two grandchildren, Mom gave us the same anticipatory smile. "Darcelle is absolutely right. When?"

Trevell and I exchanged a look, knowing there was no way out of this one, especially since my new husband was an only child. "Well, we want to have least two."

Mom's smile grew bigger. "And?"

"And we're not waiting that long," I said to Mama Ross' enthusiastic grin. "We've already started the process. We hope to become parents by this time next year."

Uncle Mel and Daddy Ross nodded in agreement. "We're glad you said that. As it happens, we have just the persons that can help your process along." Uncle Mel looked over at one of the tables where

Auntie Sandra and Madear were seated. "All you have to do is ask them."

Trevell and I quickly learned never to underestimate the power of women who want grandchildren from all their kids. Mom and Mama Ross whisked us over to the women in question with Grandma Berry hot on our heels, nudging us to speak up. When we shared our plans and desires, Madear looked around at the women surrounding us with eager grins. With a conspiratorial smile, she said, "Ladies, we have plans to make." When Grandpa Berry got wind of it, his response was, "I hope it's a boy." By January we had a surrogate secured, and on October 25, 2010, we became the proud parents of Barack Joseph Berry Delaney-Ross...

Prentice ran to the front door of the mansion while Trevell remained with the limo and spoke to the 911 operator. He pounded on it with the adrenaline rush that accompanied the fear that struck him upon seeing the still body of his grandfather. After repeated pounding, the door opened, and Mrs. Bynum regarded him with concern and bewilderment. "Prentice, what is it? What's the matter with you?"

"Grandma. Where's Grandma?" he said frantically.

"She's upstairs. But what..."

He brushed past her and bounded up the stairs with a worried Mrs. Bynum close behind him. How could this happen? His heart was pounding when he stood in the doorway, seeing the look on his grandmother's face as she sat there on the bed, dreading what he had to tell her...

By a Thread

The Kenwood neighborhood had never experienced anything like this, not in its recent history. By some miracle, Earl was still alive, but barely. As an EMT vehicle rushed him to Hennepin County Medical Center, a swarm of police cars surrounded the Berry estate. Officers cordoned off the crime scene and kept bystanders at a distance. Juanita was sitting on her bed in her nightclothes while Prentice held her, in a state of shock. It was only a matter of time before the news stations would get wind of the story and air it for their morning news, so the police knew they had to be as thorough as possible while things were fresh.

Prentice did his best to comfort his grandmother with the help of Mrs. Bynum, while Trevell called Berry family members to get them to the house and the hospital. Having completed those calls, he knew there was one other person who needed to be notified to set things in motion. As he called Douglass Welch-Edwards, the CEO of Edwards Enterprises, there was no doubt in his mind that shooting a prominent, influential, and highly respected judge, even though he was retired, was up there with the ranks of that breed of criminals known as "cop killers."

"Trevell, whatever you need us to do, just ask. We've got your back," Douglass affirmed. "How's Prentice?"

"I don't know how he's doing it, but he's trying to support Grandma Berry until some more family gets here and some of us can go to the hospital."

"Who can make medical decisions about Judge Berry if she's not there?"

200

"Auntie Sylvia. I already called her and she's on her way to the hospital. But we need you and we need Auntie Sandra on this, to help make sure the monster who shot him is caught and brought to justice. She's the new queen, and things happen when she's involved. Same goes with you."

"Done."

"Can you reach Mr. Christopher?"

"Sure."

"I know it's late, but I'm sure he and Uncle Eli will want to know."

"Done. Preston's calling Pastor Wylie, and I'll call Pastor Andrews, too. We're sending up prayers for Judge Berry right now."

A few well-placed phone calls from Sandra Harrison Edwards and Douglass were enough to mobilize the police chief into classifying Earl's shooting as a high-priority case. Having been a judge herself, that was all the motivation Sandra needed when her cousin called. Police detail was placed at the hospital as the medical team worked tirelessly in the operating room to save his life. An all-points bulletin was put out for the chauffeur, whose whereabouts were currently unknown. Meanwhile, family members arrived at the hospital emergency room to hold vigil over their patriarch.

"Has there been any news?" LaVera asked as she entered the waiting area and embraced Sylvia and Clint.

"Nothing yet. He's in the operating room," Sylvia answered.

"Where's Mama?"

"She's still at home. Chauntice and Jarvis just got there. Deshawna's on her way. Prentice and Trevell have been there since it happened and they're answering questions for the police."

"Oh, Mama," LaVera said to herself, hoping that the cruel, heartless animal who shot her father would be captured and rot in solitary confinement for the rest of his life. With no possibility of parole. "Do you think she'll be in any shape to come here?"

"We don't know," Clint said, "but don't underestimate her. That woman is rooted and grounded. Sooner or later, she'll be here. She might have a little setback, but nothing on earth will stop her from being at his side. Do you remember what it was like when the bridge collapsed, and Mr. Edwards was on it?"

"I remember," Sylvia said thoughtfully. "Madear did not miss a beat. She stayed here until Uncle Eli regained consciousness. Mama's no different."

At that moment, Derrick, Julian and Carter, and their daughters joined the family in the waiting room, sharing their concerns and what news they had. "I'll handle the media," Julian addressed the group. "Being a county commissioner does account for something. If I have to, I'll call in some favors."

"Thank you, Julian," Sylvia said gratefully after she hugged him.

Julian turned to face the concerned men gathered around him. "Derrick, Carter, Clint, let's decide what to tell the reporters so Sylvia and LaVera can focus on Daddy Berry. LaVera, has anyone heard from Linda and Mel?"

"Not that I know of, but let's not leave it to chance. I'll call them."

"And I'll see if I can find out anything more about Daddy," Sylvia added, heading to the nurse's station.

At the mansion, while Chauntice and Deshawna tended to their mother, Prentice and Trevell shared the events leading up to the shooting, answering the police detectives to the best of their knowledge. "Mr. Delaney-Ross, do you know of anyone who would want to kill your grandfather?" Detective Rita Daniels asked Prentice.

Prentice drew a deep breath to calm himself and wiped away a stray tear. "Grandpa was a judge in criminal court here in this county. Before that he was a prosecutor. I can't think of anyone in his personal life that would do it, but it wouldn't surprise me at all if someone he put away tried to."

"Perhaps someone who was released from prison might have done this," Trevell added, "or got someone else to do it."

"What about his chauffeur? You said that when you found him, he was alone in the limo," Daniels said as she jotted down notes.

Prentice looked at her in disbelief. "Mr. Boone? He loves my grandparents. He's been with them for years. I can't even imagine him doing something so horrible. Nobody could. Maybe he's hurt or something. It doesn't make sense for him to be missing like this."

The detectives continued with the usual questions in an investigation. While they questioned Chauntice and Deshawna, Trevell asked Prentice, "Why are they asking your aunties questions? They weren't even here when it happened."

"It's nothing personal, babe. It's a police matter. They have to ask them."

"Well, I hope they throw the key away on whoever did this," Trevell said emphatically as Prentice leaned on his shoulder for support.

The detectives wrapped up their preliminary questions and left their business cards with Chauntice. After they left to track down possible leads, Juanita came downstairs with Deshawna, fully dressed and with purpose in her eyes. The initial shock of Earl's shooting had worn off, and she had been the wife of a judge too long not to know the risks that came with the territory, especially in these days and times. "What hospital is Earl at?" she asked.

Prentice heard the quiet command in her voice and saw the steely determination in her face, knowing she would not be dissuaded from being at his grandfather's side. He understood; if Trevell had been the victim, the answer was a no-brainer. "They took him to Hennepin County Medical Center."

"Then if you'll get my coat, we can go."

The silence of the drive to the hospital stood out in stark contrast to the normal conversation-filled family drives as Jarvis navigated the streets in his GMC Denali SUV. Flashbacks from the evening of Eldon's murder and the subsequent trial took their place in Juanita's mind. Eldon hadn't stood a chance on that night so long ago. The fact that Earl was still alive was the hope she clung to, a life preserver in a lake of a senseless crime. She couldn't even process the question of who did it and why, with the possibilities almost as vast as online websites on any given subject. All she could think about, all any of them could think about, was getting there and being there for her husband. He would need all their strength to pull through something like this.

They wasted no time in getting to the emergency room and meeting up with the other family members. As they shared what information they had, Juanita was strangely quiet, accepting their support but with a mind somewhere off in an unseen operating room.

"What have we got so far?" Lieutenant Eddie Burrell asked, facing the two detectives in his office.

Patrick Alexopoulos Blaisdell, a veteran detective, glanced at his notepad. He had been ready to call it a night when the call came in, and his tall, olive-complexioned, athletic body gave him a silent protest. His collar-length, jet black hair that complimented his Mediterranean good looks could have used a trim, but the case load hadn't let up much lately. "Well, everyone we've interviewed thinks Judge Berry walks on water. With a record like his, he probably does. On the other hand, he's put a lot of criminals away, as a district attorney and as a judge. They want nothing more than to keep him on their hit list until he's dead."

Burrell ran a hand through his graying hair before he leaned forward at his desk. A solidly built man in his early 50s, he had the looks of Levi Stubbs of the Four Tops coupled with the authority that came with his rank and 20-plus years of police work. "No mistresses, no graft, no corruption, no scams?" he asked with his distinctive Atlanta accent.

"Nothing. What you see is what you get. He's a stand-up guy who cannot be bought. In fact, he was a prosecution witness in the Maddox case back in 2001," Detective Daniels stated.

Burrell regarded Daniels' remark. If there was one thing she was, it was thorough. Had there been anything shady in Judge Berry's background, she would have found it. She was in her early 30s now, sporting a short, dark brown, natural hair style and professionally dressed for her work, but she could make a striking presence at a police ball. In 15 years, he could see her as another Anita Van Buren from *Law and Order*—only she would probably make it to chief

204

of police. As partners, Daniels and Blaisdell had one of the highest closure rates on the force. "I remember that case. It got a lot of ink. Remind me…what happened to Maddox?"

"He was found guilty on 10 counts of larceny. He's serving 15 years for each count—consecutively."

"Check to see where he is now. Meanwhile, let's recheck the crime scene and talk to other relatives. Keep canvassing the neighborhood, too. You know the drill."

Sometime after three a.m. on November 7, a middle-aged white man in hospital scrubs entered the emergency waiting room and approached the anxious group. "Mrs. Berry?"

All eyes turned in Juanita's direction. She looked up from her seat in anticipation. "I'm Mrs. Berry."

"I'm Dr. Wallace. I'm part of the medical team that performed surgery on your husband. I only wish we could have met under different circumstances."

"I know. How is he?"

"He came through the surgery. We removed two bullets; they're being taken straight to the ballistics lab. However, he lost a lot of blood, and he's in a coma," Dr. Wallace said. "I assure you, Mrs. Berry, we're doing everything we can for your husband. All we can do now is wait."

Juanita grew still as the gravity of the situation weighed upon her. A couple of tears rolled down her cheeks, which she wiped away with an embroidered handkerchief. Her spine stiffened as she asked, "When can I see my husband?"

"As soon as he's transferred to intensive care and a police officer is stationed outside his room." The doctor paused for a moment before he spoke. "You may not know this, Mrs. Berry, but when Judge Berry was a district attorney, he prosecuted a rape case and won it. I was 13, and the victim was my sister." He took Juanita's hand and looked into her eyes. "My family has never forgotten what your husband did for us. No one is going to rest until the person who did this is brought to justice."

"Thank you, Dr. Wallace." After acknowledging the other relatives in the room, the doctor returned to the emergency area. Juanita quietly took her seat, while her family mulled over this example of the impact Earl had on so many lives during his career. However long it took, they would be there.

By morning news of the shooting had hit all the local television stations, the *Minneapolis Star-Tribune*, and the *St. Paul Pioneer Press*, second only to the coverage of President Obama's re-election. Reporters had camped out at the hospital, the Berry estate, and the police department, all eager for any new development in the crime. At the hospital, Juanita's children ran interference for her, with Carter and Julian giving statements and fielding questions from the media so that Juanita could have privacy with her husband.

Member by member, the police detectives questioned the Berry family regarding their whereabouts and possible suspects, including the whereabouts of Marvin Boone, the missing chauffeur. Deshawna was puzzled. Mr. Boone's disappearance didn't make sense, given his deep devotion and loyalty to her parents. In her mind, the only thing that could account for his absence was either fear or his death. The longer he was missing merely strengthened her suspicions.

"Mama, I know the police didn't question you last night about Daddy because you were really out of it at the time," she said quietly, "but I know it would help if you could tell them something, anything you remember. That could give them a lead to help them find the person who did this to Daddy. It could also help them locate Mr. Boone. He's missing."

Juanita paused, taking her eyes from Earl, her ears immersed with the sound of machines giving him life support, before she faced her daughter.

"Mama, if you don't want to talk to them, just tell me and I'll tell them."

Juanita's voice was subdued when the words finally came out. "Deshawna, you know how your daddy is about his Starbucks."

"Yes, I know."

"Last night wasn't just Election Night. We were at the Edwardses for their anniversary party."

"Oh, that's right. 63 years, isn't it?"

Juanita nodded. "Well, after we came home, your daddy wanted Mr. Boone to drive him to the nearest Starbucks for coffee and a cinnamon roll. He gave me a kiss—just like he always does—and he said they'd be back in a bit. Then I went inside and got ready for bed." She took a handkerchief to dab at a couple of tears. "That was the last time I saw him before it happened."

Deshawna held her mother's hands, wishing she could take the pain away even as her own heart was heavy. "Mama...do you know which Starbucks he would have gone to?"

Juanita forced herself to concentrate. "It...no, it couldn't have been the one downtown. That one closes early. It would have to be the one on Hennepin Avenue, going toward Uptown. Where is... Detective Daniels?"

"She's in the waiting room, questioning everyone who wasn't at the house."

"Tell her I'll speak to her in a few minutes. The police are going to need all the information they can get in the next 39 hours."

Juanita's statement was enough to send Daniels and Blaisdell to the Starbucks coffee shop in the Lowry Hill neighborhood, where they found an unconscious Mr. Boone in the back behind a dumpster. According to the ER staff after he was admitted, he had been pistol-whipped and left for dead, with brain trauma that left him in no condition to answer any questions. Faced with the possibility that the chauffeur was a witness who could identify the perp--should he regain consciousness--protective measures were implemented.

Jarvis, upon hearing the news of Mr. Boone's attack, was concerned. "Who can we contact about Mr. Boone?" he asked the group.

"His niece Sherilyn lives in town," Carter said. "I'll call her and let her know about this, if she hasn't already heard about it on the news."

"I don't think this was a random occurrence," Jarvis concluded. "It may be conjecture, but the perp must have known about Daddy Berry's Starbucks run."

"Everyone in the family knows that," LaVera threw in, "but I think I know what you're getting at."

"Exactly. He must have been studying Daddy Berry's routine for some time."

"How can you be so sure the perp is a man?" Chauntice countered. "Unless…wait a minute. Daddy was shot in front of the house. That means the perp could have taken Mr. Boone's place at Starbucks."

"I would say the perp followed them there and attacked Mr. Boone. From there he must have held Daddy Berry hostage on the drive back."

"And no one would have heard any shots if the gun had a silencer on it," Carter added. "Well, that tells us the how, but it still doesn't tell us the why or the who."

Jarvis stroked his chin, his eyes serious with conviction. "Right now, this could be either a flat-out murder attempt, or a murder-for-hire. Either way, it was premeditated. Let's hope he left fingerprints, any kind of evidence that could connect him to the crime."

"Or the person who hired him, if that's the case," Sylvia said grimly. "I was thinking about something else last night when we got the news."

"What is it?"

She was quiet for a moment. "Well…what happened to Daddy sounds like a murder plot in one of my novels."

Everyone perked up their ears at the revelation. "Can you remember which one?" Deshawna asked quickly.

"Not at the moment, but I'll check it out as soon as I can." Sylvia grabbed a note pad from her purse and made the notation. "I really have to wonder, with the way this happened, just how much research this guy has been doing on our family."

Chauntice looked around the group, each person processing the facts and clues they had gathered. "When Daddy became a judge, that made him a public figure. With the Internet, our perp could have done quite a bit of background work before he struck. I think it would be a good idea to keep this between us for now. Mama doesn't need any more on her plate at the moment, so unless she asks, mum's the word. Just make sure we keep Linda and Mel in the loop."

The group nodded in agreement. "We do, however, have to help the police any way we can," Julian reminded them. "This is now an ongoing investigation, and they're going to be all over it. Anything we come up with could be a lead."

"Speaking of motive," Jarvis broke in, "what about the standard motives for murder? Love, money, revenge?"

"Well, we can rule out love," LaVera said emphatically. "This certainly wasn't a crime of passion. So that leaves money and revenge."

"In other words, we've got our work cut out for us," Jarvis concluded.

"Maybe so, but while we're searching for answers, let's remember one thing Daddy always says," Deshawna said.

"What's that?"

With determination in her voice, Deshawna replied, "Never give up."

With the intended murder victim and another possible witness unable to testify, no other witnesses available or forthcoming and pressure from above to solve the case, Burrell, Daniels, and Blaisdell felt the frustration. Burrell fielded numerous calls from his superiors while his detectives started preparing the initial paperwork. Forensic evidence had yet to turn up any clues. The bullets removed from Earl's body were identified by ballistics as those used for a .9 mm. Fingerprints on the limousine were checked, but all had been identified and ruled out. The crime scene was still being examined for evidence, possibly the gun. And yet there was nothing.

Jarvis and Chauntice had gone to the police station to see them with the information they had come up with, and the detectives promised to check it out. With their window of opportunity down to 30 hours, the effects of fatigue set in as they filled out the seemingly endless forms. It was a tedious job, but they knew cases had been won

209

and lost because of the handling of those very forms, accompanied by the chain of evidence.

"I almost forgot how many guns fit the description," Blaisdell said after getting off another phone call.

"Tell me about it," Daniels agreed. She stretched in her chair for a few seconds before she grabbed her mug of black coffee, putting just enough Coffee-Mate in it to match her yellowish-brown complexion. "What do you think of the Varnells' theories?"

"More than plausible." Blaisdell tapped his pencil. "You know, what happened to the chauffeur could mean something else."

Daniels took a sip of her coffee and added a packet of Sweet 'n Low to it. "Like what?"

"That there were two people involved in this shooting."

"Sure. They could have followed Judge Berry to Starbucks, stayed out of sight, and coldcocked Boone. Then one of them commandeered the limo with the judge inside, while the other perp followed them back to the estate. His grandson said they saw a car leaving there at high speed just before they arrived. That was how they made their getaway."

"Hmmm. The shooter wouldn't have wanted to arouse Judge Berry's suspicions, so he—or his accomplice—would have had to take Mr. Boone's place."

"Which means that he would have needed a chauffeur's uniform to match Boone's."

"Let's start checking the uniform supply stores in the area."

Carter and Julian entered their home, falling into easy chairs in the family room while they waited for Lilly to come home from school. Their respective staff members at Ujima and Hennepin County had vowed their support in keeping things going and fielding telephone calls, leaving them free to deal with the crisis before them.

"Do you want it on?" Julian said, holding the remote in his hand.

Carter shook his head. "All I want now is to rest and regroup before the girls get here."

"Donna Jo's coming over?"

"Yeah, she called and said she'd be by. She couldn't focus on her studies very well. Besides, they'll want to know what's going on."

The couple lapsed into the netherworld between sleeping and waking, each having an ear alert for the sound of a telephone or the door. Half an hour later, Carter heard the back door open and close, rousing himself as Lilly entered the family room, followed by Donna Jo. Through the luck of the genes, 14-year-old Lilly was the spitting image of her grandmother Juanita, as 20-year-old Donna Jo was a feminine version of Julian. At the moment, their beauty was clouded with the distress on their faces.

"Dad," Lilly said after Carter and Julian hugged them, "how's Grandpa Berry?"

"He's out of surgery, but he hasn't regained consciousness. We just have to wait and pray he pulls through," was Carter's response.

"What about the police? Have they found out who did this to him?"

Not knowing the why or who in this case tore him up inside, but Julian knew he had to be strong for his daughters. "They're doing everything they can, Lilly. Your Uncle Jarvis has his operatives on the case, too, not to mention all the news coverage it's getting."

"I couldn't concentrate on my classes," Donna Jo said somberly, her 5'10" body slumping onto a sofa. "Students on campus I don't even know kept asking me questions, and all I could think about was Grandpa Berry. He has to make it. He just has to…"

"Donna Jo? What is it?"

"He's not going to stop," Donna Jo said in a tone unmistakable to Julian and Carter. "Not until he finishes the job."

"What do you mean?" Carter asked his daughter.

"Grandpa's not safe. He's going to try again if we don't stop him."

Julian was filled with the dread of Donna Jo's vision. "We'd better call the police. I don't care what they'll say about it, this perp must be captured before he strikes again. You're absolutely certain our perp is a man?"

"Yes, Papa."

"Well, you know what your grandpa says." Carter grabbed the car keys from the coffee table. "We can't just call them; we need to go down there now. The first 48 hours are crucial in any crime investigation. And time is running out."

The Ticking Clock

"I would appreciate it if you stopped looking at me like I was a nut job," Julian said in a stern voice during their meeting with Lieutenant Burrell and Detectives Daniels and Blaisdell. "Granted, you've probably gotten your share of them since this case broke, but our daughter is *not* one of them. She has this gift. My father has it, and my great-grandfather had it. If she says this man is going to strike again, you can take that to the bank."

"Unless you want us to take this up with Chief Matheson, I would suggest you listen to what she has to say," Carter added. The lieutenant suppressed a flinch at the mention of the police chief and nodded while Carter looked at his daughter, whose worried expression carried a sense of urgency. "Go ahead, Donna Jo."

After Donna Jo shared her vision, the police regarded her with unreadable expressions. Finally, Burrell asked her, "Can you describe what the perp looks like?"

"White, maybe 35, 5'11". Average build, short nothing-brown hair."

"What about distinguishing features? Marks or scars?"

Donna Jo wracked her brain for any visual image in frustration. "He has a...dead look in his eyes. Other than that, he's not a person that people would take notice of." At that moment the familiar look came across her face, and Julian motioned for the officers to be silent. "Cheetos. He threw an empty bag of Cheetos away. Starbucks... under the dumpster...straw...fingerprints."

Daniels and Blaisdell exchanged a look. Though they were skeptical of psychic phenomena, the young woman's vision could be one of the few solid leads they had. "We'll get on it," Blaisdell said as Donna Jo came back to herself.

"Please protect Grandpa," she pleaded in earnest.

"We'll do our very best, Ms. Berry-Edwards, Commissioner," Burrell said as the family got up to leave.

"Before you go…" Carter broke in.

"Yes, Mr. Berry-Edwards?"

"There's someone else you might want to check out."

"Who's that?"

"A guy named Jackson Trent. He was the last person my father sentenced before he retired. He got 25 years for murder-two."

"And?"

"Check out the case. He was released on parole two months ago," Carter stated as the police officers exchanged looks again. "He doesn't fit the description our daughter gave you, but I'm sure he's mixed up in this somehow."

After the family left, Burrell faced his lead detectives. "Whether they pan out or not, it's better to run down these leads. Go over to Starbucks first. And Daniels, get everything you can on Jackson Trent."

"Got it," she said as they rose to leave his office.

"So, we have a perp and his accomplice. From the way Ms. Berry-Edwards described him, the perp looks pretty ordinary, but the accomplice would have to look something like the chauffeur to pull it off. In short, we have a salt-and-pepper team," Daniels noted. "What do we have in our records?"

Blaisdell studied the photo of Marvin Boone on the white board and the notes on his description. He made entries into his laptop computer, his expression thoughtful as the search results were displayed. "We have three possibles. One did time for armed robbery, one for manslaughter, and the third for assault and battery. They all have a general resemblance to Mr. Boone. Any one of them could have made the switch at Starbucks."

"Speaking of which, let's go check out the girl's...whatever you want to call it. We don't need the chief and the commissioner breathing down our necks. Let's just hope it gives us evidence."

If the detectives were astonished at their discovery of the empty Cheetos bag, they didn't say so, not even when they found a straw inside the bag. While Daniels bagged the evidence and took it to the crime lab, Blaisdell questioned the Starbucks employees again about the Berry chauffeur and the events of November 6.

When Blaisdell returned to the station, he found Daniels studying the chart on the white board, which now included photos of Jackson Trent and Benjamin Maddox among the list of suspects, plus a new photo. "Who's that?" he asked her.

"His name is Glendon Price," was her reply. "Judge Berry's daughter, Linda Delaney Edwards, had trouble with this guy – enough to have a harassment restraining order placed on him in Milwaukee. She called me while you were out. From what I learned, he blamed her father for interfering with his so-called relationship with her. The relationship, of course, was all in his mind. He was facing charges and served some jail time in Wisconsin, but he violated his parole and followed her here last year. He was captured and taken back there."

"What do you hear from the prison?"

"As of today, Price is in the wind. He escaped from prison. There's an APB out on him."

Blaisdell's concern showed up in a frown. "The dude does have motive. If he's here and he did this, that gave him opportunity. This Price character may not stop with Judge Berry. He could go after his daughter."

"I've already brought Burrell up to speed on that," Daniels said. "As of now, we're working with Wisconsin to apprehend Price."

"Got it. So, what's the deal on Trent?" he asked her.

"He hated Judge Berry. He's a real piece of work. He didn't believe he deserved prison time for murdering his boyfriend, much less 25 years. His wife divorced him after the trial, too, so all that gives him motive. Trent is a blame-it-on-the-world type. And being out on parole, he'd have the opportunity to do it."

215

"That would make him a suspect, but it's still circumstantial. There's the question of the gun, too. Anything on that new evidence?"

"The DNA on the straw is contaminated, but we've got prints from the Cheetos bag. On points, they're similar to one of our suspects."

"Which one?"

"Benjamin Maddox, the con man Judge Berry helped convict in 2001. But I don't see how it's possible."

"What do you mean?"

Daniels looked at the mug shot in question and frowned. "As of today, he's still in prison."

"In other words, we can rule him out. He couldn't be in the slammer and shoot Judge Berry at the same time."

"No, but there's still something about that fingerprint that points to him. And that straw...." Her eyes lit up in a moment of intuition. "Hold on. What about children?"

"You might have something there." Blaisdell furiously went back through his notes until he found a page. "Here it is. Maddox has two sons, Grady and Theodore. But get this. Theodore—or Ted—did time in Stillwater for man-one."

"Hmmm. Pull up his mug shot."

Daniels raised her eyebrows at the image on the laptop. "Yep. It's just like the young woman said. He is so bland you wouldn't give him a second look...hold on a minute." Daniels picked up the ringing phone and listened intently. "Detective Daniels...Mmmhmmm... that's the one...thanks. I owe you one." She disconnected the call and turned to Blaisdell. "It just gets better."

"Oh? How is that?"

"Ted Maddox and Jackson Trent were cellmates at one point. Do you think they were comparing notes while they possibly were knocking boots?" Daniels speculated as she made the notations on the white board.

"It wouldn't surprise me one bit. I guess what young Mr. Maddox lacked in looks he made up for in other areas, especially where someone like Trent is concerned."

"Speaking of which, I say it's time we brought Mr. Trent in for questioning. And let's run those prints and see if we get a hit on Ted Maddox."

Jackson Trent was most uncooperative when initially questioned about Maddox, looking like an Abercrombie and Fitch model with high mileage and a healthy dose of petulance. Unable to account for his own whereabouts at the time of the murder attempt, only when faced with an accessory charge against him and a parole violation as instructed by ADA Johnetta Scott did Trent finally confess his involvement with the perp.

"Now, you promised me a deal," Trent said as they sat in an interview room at the Fifth Precinct police station in south Minneapolis. The precinct handled crimes committed in the near west and southwest portions of the city, which included the "chain of lakes"—Cedar Lake, Lake of the Isles, Lake Calhoun, and Lake Harriet.

ADA Scott, a biracial, middle-aged woman with a zero tolerance level for foolishness, held the deadpan, all-business expression of Sergeant Joe Friday from *Dragnet*. "That depends on what you tell us."

"Well, you already know Ted and I were cellmates for a while. I was his prison b...well, you know what I'm talking about."

"Go on."

"Anyway, I got a visitor who wanted to know if I could recommend someone who could do some handyman work for him. I knew what he meant—he wanted someone knocked off. Ted was getting out soon, and so I told my visitor about him."

"How long ago was this?"

"Oh, around six months ago."

"And who was your visitor, Mr. Trent?"

Trent stonewalled ADA Scott with silence. She merely stared him down and said, "Ted Maddox isn't the only one who wanted to kill Judge Berry. You had every reason to want him dead. He may not have outed you, but he sent you up for 25 years. You could have just as easily hired Maddox to do it, which leaves you wide open for

217

a charge of murder-one if Judge Berry dies. Now either you tell us who visited you or the deal's off the table."

"All right, already," Trent said hastily. "It was this guy I'd never seen before. He called himself Sean Jamison. Looked like a mouthpiece at first, but not when you talked to him. While he was talking, I kept getting the impression that...that..."

"What?"

"Well, that he was a front man for somebody else. I didn't really think about it long, because he offered me $5000. Said it would be waiting for me when I got out."

"And was it?"

"Yeah."

"Have you been in contact with Ted Maddox since you were released?"

"No. I haven't heard a thing from him. Honest."

"Describe this Sean Jamison."

After Trent gave her the description and was returned to his holding cell, ADA Scott contacted Daniels and Blaisdell. They wasted no time in checking the visitor roster at Stillwater State Prison for the months of May, June, and July, finding an entry for June 2.

"Thank you," Daniels told the corrections officer on staff as she and Blaisdell left the prison. "That takes care of how Maddox found out about it. Let's see...Jamison visited Trent on June 2. Maddox was released on July 2, and Trent was released September 7. If Trent's telling the truth, Maddox must have contacted Jamison shortly after he got out."

"And from the way the murder attempt went down, this was something that involved planning," Blaisdell concurred. "They had to have been studying Judge Berry, his habits, his routines..."

"Exactly. Let's check and see if Sean Jamison is in the system when we get back."

They got into their unmarked car and headed west on Highway 36 when a cell phone rang. "It's mine," Blaisdell said. "Detective Blaisdell... When?... We'll be right there."

"What is it?" Daniels asked after Blaisdell ended the call.

"Officer Fitzpatrick over at Hennepin County Medical. We've got our perp."

Donna Jo was still shaking with relief as Ted Maddox was hauled away in handcuffs. "It's all right, Donna Jo. It's all right," Juanita said reassuringly, holding her granddaughter while Carter and Julian spoke with the police detectives. The last thing they'd expected was to see the man in question walking down a corridor not 20 feet away from Earl's hospital room, dressed in an orderly's scrubs. He'd blended in so well, seemingly going about hospital business and unnoticed by the busy staff members. Only because of a chance glimpse at him earlier, when she left the cafeteria, did Donna Jo recognize him in her psyche. She quietly warned the police officer stationed outside her grandfather's room, which gave the police enough time to set a trap. Caught in the act, Maddox was quickly captured and subdued, and the syringe Fitzpatrick confiscated was found to be filled with deadly poison.

"What's the latest on our prisoner?" Burrell asked his detectives when they returned to the station.

"He lawyered up, of course," was Blaisdell's dry response.

"We have enough evidence to convict him for this attempt on Judge Berry. Now we have to find the gun for the previous attempt and get the person who hired him."

"The prints from the Cheetos bag are a match for Maddox, so that places him at Starbuck's. That should get us a warrant to search his place. Let's hope it turns up more evidence."

"All right. Daniels, what do you have on this Sean Jamison?"

"He's not in the system—no juvenile record, nothing," Daniels said. "Lives in Woodbury, has an ex-wife, Nevaeh, and a son, Neville."

"Anything else?"

Daniels thought for a moment. "There is one thing. He's heavily in debt. He's facing foreclosure, car is leased, behind in alimony and child support, etc., etc. There's no way he could have paid Trent out of his own pocket. He has to be the go-between for someone else."

"All right. Daniels, you follow up on Jamison. Check if there were any large deposits to his accounts in the past six months. Blaisdell, go back to the hospital and see if Judge Berry has regained consciousness and is able to make an ID on our perp."

When Blaisdell returned to the hospital, it almost seemed like a typical day there—if one didn't count the uniformed officer fiercely standing guard outside Judge Berry's hospital room. After showing his badge, he entered the room, where the judge laid in his bed with his wife by his side. He was grateful that Judge Berry had finally regained consciousness. He was also sure the family had even more reason to be thankful, although there would be a long recovery process.

"Judge Berry, I know you've gone through an ordeal, but it's important we have evidence that links our suspect to the first attempt on your life." Blaisdell pulled out an array of photographs, laying them out on the tray while Earl put on his glasses. "Now, look at them carefully and see if you recognize anyone."

Earl slowly scanned the photographs, looking them up and down. As his eyes fell upon one of them, his mind went back to that night. Even though it had been late, the streetlamp was on where the limo was parked. The eyes...the eyes...everything else about him was forgettable, but those eyes. They were on a younger man, but the eyes were the same. That cold, dead look he'd seen before, 11 years ago...

"That's him."

"You're positive?"

"There's no question in my mind. That's the man who shot me. In fact, he reminds me of someone I testified against some years ago."

Blaisdell picked up the photo of Ted Maddox and inwardly exhaled with relief. "Will you be willing to testify to that when this case comes to trial?"

"You just tell me when."

"Out of curiosity," Blaisdell said, pulling out another photo, "do you recognize this man?"

Earl's eyebrow arched. "Benjamin Maddox. It all figures. Father and son. Where's the father?"

"Still in prison."

"Do you think he did this on his father's orders?"

"We're checking out all the possibilities."

"Where is he now?" Juanita asked.

"He's in a holding cell, waiting for arraignment."

"I know you'll do your best to see justice served, Detective." Earl gently squeezed Juanita's hand.

"Yes, Judge. You have the whole force behind you on this." Blaisdell paused before he spoke. "There is something else that came up you need to know about."

"What is that?"

"Do you know a man named Glendon Price?"

Despite his weakened condition, Earl's spine stiffened. "That man was obsessed with my daughter Linda, to the point where she had to take out a harassment restraining order on him. She had no interest in him, but he didn't take no for an answer and stalked her. He was all wrong for her as it was, with everything we discovered about him. Why?"

"He escaped from prison in Wisconsin, and presently his whereabouts are unknown."

Earl and Juanita exchanged a worried look. "Then he could come after me and Linda. You will see to it my daughter and her family are protected until he's captured?"

"We'll do everything we can, Judge."

After Blaisdell left, Earl and Juanita looked at each other for timeless moments, silently professing their abiding love, that comfortable silence of couples who have been together for many years. As Earl squeezed his wife's hand again, he became aware they were no longer alone.

"Eli, Donna," he said in gratitude as their best friends approached them. "It's so good to see you."

"We wouldn't be anywhere else," Donna said warmly.

"Douglass told us about you the morning after you were shot." Eli regarded his friend with the care of concern. "We knew your kids

221

would be here at the hospital, and they've kept in touch with us about your condition. You've been in our prayers."

"And you know that if you need anything, you only have to ask," Donna added as she squeezed Juanita's hand in support.

"Thank you, thank you," Earl beamed weakly. "I'm sure you want to know what's been happening with the case, so have a seat."

"We don't want to tire you out," Donna cautioned as she sat down.

"You won't. In fact, I really need to talk about this, and you know us better than anyone. First, the good news. The man who shot me is now in police custody…"

Back at the station a few hours later, Blaisdell and Daniels were busy with the added paperwork on the case when Burrell called them into his office.

"Judge Berry made a positive ID?"

"Yeah, I have his statement," Blaisdell replied. "And that eliminates Price as a suspect in the first murder attempt."

"What about the search of Maddox's place?"

"We found a digital camera and photographs of Judge Berry and Mr. Boone. The photographs were taken in different locations around town. It fits the profile that they were following him, learning his routine. I just wish we had found the gun."

"I know. Daniels, anything more on Jamison's finances?"

"Nothing we don't already know. He may be a front man, but he's not benefitting from this. I would say our mastermind has something on him to keep him in line."

"Dig deeper on that guy," Burrell advised her, leaning slightly forward in his seat, "and then we bring him in for questioning. What about Maddox's accomplice?"

"Of our three possibles, Joe McIntyre is dead, Elmore Chase has been in St. Cloud Pen for the past year, and Thomas Ward is out on the streets."

"Put out an APB on Ward. Let's hope we get to him before Maddox."

Late in the afternoon of the following day, the family came to see Earl, encouraged by the capture of Ted Maddox and concerned for their patriarch's welfare. They had no wish to tire him, but Earl insisted on knowing what progress was made on the case, now that it had passed the 48-hour mark. The police made good on their word regarding Linda, as did Mel, who was adamant that she not go anywhere alone. She wasn't thrilled about it, but under the circumstances, she accepted the protection. While the family shared what they knew, she went through the mail she'd brought from the mansion for her parents.

"Mama, there's a letter here for Daddy," Linda said, stopping at the pale blue envelope that stood out in contrast to the white ones in her hand.

Juanita looked up from her husband's side. "Who's it from?"

Linda studied the neat but fragile handwriting. "The only thing on the return address is a last name...Madsen."

Earl's gaze shifted, as if searching for some faraway memory even as his body struggled with the pain of his recent trauma. "Madsen... Madsen...where have I heard that? Would you read it for me, Linda?"

The family grew quiet as Linda opened the envelope and started to read. "November 7, 2012...this was just written a couple of days ago." As Linda continued reading the contents, Earl's face registered shock, then sadness.

"Oh, no. How could we have missed this?" Chauntice said in astonishment.

"It never occurred to anyone that Sheree Madsen had committed perjury," Deshawna concluded. "She must have been very convincing on the witness stand."

Earl nodded slowly. "She was. Her testimony was a crucial part of getting the conviction on Malcolm Wesley."

"What else does the letter say?" Jarvis asked.

"She names the real molester, who was her next-door neighbor. Her mother forced her to lie about it. The guy's been dead for 20 years, so we can't even go after him." Linda finished reading and met the eyes of her family. "Sheree must have been carrying this inside her for over 40 years. I guess she couldn't take it anymore."

"Makes you wish we could have done DNA back then. What about the mother? Where is she?" asked Deshawna.

"The letter says she's in a state institution. Her mind's gone. What kind of a mother does that?"

"Put up by the mother to get even with the mother's boyfriend, who apparently was cheating on his wife. An innocent man went to jail and died there because two women lied," LaVera spat.

Carter nodded in agreement. "Unfortunately, that was a case Daddy prosecuted. That's the case that made his career."

"So that would make this a confession." Mama grew quiet for a moment. "We may have been looking in the wrong direction."

"Of course. Ted Maddox had a strong motive for wanting to kill Daddy because of his father, but this letter gives someone else an equally strong motive," Sylvia stated.

"We know Maddox was hired by someone," Chauntice added. "If this is true, that person had to know facts about that trial. How long ago was it?"

Sylvia thought for a second. "1965. I remember it because I'm the same age as Sheree."

"Well, I'd say the common thread here is revenge." Linda handed the letter to Jarvis and sighed. "Where do we start looking for suspects?"

"Start with the most direct route. Follow the money. I'm sure the police are thinking that now," Earl said quietly. "In light of this letter, our mastermind is most likely someone very old, or a descendant of Malcolm Wesley."

"In the meantime, this is evidence that could give us a strong lead, but it has to go to the police—now." Jarvis scanned the room as heads nodded in agreement. "Let's hope they can find her before she…"

"It may be too late," Chauntice said with dread in her voice.

Sheree Madsen's lifeless body was found in a rooming house on the edge of downtown St. Paul, with empty bottles of alcohol and barbituates on the kitchen table. Handwriting experts confirmed that the letter was indeed written by her, and with the lethal combination of drugs and alcohol in her system her death was ruled a suicide.

Heaviness and guilt set upon Earl's heart when he received the news, wondering if she even had any family left to mourn her passing. *I should have pressed harder. I was so quick to believe them. Why didn't I see? Was I so zealous to convict Malcolm Wesley that I overlooked the possibility he was innocent?*

That night, Sylvia sat at her laptop in the den, unable to sleep as the facts and clues gnawed at her. Clint finally went to bed out of sheer exhaustion but sleep simply eluded her. She grabbed her notepad and glanced at it, seeing the notation, "Which novel is murder attempt patterned after?" She went to the bookshelves where each copy of her novels was neatly shelved in order of publication. She grabbed the mysteries and took a seat in her favorite chair, one by one reading the synopses for a clue.

She was three-quarters of the way through the twenty mysteries when she paused and reread the synopsis of one. *This one...this one could be it, but I'd better be sure. The Case of the Judicious Justice.*

"Oh, no," she breathed, shivering by the time she finished speedreading her way through the novel. "Oh, no..."

Never Give Up

With Ted Maddox behind bars, awaiting trial for the attempted murder of Judge Berry, Daniels and Blaisdell felt some of the pressure ease, but they weren't out of the woods yet. It was progress to have him dead to rights on one count; it would be even better to have him on two. Judge Berry's testimony, they knew, would solidify their case, as well as the supporting evidence from Jackson Trent. Still, having the murder weapon would make the case against Maddox a slam-dunk, not to mention collaring the brains behind it all.

Burrell, however, wanted more. With everything he learned about Judge Berry and his family in the past 72 hours, he wanted a solid case against every member of what had turned into a conspiracy to end the man's life, and eliminate the threat of Glendon Price.

"Anything more on the gun?" Burrell asked them.

"Nothing. We've searched the crime scene, we've searched inside and outside Maddox's apartment, but nothing yet. And there's nothing linking Maddox to his father for this crime," Daniels vented in frustration. Although she had only been in her teens when Judge Berry retired from the bench, her research on him in this case had filled her with a hearty respect for him and what he stood for in this state.

"What about his accomplice?"

"The owner of the shop was out of town before. When we went back and talked to him, he recognized Thomas Ward as the man who bought the chauffeur's uniform."

Burrell rubbed the back of his neck, feeling the tense muscles there. "You know ADA Scott. She wants an airtight case against this scumbag."

"We all do," Blaisdell said, reflecting on the days when his father and grandfather were on the police force and Judge Berry was a prosecutor. There was no shortage of officers who had offered their assistance and support to this case, eager for everyone involved in this crime to be convicted.

With continued police protection, Earl laid in his hospital bed quietly, mulling over the events of the past two days. Though Ted Maddox had been captured, Burrell left nothing to chance with Earl's safety. Earl insisted Juanita go home and get some rest. She was reluctant at first, but between Dr. Wallace and their children, she finally left.

Given the medication in his system and the slow recovery process from his surgery, it was difficult at times for him to focus. Two facts, though, were crystal clear and inescapable: he had gotten an innocent man convicted, and someone other than Ted Maddox was out there with a powerful motive for murder. It grieved him to think about it. It went against everything he stood for. It was too late to tell Malcolm Wesley, but Sheree Madsen's suicide letter would at least provide some closure for his family and clear his name—provided they could put the final pieces of the puzzle in place.

His thoughts swirled as sleep began to overtake him. *I hope you can find something, Jarvis. As the youth say, it's crunch time...*

Armed with the knowledge of her novel's contents, Sylvia went to Jarvis' offices in the IDS Tower, Minneapolis' tallest skyscraper, where he and Chauntice were conferring about the latest developments.

"It's all here," she declared, handing the book to Jarvis. "A murder-for-hire plot to get rid of a judge, and an innocent man convicted for the crime. Only in my novel, Sherry Payson uncovers the killer and the wrongly convicted man is released."

"It sounds like our murderer is an avid reader of your mysteries." Jarvis accepted the book while finishing some notations. "It could be part of the overall research this perp has done on the family."

"Do the police have Sheree's letter?"

"I gave it to Detective Daniels," Chauntice said.

Sylvia sat down, frowning slightly. "I know we don't want to interfere with an ongoing investigation, but we need to do something. I mean, that evidence gives them a whole new avenue to check out."

"Maybe there is." Jarvis got up from his desk and paced. "Chauntice?"

"Before I left the station, I happened to overhear Detective Daniels and Detective Blaisdell mentioning someone by the name of Sean Jamison. They sounded very interested in getting more info on him."

Sylvia was pleased that the eavesdropping trait among Berry women had once again born fruit. "Well...Jarvis could set up surveillance on him."

"I have Rashid getting everything we can on him online." Jarvis continued to pace as he mentally organized himself. "I sent one of my operatives to watch him, too. I'll be taking his place in a few hours."

Stakeouts are considered part of a private investigator's job description. The personal aspect of this case lent it a sense of urgency, but Jarvis knew only patience would pay off. All his senses were on alert when his cell phone vibrated.

"What's going on?" Chauntice asked over the phone.

"He just went inside," Jarvis replied, watching discreetly from his parked SUV as Sean Jamison entered the ultramodern Loon Lake Casino in northern Pine County. "The bug's got him."

"What did the staff say?"

"Oh, they know him, all right. No sooner does he pay off one debt than he's back again. Lately, each time he comes, he's losing more money than the last time."

"That could be the hold our perp has on him—his gambling addiction."

"Could be. If he taps out, he could get just desperate enough to lead us to our murderer. How's the book?"

"There's no question about it, our perp used it as a blueprint. The main difference is that in the book, the perp was someone who worked for the judge at one point. My intuition says it's someone outside the judicial system connected to that Madsen case. Just be careful, honey."

"You know I will. I'll call you as soon as I can." He ended the call, watching the area and wondering why the casino was given that name when the actual lake was two counties away. *Oh, well. To somebody it must have seemed like a good idea at the time.*

Donna Jo found herself feeling restless during her economics class the next morning. She took notes, but her level of participation in class was lower than normal. She chalked it up to her concern about Grandpa Berry, since he was still in the hospital, and yet... images began to flash in her mind. She wished they would stop.

Not here. Not in class. Someone taking something in his hand. Walking. No, not walking—hiking. Where is this place? The building he's hiking away from. It seems so out of place. A glint of metal, just before it was covered over with dirt and leaves. But it's more than just metal. What is it about those strange bird calls? And the...

"Ms. Berry-Edwards? Are you all right?" the instructor said, regarding Donna Jo's blank stare and slightly parted lips with concern. Getting no response, she shook her gently, which seemed to snap her out of it.

"What? What?" Donna Jo asked, aware of the entire class staring at her while her instructor stood over her.

"I said, all you all right?"

There was no way she was going to tell them what had just happened to her, so she fell back upon the most readily available answer. "I'm sorry, Ms. Evans. It's just been hard....my grandfather. I can't seem to concentrate."

"We understand. Do you want to talk about it later?"

"Yes. I'll try to do what I can. Sorry to interrupt the class."

When class ended, some of her friends and classmates asked about her grandfather's condition. It was unavoidable, given the media's attention to the case. If it was hard for her as a college student, what was it like for Lilly, who was a freshman in high school? She gave short but polite answers, soon claiming an imminent visit to the hospital with her family. With haste, she made her way to one of the student parking lots, promptly getting into her Toyota Prius and pulling out her cell phone.

By mid-afternoon police were combing the woods behind the Loon Lake Casino. It took them just over an hour to find the tree Donna Jo had described—and the .9 mm pistol buried there. Blaisdell could only shake his head. He had always been a skeptic when it came to psychic phenomena, but something about this young woman was causing him to rethink his viewpoint. So many so-called psychics wanted—craved—their 15 minutes of fame. Donna Jo, however, had no desire to call attention to her "gift," as she called it. Her fathers had even insisted it not be leaked to the media during that first meeting with Burrell, himself, and Daniels, and the detectives had kept their word. Who would have even suspected the gun would turn up a hundred miles away from the crime scene?

"The ballistics match. It's the gun," Daniels stated as Blaisdell was completing more of the endless paperwork at his desk.

"Good," Blaisdell said with satisfaction, hoping when all this was over, Donna Jo Berry-Edwards would let him take her out to dinner. Meanwhile, first things first. "What about prints?"

"Wiped clean—except for a partial thumbprint. Whoever disposed of the gun got careless."

"Or nervous."

"Whose print is it?"

"Maddox's accomplice—Thomas Ward. And forensics found traces of blood on the gun handle. It was a match for Marvin Boone."

A knowing smile crossed Daniels' face. "Let's hope that carelessness is one of Ward's character traits. Who knows what else is waiting to be found at his place?"

230

"I'll have Scott get a warrant. You know, that woman is amazing," Blaisdell said with appreciation in his voice.

"Tell me about it. Now let's hope forensics can find something else that links Maddox to Judge Berry's shooting."

The search of Ward's apartment on the near North Side seemed fruitless at first. The detectives ran his financials and found a substantial deposit to his checking account the day after the murder attempt; when combined with the forensic evidence and the ID from the supply store, it was enough to secure the warrant. Bags and packed moving boxes were scattered about, along with dirty dishes from what looked like last night's dinner. Daniels, however, refused to rest until every square inch was covered, including the trash outside.

Yes, Ward, carelessness is one of your character flaws. She noted the rumpled, wrinkled, balled-up chauffeur's uniform stuffed behind the refrigerator. "Bag this," she told one of the uniformed officers. Spotting a matching pair of gloves underneath, she added, "And these." Satisfied with the search results, Daniels stepped out of the apartment and headed for the building entrance—in time to see Ward fleeing up Glenwood Avenue with officers in hot pursuit.

Faced with charges of aggravated assault on Marvin Boone and accessory to the attempted murder of Judge Berry, Ward sweated it out in an interview room before he and his attorney asked for a deal. ADA Scott, mistress of the poker face, calmly told him, "That depends on what you tell us."

Ward took a deep breath, knowing in his heart he was toast if he took his chances in a trial. "I didn't know he was planning to whack a judge."

"Who?"

"Maddox. All I knew was that he needed me to pass as a chauffeur, and I looked something like the real one. We followed the limo to Starbuck's, I knocked the guy out with the gun and took his place."

Scott, having seen the results of Ward's handiwork on Mr. Boone, resisted the urge to purse her lips and narrow her eyes as Ward continued. "I kept my face out of sight while I gave the old man his coffee. Maddox followed us back to his house. That's when he got out, walked up to the limo, and shot him. Then we took off."

"We checked your bank records. Who paid you the $5000?"

"Maddox said some dude named Jamison was putting up the money for the hit. Said he was getting $20,000 from Jamison to be the trigger man."

"Whose idea was it to get rid of the gun behind the casino?"

"Maddox thought it up," Ward said in disgust. "He figured no one would ever think to look up there."

Burrell, Daniels, and Blaisdell were grateful for the roundup of perps associated with the crime, even as they were hoping for that final break in the case, while the media fed on it with the relish of *Jaws.* Having Sean Jamison implicated was one thing, what with the evidence Ward and Trent had provided. Could they get him to roll on the person who hired him? If so, how?

While they were pondering this, their attention was grabbed by the appearance of a tall, elegantly dressed, white-haired man in his 80s, whose steps were supported by an understated but expensive walking stick. He possessed a quiet aura about him that made people stand up and take notice, a man who commanded great respect without even uttering a word. "Excuse me. I'd like to speak to Lieutenant Burrell, please."

"I'm Lieutenant Burrell," he said, his curiosity piqued by this man. "Would you like a seat?"

"Yes, thank you," the man replied as he accepted the chair Blaisdell offered him. "I'm here because Judge Berry is still in danger."

"Go on."

"A man is coming here for him. He is on I-94 between Menomonie and Hudson right now. He is driving a blue 1998 Camry with Wisconsin license number 559 XCV. One taillight is burnt out, but he doesn't know it. He is armed with a .380 that someone gave him when he escaped from prison." The officers' ears perked up with the eerie feeling of *déjà vu* and the tone in the man's voice as he continued his story. "He is planning to kill Judge Berry and Melvin Edwards. He

232

is after Judge Berry's daughter, Linda, and he will stop at nothing to get her. You must stop him."

Burrell squirmed with the unsettling news, but he asked with his most professional voice, "How do you know all this?"

The man sighed. "You probably wouldn't believe me if I told you. But this will happen if you don't take action."

"We'll check it out. And your name is?"

"My name is Elijah Edwards. Judge Berry is my best friend, and Melvin Edwards is my son."

In the meantime, Jarvis continued his surveillance of Sean Jamison. He had discreetly stayed out of sight when the police combed the wooded area behind the casino earlier, resuming his post after their departure. He wished he was home with his wife, but he had been in the business long enough to stick it out. Besides, he knew Chauntice would be there for him when it was all over, when he would waste no time taking her in his arms.

He sipped some black coffee, alternately watching Jamison's late-model Acura TSX and the casino entrance, trusting his instincts.

An hour later, Jamison exited the casino. Jarvis checked out the nervous tension in the walk as his quarry, a watered-down version of actor Michael Beach, headed to his car and grabbed a cell phone from his pocket. From what he could see of the body language, the conversation wasn't that of a person who had struck it rich at the tables. Jarvis could almost smell the desperation as Jamison ended the call, started his car, and left the parking lot. Putting his phone in hands-free mode after entering a phone number, he continued in pursuit, maintaining a safe following distance as the cars headed south on I-35.

"Detective Daniels? Jarvis Varnell here. I don't know how soon you can check LUDs, but something strange happened up here at the Loon Lake Casino with a guy named Jamison. I'm following him back to the Cities."

Daniels wasted no time contacting the precinct's IT department. Previous LUDs on Jamison's phones were obtained, and every number was verified. In the early evening hours, one of the techs called Daniels. "We've got a hit on his phone records."

Sean Jamison sat in a police interview room, somewhat disheveled after a night in the city jail following his arraignment. Devoid of funds, he glanced over at his court-appointed attorney. ADA Scott took note of his eyes, eyes that spoke awareness of his impending doom even as his lips denied it. "I don't have anything to say to you. I don't understand why I'm even here," he said.

ADA Scott stared Jamison down. "We have enough evidence on you to charge you as an accessory—more than enough, in fact. You're in it up to your eyeballs. Now, unless the prospect of 40 years in prison for attempted murder is highly appealing to you, it's in your best interests to start talking. Your accomplices have already given their statements, and it doesn't look good for you."

15 seconds of silence ensued, after which Jamison whispered something to his attorney. The attorney then said, "May I confer with my client?"

Scott left the interview room before Jamison and his attorney engaged in a heated discussion. When she returned, Jamison's shoulders were slumped in resignation as he glared at Scott. "What are you offering?" his attorney asked.

It had seemed like a long road, but in retrospect only 96 hours had passed from the time Judge Berry was shot. As Daniels and Blaisdell walked down the 33rd floor hallway in Capella Tower to their destination, Blaisdell knew it would be a bittersweet moment for Judge Berry. Still, he knew the case, like others before it, had to be seen through to whatever the outcome would be.

The receptionist was slightly unnerved when they walked into the office and flashed their badges, walking past her and into the conference room without a word. *This one's for your grandpa, Donna Jo,* Blaisdell thought as they faced the cold, poised, confident Barbara Stanwyck lookalike seated at the head of the table conducting the meeting.

"Noxzema Jordan, you're under arrest for the attempted murder of Earl James Berry," Daniels stated with grim satisfaction as Blaisdell pulled the woman out of her seat and handcuffed her. "You have the right to remain silent…"

EPILOGUE—MAY 14, 2013

Although it was an unseasonably hot 98 degrees, nothing could keep the Berrys and the Edwardses away from the crowds gathered outside the State Capitol in St. Paul to witness history in the making. Gov. Dayton was signing marriage equality into law, the culmination of the largest grassroots movement in Minnesota's history. Several family members, like Jason and Deshawna Randolph, were recording the event with cell phones and camcorders. James and Jonathan Varnell-Bradshaw took turns with their five-month-old son Jonah, Jonathan holding him while James held an umbrella to shield them from the afternoon sun. Even Kira Varnell Hendricks, now an attorney in her mother's law firm and due to deliver her first child in a little more than two weeks, was on hand for the ceremony with her attentive husband Keith beside her.

Earl and Juanita sat comfortably in lawn chairs near the front of the festive crowd, joined by Eli and Donna Edwards. As they listened to the speakers, Earl looked over at Juanita and squeezed her hand, once again feeling gratitude for her and for being alive. He gazed into eyes that had grown old with his. Eyes that had lived to see history continue to be made. Eyes that shared positive energy and gratitude after the ordeal of the past months. *When everything looked hopeless on that night six months ago, she never gave up, and neither did I.*

He and Juanita had attended every day of the trial, supported by their family and close friends as the facts unfolded. Noxzema Wesley Jordan had only been a child in 1965 when her grandfather, Malcolm Wesley, was convicted of statutory rape, sending her grandmother into a depression she never recovered from. The desperation—and later bitterness—her father experienced in his fruitless efforts to clear the family name before he died had been passed down to her. When her grandfather died in prison and her grandmother passed away a few days later, the bitterness inside Noxzema turned into a desire for revenge that had simmered, festered, for years.

Only through a chance meeting with a drunken Sheree Madsen, on a rainy spring day in 2012, did Noxzema unexpectedly learn the ugly truth. Instead of going to the police or the courts, and unable to bring the real perp to justice because of his death, her warped mind blamed Earl for railroading her grandfather. With the resources of her company at her disposal, she quietly hatched her plot with the help of the Sylvia Berry Lewis novel she had borrowed from her daughter.

Her former son-in-law Sean made it easy. His gambling was out of control, and the threat of turning him over to the casino's enforcers insured his cooperation in her plan. Besides, she had the ear of her daughter, Nevaeh Jordan Jamison. Noxzema had stirred the pot of discord with indirect references to the negative impact Sean's addiction had had on both their marriage and their son, encouraging Nevaeh to limit any contact with him.

Even if Ted Maddox and all the others had been convicted of the crime, Noxzema's skirts would have been clean, and her family would never have known of her involvement. If only Sean hadn't gotten scared and phoned her that night. If only her nosy maid hadn't been outside her bedroom and overheard the call. If only that stupid Ward and Maddox hadn't decided to dispose of the gun near the casino, of all places.

Even after the trial that sentenced Noxzema to 30 years in prison and Maddox to 60 years, it had been hard for Earl to forgive himself. Self-recriminations of overzealousness caught him at the most unexpected times while he was recovering. He couldn't undo what he'd done to Malcolm Wesley—even though he made sure the state issued a public apology and cleared his name, it seemed inadequate. Sheree Madsen's suicide and her mother's insanity wouldn't bring him back, although they ultimately paid the price for what they had done. However, to have Nevaeh forgive him instead of vilifying him was humbling.

"Where were you just now?" Juanita asked him.

He shifted to a more comfortable position in his chair. "Still trying to make sense of things."

"Give yourself time, honey. You may have spent your life in the world of law, but not every reason is going to be clear to you—only to Him. And like it or not, this is a reminder that we all have flaws. If we didn't, God wouldn't have anything to work with. We're a constant work in progress."

"You're right, Juanita. And the best thing I can do is forgive her and forgive myself for our errors in judgment."

"Exactly. You're alive, you have us, and you're still around to see history in the making again."

Earl nodded, smiling in agreement and looked over at Eli and Donna. As the respective speakers came forward, Eli happened to catch his eye and they exchanged a meaningful expression, one of understanding of a shared history as African Americans in the state. So much had been said about being on "the right side of history," and in Earl's mind that could be expanded to include being on "the right side of justice."

He had been asked to be the keynote speaker at the U of M law school in a week, and in that instant, he knew what his topic would be. "The Right Side of Justice." So many challenges would face the latest class of law students, but his own experiences of the past six months would, he hoped, give them a different perspective.

His daughter Linda and his son-in-law Melvin were standing nearby with their children and grandchildren, and he felt that ongoing sense of relief that Glendon Price had finally been eliminated from their lives. Thanks to Eli's vision, Price had been recaptured by the Minnesota Highway Patrol when he crossed the St. Croix River into the state and shipped back to prison.

Marvin Boone, who had achieved a nearly complete recovery from his injuries, was there with his niece Sherilyn and her soon-to-be wife, grateful for their care of him during his convalescence, thankful to support them and for being alive to bear witness to the occasion.

Donna Jo and Blaisdell—Earl still hadn't gotten used to calling him Patrick—were holding hands behind him along with Carter and Lilly, beaming as they heard Julian say a few words to the crowd before he took his place behind the governor.

"So how does it feel to be part of making history, Juanita?" Earl's face was a mixture of awe and pride.

"You mean again?" she asked with a little laugh.

"Yeah. You think Blaisdell knows what he signed onto in becoming part of this family?"

"Maybe not everything, but he's getting there. And yes, it's good to know we're a part of history changing for the better."

"And for a lot more people than we know, honey. Look."

Juanita's eyes followed the direction Earl was pointing, where Lieutenant Burrell stood with a tall, handsome man in his late 40s who reminded her of Nat "King" Cole. Though they were watching the ceremony, the chemistry between the two men was unmistakable. The lieutenant happened to look in their direction, and Earl invited them over with a wave of his hand.

"Hello, Lieutenant Burrell."

"Judge Berry," he said with a smile, shaking his hand. "Glad to see you're better. I see you're out here for the big day."

"We wouldn't miss it. Is this your husband?"

"Yes, he is. Well, he will be in September. Rahkeem, this is Judge Berry and Mrs. Berry."

"Glad to meet you," Rahkeem said. "Your son-in-law is making a huge difference in the community. From what I've learned, so have you."

"Thank you, Rahkeem," Earl replied. "I'm sure Julian would appreciate hearing that. And Lieutenant…"

"Eddie. Off duty, I'm Eddie."

"Eddie, again I want to thank you for everything you and your division did to bring the conspirators to justice last fall. If you need anything, anything at all, just ask."

"Thank you; all part of the job," Eddie said humbly. "Well, if you'll excuse us, we'll just go..."

"Please. Stay. In a way, you're part of the family now, just like Patrick," Juanita beamed gently.

"OK." Eddie nodded as Rahkeem whispered something in his ear. "Judge Berry, Rahkeem and I would consider it an honor if you and your family would attend our wedding."

Earl gave the couple a heartwarming smile. "It would be our pleasure."

Watching the latest chapter in history unfold as the governor signed marriage equality into law, Earl felt a sense of accomplishment. Surrounded by his family, old friends, and new friends, he remembered those days as a young man, eager to make a difference in the world as an attorney, and later his tenure as a judge working in the interest of justice. Justice, though, was something that was ever-evolving, and even at his age he was still learning something new. And though justice and equality at times could take years to come to fruition, one never gave up.

CPSIA information can be obtained
at www.ICGtesting.com
Printed in the USA
LVHW091620071020
668212LV00002B/326

9 781728 367989